VARED

SVESTI FATED MATES BOOK 1

WAVY MARTIN

Catalyst Publishers
P.O. Box 1232
Aliquippa, PA 15001
publisherscatalyst@gmail.com
Author website: wavymartin.com

Table of Contents

Chapter 1

GOOD DAY, FELLOW citizens of the United States and of the world. My name is Talia Sullivan. On Thursday, April 2, 2037, President Furman appointed me to the position of United States Ambassador of Interplanetary Relations. Yes, you heard me correctly—Interplanetary Relations.

Earlier this week, Commander Vared Durek of the Svesti race made first contact with President Furman and top officials from several other countries. We are not alone in this universe; there are thousands of other alien races we have yet to meet. As humans, now that we have this knowledge, we will need to adjust our worldviews and actions accordingly.

The Svesti is a warrior race, and the technology they use is well beyond Earth's capabilities. They protect many regions of space, including ours, primarily from the Zuvgran. The Svesti have informed us that the Zuvgran is a destructive race—violently invading planets, stripping natural resources and harvesting the remaining inhabitants of those worlds to use as slaves. The Zuvgran leave nothing living or useful behind. Three Earth decades ago, the Zuvgran utilized a biological weapon on the Svesti home world, Costonia, that killed most of their women and rendered the remaining females infertile. They did this in an attempt to commit a slow, emotionally painful genocide of the Svesti and remove them as the primary deterrent to the Zuvgran's intergalactic expansion plans. Even with their superior medical knowledge and technology, the Svesti have been unable to reverse the virus' effects on its people.

Svesti scientists have determined that the human race is biologically compatible with the Svesti race. As such, the Svesti would like to begin negotiations on how to integrate what they call a breeding program with human women. One of my first tasks as Ambassador will be to ensure the Svesti understand that the term breeders, in any iteration, is offensive to all human women.

Our initial reaction may be to reject outright the Svesti's requests. In my opinion, that would be shortsighted. The Svesti have been protecting us from the Zuvgran for many years now, but the undeniable fact remains that warriors die in battle. As the Svesti population decreases, at some point they may have to determine which areas of space are more important to concentrate their dwindling resources. Humans are not yet at the point where we can protect our world on our own. And we already know because of Earth's own turbulent history that insisting on racial purity, in any form, is divisive and creates great pain and suffering.

Tomorrow, I will join Commander Durek on his space cruiser to learn more of what is truly occurring in intergalactic space and the Svesti culture, as well as educate them on our ways. I will note cultural differences that may need to be addressed to avoid or reduce confusion and fear between our peoples. The plan is for me to spend eighteen Earth months with the Svesti to determine what the American response should be to their request. The President's intent is that my mission is to remain top secret until we know more.

I have to be honest; President Furman did not choose me as Ambassador because I have a political science, law, or any other pertinent degree or experience which qualifies me for this position. I was a teenage mother and am currently a divorced mom to a son in college. I am a moderately successful author. But the real reason behind my selection lies in my DNA. The Svesti have informed President Furman that I have a specific DNA strand that will allow for the best chances of compatibility with their technology. This compatibility should make it easier and significantly faster for me to learn the knowledge that will be necessary to interact in an intergalactic environment. Given the ages and life circumstances of the other Americans who also share this DNA strand, I felt compelled to accept President Furman's appointment. I have a deep love of country and humankind that will guide my actions, decisions, and recommendations.

If you are viewing this broadcast, that means security has been breached, either here in the United States or in one of the other countries that the Svesti have also contacted. I am recording this now, hoping to provide accurate information to the world if that has happened. With that in mind, I will encode additional data streams into this video—math, literature and science. It will require all three data streams to reveal another message. My intention is that no one can alter this video and my message today reaches you as complete and secure as I can make it.

In the next few decades, the world as we know it will transform. I do not know what our world will ultimately look like. The human race must adapt quickly. We must think and act globally in a way that has not yet been reliably achieved so we can take our place in the intergalactic community. It is time to educate ourselves and prepare, not panic.

May lasting peace here on Earth and in all galaxies be our goal.

Translated data streams:

I wish I could say this video is a belated April Fool's Day prank, but it is not. Rest assured, I will do my best to discover the truth and keep Americans and all humans as safe as I can. I hope my mission is successful and an age of prosperity follows. But, Joshua, if something unexpected should happen to me, your father and aunt will be there for you in my absence. Please remember, I have always loved you with all my heart. Space and time cannot diminish our bond. My only regret is that we could not say goodbye in person. Be safe, be well, and achieve your dreams. I have forever been proud of you and will miss you more than you can know. I love you. Mom.

Chapter 2

PERSONAL JOURNAL - DAY 1.

I was happy leading a relatively boring life. Then the Svesti, an alien race of warriors, showed up and now I'm the United States Ambassador to the Stars or some other happy horseshit title. How the hell did I get picked for this spaceship ride? I'm still trying to figure it out.

I'm writing this longhand to keep a record for myself. If I ever make it back to Earth, maybe I'll edit my journals and publish the first tell-all book documenting my meeting and living with aliens. Or maybe I'll just curl up into a little ball and end up in a rubber room. Only time will tell.

Before I continue, I guess I should talk about earlier today. It was spring cleaning day, so I was in my black leggings paired with an oversized T-shirt—you know, the ratty one with paint drippings on it—hair pulled up in a messy ponytail. I had just finished cleaning the baseboards and had started scrubbing the floors when a whitish-blue light surrounded me. The next thing I knew, I was on my hands and knees staring in shock at the Presidential seal on the carpet in the Oval Office with the scrub brush still in my hand. I looked up and saw President Furman leaning against his desk with some Secret Service people behind him. The only reason I knew it was the President is I recognized him from the news and, duh, the Oval Office.

As I cautiously moved my gaze around, I saw two other men, one in military uniform—I later learned it was General Abram Johnson, the Secretary of Defense. The other was Rick Newell, the President's Chief of Staff. I didn't like him at all; my avoid-the-creepy-guy vibes were on full alert.

Then I looked to the other side of the room. Still in a crouched position, I saw six muscular legs in black leather-like boots. Those long toned legs were in black, form-fitting uniform pants of some material I didn't recognize and belonged to three very tall and very large beings. One was wearing a Cobra Kai-ish, form-fitting black top that showcased his incredibly large and lickable biceps. There were criss-crossing straps across his torso with sheaths for various weapons. Golden bronze skin, lavender eyes and short, dark, wiry hair made a striking combination. One long scar on his cheek interrupted the harsh planes of his face. That was my first look at Commander Vared Durek. My fingers itched to touch his skin, his hair, even his scar.

With him there was another being, this one's skin a more caramel bronze with no shirt to hide his pecs, but he had a weapons harness as well. From what I saw, he had at least an eight-pack of abs. His eyes were a light teal color and his dark hair was in longish braids. I noted a tattoo of some sort near his collarbone. That was Lieutenant Devik Tolvex.

The third set of legs belonged to Lieutenant Karid Wurvez. His skin was a deep reddish bronze and his eyes were gray. His long hair was light brown and pulled back into a ponytail. Wurvez wore a black, short sleeve top underneath his weapons harness. I have to say that black was an excellent color on all of them.

All three Svesti towered over the humans in the room. I estimated they were about seven feet tall and all were insanely handsome in an unusual sort of way. Their skin looked like it had a furry texture, a bit like a short-haired cat. The aliens were sporting some impressive packages that looked like their pants were about to burst at the seams. Hey, I couldn't help but notice. I may not have had any sexy time in so long that I'm a born-again virgin at thirty-six, and while I suspect there may be a "Permanently Closed" sign in the vicinity of my vagina, I'm not dead yet. I freely admit to admiring the alien man candy. No little green men with oversized craniums to see there.

Tolvex turned toward Durek, and I contained my shock. *A tail above that tight butt! No freakin' way!* You'd think that would be a major turnoff, something about it was sexy...alluring. I just wondered if their tails did anything other than help keep them balanced. In their rumbling, deep voices, they spoke in their native tongue—a lyrical-sounding language similar in tone and rhythm to Earth's romance languages.

Now I don't normally get embarrassed easily, but I have to say when my brain started working again, I'm not sure the redness of my face was from the exertion of cleaning or from my realization that my ample ass was on full display in the Svesti direction with me looking back over my shoulder at them. Especially given the highly inappropriate thoughts I'd been having about their appearance. A shiver ran down my spine when I saw the

Commander looking at me. Holy hell, if he were human, I would've revisited my stance about refraining from one-night stands and wiggled my butt, just to see what happened.

Slowly, I stood. *You have got to be kidding me* echoed in my head when I remembered I was also wearing my purple, fluffy unicorn slippers with the huge googly eyes that Joshua had given me years ago.

"I sincerely hope I inadvertently mixed some cleaning chemicals and I am currently hallucinating," I said, pretending that this type of crap happened to me every day.

"Ms. Sullivan, thank you for joining us on such short notice," President Furman said with a tight smile. I transferred my scrub brush to my left hand so he could shake my right.

Okay, I'll play your game. "I wasn't aware we had a meeting on the schedule, Mr. President." He shot me a look that let me know he heard my underlying sarcasm and was choosing to ignore it.

"Let me introduce you to everyone and let you know why you're here." I did my best to act like I meet the President and huge alien beings regularly. I've always known there had to be other life out there. The universe is just too damned big. I'm not so arrogant as to believe humans are alone. And the books I write don't always take place on our planet, so it's not like I haven't imagined all sorts of aliens. But I have to admit, meeting some was a huge surprise.

The Svesti spoke English, haltingly, explaining that they have been protecting our region of space for over a century. Their sadness and anger was evident when they told me of the Zuvgran virus that had decimated their female population. I couldn't help but feel empathy for them. I kept my face impassive as they put forth their request for a "breeding" initiative with Earth.

President Furman spoke up, "And that leads us to why you're here." He explained the Svesti had provided him a list of individuals in the United States who have a particular DNA strand that is the most compatible with some technology or other. Get this, the Svesti compiled this list by hacking into a genealogical database. I was on this list. Just goes to show that you never know who will access your data.

The Svesti stated they had to speak with other nations' leaders and ported out, leaving us humans alone. That's what they called the technology with the whitish-blue light—porting. Which was pretty cool to experience from the observer's point of view; the Svesti just dissolved in the light.

"I'm still not sure why I'm here, Mr. President."

"Ms. Sullivan, we did a quick background check on everyone on the list that might be suitable for the task at hand. We eliminated everyone who is married, pregnant or has young children, elderly, under eighteen, ill, or has a criminal record. We disregarded those who had pressing commitments—sick family members and things like that. Of the remaining few from the list, you are the only one who hasn't publicly expressed radical views and is in a profession that can take an extended leave of absence."

"Leave of absence?"

"The Svesti would like us to send an emissary with them to negotiate terms. I would like you to serve as an ambassador representing our country. Observe and interact with the Svesti and report your impressions and recommendations back to me."

"How long are we talking?"

"Eighteen months."

"A year and a half away from my family?"

"Ms. Sullivan, your son is in college and his father is still alive and involved in his life. Your sister is also available to help if your son requires it."

"How long do I have to decide?"

President Furman appeared uncomfortable. "The Svesti leave tomorrow and I would like you with them."

That's when I lost it. "Are you freakin' serious? I don't even have a day to decide and make arrangements to be gone from Earth for an extended period of time if my answer is yes? That doesn't even give me time to see my son beforehand."

"All of what has been discussed here is considered beyond Top Secret and can't leave this room, Ms. Sullivan," General Johnson spoke up. "You can't tell your family or friends anything beyond you've accepted a short-term, confidential position with the government that will have you out of contact for an extended period for your safety and the safety of the mission."

"There is no one else?"

"No one whose life would be less affected than yours or that I would feel any confidence in trusting, Ms. Sullivan," the President said. He didn't look like he was any happier about the idea than I was.

It took a little while, but obviously I caved and agreed. But not until I negotiated a deal of my own. A decent paycheck so

Joshua's college would still be paid for, my house paid off, standard government health insurance to cover my son, a hastily drawn-up power of attorney for my sister to use in my absence, several cases of notebooks, journals, a case of my favorite pens, chocolate, and coffee to take with me, as well as a few other things were agreed to.

I was sworn into my position still wearing the stupid slippers. I bet that's something for the history books.

Then there were the high-level discussions on what our government wanted to know beyond the breeding initiative. That's when the creepy-guy vibes from Newell really ramped up. You would think it was the General who would be the most interested in the Svesti military technology, numbers, and capabilities, but no, it was Newell who incessantly harped on it. I'm not sure Newell really internalized that between humans and Svesti, the Svesti are the alphas, even without their technology. Newell himself is a Chihuahua in comparison.

Anyway, Joshua, my sister and I had a video chat where I passed along my cover story, made arrangements for the house and finances and did my best not to tear up and sob when I said goodbye to my son. I called my ex-husband, Tim, to let him know he was going to be parent-in-charge for the foreseeable future. Then there was a shopping trip with Secret Service to purchase clothes and toiletries. They weren't happy when I gave them the slip and headed to an internet cafe to make a secret video explaining to the world what was going on—just in case. Fortunately, I had finished and was just picking up a latte when they finally found me. Good thing I made a point of getting some cash from the President's secretary, since I couldn't use the White House credit card to pay for the internet or latte like I did for everything else.

So now here I sit in a secure location writing this while awaiting tomorrow. Part of me is excited, but part of me is terrified. What if I screw up and subject Americans and humans to something that isn't in our best interests? What if the Svesti are lying? So many questions.

Aw, hell, I really need to get some sleep. Tomorrow's a big day.

Chapter 3

O N THE BRIDGE of the space cruiser *Invictus* orbiting Earth, Vared asked, "Impressions?"

"Most of the leaders we met today seemed as if they might be honorable, but some of their subordinates, not so much," Karid Wurvez said.

"Agreed." Devik Tolvex gave a curt nod. "While not a match for us, I recognized the same dedication in their security personnel for the protection of their people. It's in the stance and the eyes. I had more respect for those warriors than some of their leaders."

"The females were...unusual," Karid grumbled. "Tiny beings with odd clothing and mannerisms."

"I believe the females were not prepared to meet us." Vared smiled, his fangs showing. "We shall see how they act tomorrow."

"They are so small and weak. No fangs, claws or tails for defense. Our scientists are certain they can breed with us and bear our younglings safely?" Devik asked.

"So the Council says." Vared brought up the relevant report on his tablet. "The biggest uncertainties are the length of gestation and the potential size of the young at birth. Human, what is their word, ah, babies are not as large as Svesti young. Humans average a nine-month gestation period, while Svesti average five lunars. We can confirm with Rivezt if there are any other issues we need to be aware of after he conducts their medical examinations."

"I still don't believe their bodies can survive mating with us," Devik said.

"Their mammary glands surprised me," Karid said. "What use are they if they have no young to feed?"

Vared hid his smile. "Perhaps you need more time in an erotica establishment or on a pleasure planet. I'll see if we can arrange that for you." The bridge crew laughed and made ribald suggestions.

"Do you think there will be any fated mate pairings with the Earth females?" asked Triv'n Brauvix, the communications officer on the bridge. Brauvix was the youngest member of the *Invictus* crew and had only been with them for three solars.

"There hasn't been a case of fated mates on Costonia in over a century. It is unlikely that the Earth females will spark the bonds." Vared frowned. "It is best to keep our hopes on something attainable like breeding and troth contracts, if the females are willing. However, these females are not for us. Their Choosings will be at the King's court."

Vared let the camaraderie of the bridge crew settle over him as he reviewed the day. As their commander, he needed to project confidence in the Council's plan to breed human females, but he silently shared the same doubts as his trusted males. Their species was dying without new young being born. Most of the males he knew had settled on the expectation that they would die in battle without ever having younglings to carry on their lines.

The females they had met today *were* strange with their unusual skin and coloring. Most did not appeal to him. However, his tail had tried to reach out to the one with her soft, plump ass and her face red from exertion. Only wrapping it around his ankle had kept his unruly appendage under control. Involuntary tail movement to touch another hadn't happened to him since he was a youngling. Fortunately, Devik and Karid did not notice or his old friends would harass him incessantly.

He wondered if she would look the same after mating—skin flushed, damp and dewy. Her brown hair had shimmered with a red that reminded him of the *woolah* flower during Harvest season on the home world. Her brown eyes were bright with intelligence. Interestingly, she had exhibited no fear or distress at being ported and thrust into an unusual situation—not like the other humans. Males and females alike had initially reacted with distrust, fear, or belligerence when he and his warriors contacted them—all but her. Beneath the chemical smells, her natural scent reminded him of *leringa* fruit—refreshingly sweet with a hint of spice. It brought to mind his youngling days on Costonia before he started his warrior training. That time that was before his mother and sisters died from the Zuvgran virus and he and his father lost their love and laughter. Shaking his head to dispel the memories, Vared interrupted the banter.

"Arrange for private quarters for each of the females. Gather some human food for our stores. Remember, most Earth humans do not know we exist; let us keep it that way. When we have a better idea of what the females like to eat, have the master synthesizer programmed with some of their favorites. Ensure there is appropriate clothing waiting for each female. Given their fragility, they should have nanosuits for added protection. They will require comms. When we port them tomorrow, we will depart for Costonia. We will resupply at Theron before continuing on to the home world. The *Defiant* will continue to patrol this sector while we complete our mission. It shouldn't be necessary to remind them, but I will speak to the crew before the females arrive and reiterate that these females are to be treated will the same respect and care as a Svesti female."

"Yes, sir."

"Any suggestions or questions?"

"No, sir."

"Sir, incoming message from King Sovex, coded private for you," Brauvix said.

"Send it to my on-call room. I'll take it in there," Vared said as he walked away.

The holographic image of King Traxen Sovex of House Davelk appeared above Vared's desk. Vared thumped a fist over his heart and bowed his head. "Good day, Sire."

Traxen grunted, "It's just us, Vared. How many times have I told you formality is unnecessary?"

Vared grinned and sat. "How are you, cousin?"

Traxen leaned back in his chair, a grimace on his golden bronze face. "I'd be better if the *crekkin'* Council would behave. It's like herding wet *rulahs*, each going a different direction. There are some who want to just invade Earth and take all their females. They do not understand it uses fewer resources and creates more goodwill when the females are offered willingly. There are others who complain we will dilute our genetic pool by breeding with another race. There will be no Svesti race at all if we cannot have any young. I will not be the King who let our race die out."

"Which Houses are in favor of invasion?"

"Houses Troliv, Glixon, and some outliers of Kreliz. Midnar is playing all sides, as usual. Your House of Ruxila, as well as Vramel, Fresida, Binova, and Yula will most likely follow my lead. Nuxar and Srotix are firmly on the racial purity side."

"Troliv and Glixon only want war for profit. Too many of their merchants and traders see it as an opportunity to fill their coffers. Kreliz surprises me a little." Vared frowned.

"Kreliz lost most of their younglings in addition to their females. Those in favor of invasion may be desperate to populate their lines as quickly as possible. It's understandable, but I must make this decision with a cool head. Enough about the Houses. How is your mission progressing?"

"Earth does not have a central government for their planet. They have what they call countries that divide them. Each of these countries governs themselves in various ways. Based on our observations, we contacted six who appear to be the largest in territory or influence. We met with their leaders and all have agreed to send a woman to present for the Choosing.”

“Wonderful. What are the females like?”

“Smaller and more fragile than Svesti females. A wide range of skin, hair colors, and body types appear to be the norm on their planet. All appeared to be healthy. We will bring them aboard the *Invictus* tomorrow and begin traveling to Costonia. We’ll stop for a resupply on Theron.”

“Good. Are the women eager to volunteer?”

“I do not know, Traxen. We were not privy to those conversations with their leaders.”

“Well, their leaders have agreed.” Traxen leaned forward; his long braid swayed and his lavender eyes narrowed. “Our intelligence has identified four potential locations for Zuvgran laboratories. Hopefully, one will have information on the virus that we can use to find a cure.”

Vared’s back stiffened and his face hardened. “Where? If any are on our way, I can send teams to investigate.”

“No, Vared, the human females are to be protected at all costs. They may be what saves our people. I do not want them put in harm’s way.”

“Traxen, the *Invictus* can investigate and protect the females. They would remain onboard.”

“We do not know what security measures the Zuvgran may have in place. Your mission remains the same. Escort the human females to Costonia.”

“Cousin,” Vared growled.

"I have decided, Commander Durek. I expect you to follow orders." Traxen stared at Vared, lips tightened. After a moment, Vared sighed.

"At least send me the intelligence so I can review it and offer suggestions."

"That I can do. Obviously, this information must remain closely guarded. We do not want the Zuvgran to be forewarned of our knowledge and abandon any labs. We need their research."

"Are you concerned about traitors?"

"I am always worried about traitors, Vared. That's how I stay alive." Traxen grinned, his fangs visible. "Now, bring those females here. I want to meet them. Perhaps some troth or breeding contracts with willing females will settle down the Council members."

"From your mouth to the Goddess' ears, Traxen. Many of the Council are as useless as *mentoks*—flashing their plumage and chattering incessantly about nothing."

Traxen laughed. "True, but others are dangerous, Vared. They play their little games for personal gain, riling up others with lies and misdirection. Do not discount them."

"There are many reasons I am glad you are King, cousin. I could not do what you do. I'd be tempted to sever heads from bodies." Vared grinned.

"So I should not name you my heir?" Traxen's eyes twinkled.

"Oh, Goddess, no. Do you hate me that much?" They both laughed.

"I will contact you tomorrow to get an update on the females. Keep your temper under control, Vared. They are not warriors. Do not treat them as such."

"As you wish, cousin."

After they terminated their link, Vared reviewed the intelligence in the encrypted data Traxen sent. A small smile tipped at the edges of his lips. "Wurvez," he said into his comm. "Report to the on-call room."

"This is need-to-know information, Karid." Vared showed the data to the *Invictus* tactical officer. "As we approach Theron, I want you to run deep-level scans in this sector." Vared pointed to an area on a holographic map. "Send me the data."

"What are we looking for?" Karid skimmed the map, his gray eyes glinting.

"Signs of the Zuvgran. Specifically laboratories, power usage, anything unusual. The labs may be underground."

"If we find anything suspicious, will we be sending a scout team?"

"Unfortunately, no. King Sovex has made it clear that our only mission is to escort the human females to Costonia safely. However, any information we gather will be helpful to the cause. Supposedly, that planet is uninhabited. It's outside normal travel lanes, so if the Zuvgran are using it, there should be some signs of them. Brief Tolvex separately, but we will be the only three onboard who will have access to this information."

"Understood." Karid clenched his fist. "I would like a chance to take down one of their labs. What if the human females are susceptible to the virus too? Are we dooming them as well?"

"Our scientists say the humans are not, but no one knows if their female younglings will be. We must find a cure or vaccine."

Sweat dripped down his face, but Vared ignored it. He narrowed his eyes, remaining motionless as he watched Devik. When Devik's teal eyes minutely signaled his intent to move left for a strike, Vared moved into it and rapped his staff into Devik's ribs. Simultaneously, he raised his right arm and took the hit from Devik's staff. Stepping back, he abruptly spun and landed a kick on Devik's thigh. Devik retaliated with a surprise punch to Vared's face. Both grunted with their exertion.

"Nice move, Vared." Devik grinned ferociously. "I hope you didn't break my ribs."

"I think you loosened a fang, you overgrown *naroon*."

"When did I turn blue?"

"You will when I cut off your air," Vared countered with his own ferocious grin. Their staffs spun rapidly, intermittently striking the other. The loud whacks of wood hitting wood echoed in the training area.

"My commander says such sweet nothings to me. Is it any wonder I feel so valued?"

"Your prattle does not distract me, Devik." Vared swept his staff at Devik's legs, but Devik leaped over it. Vared continued his turn and sidestepped to hit Devik on his back.

"Ooomph. *Crek!*"

"Would you like me to continue with my sweet nothings?" Vared chuckled.

"No. I think I've had enough for now." Devik grabbed two towels and tossed one to Vared. They both began wiping the sweat from their faces and bare torsos. The clan markings below their collarbones showed slight differences from each other. "I plan to put the females in the residential section closest to the bridge. Those are the nicest quarters and will keep them nearer to senior crew."

Vared handed a water pouch to his friend. "That makes the most sense. You've set up the parameters for their access to areas of the vessel?"

"Yes. For now, they will be restricted to the six upper decks. No independent access to engines, cargo bays, hangars or the lower residential areas."

"Very well. I'll have Brauvix explain some of the technology they may use regularly. He's competent and eager."

"He's coming along." Devik took a long gulp of water. "Were we ever that young?"

Vared smiled. "Are you saying we're old?"

Devik shook his head, a serious look in his eyes. "I admit with all this talk about the human females, I've begun to wonder."

"Wonder what?"

"If there is something more than serving our race. There is hope now that we may be able to have younglings and continue our lines. Female companionship. Families consist of more than males. I did not think about it when there was no hope, but now the change excites *and* worries me."

Vared glanced at Devik, then watched the other males training in the large space. Some were training alone, others sparring with each other or training bots. No one was nearby. "I think the change will come with its own set of problems—larger than the personal considerations. According to the king, there are those who wish to invade Earth and take their females, while others believe the younglings will no longer be Svesti. The Council is divided, which does not bode well."

"Do you believe the females may be in danger?" Devik growled.

"Unknown, but we must proceed as if they are."

Chapter 4

PERSONAL JOURNAL - DAY 2.

I am livid. I don't care what species they are, men are the same everywhere! I can't even write about it just yet. The only good news is that the other women from Earth and I have definitely bonded.

When the porter beam surrounded her to take her to the Svesti space cruiser, Talia expected to see a porter room similar to those in her favorite science fiction movies. However, she woke up on a single bed, wearing some sort of medical gown and wondering why her head ached.

"You did *what*?" she heard. Talia sat up and saw the owner of the voice was a human woman dressed as she was. The tall, lean blonde was yelling at a Svesti male. Scrambling off the bed, she noticed four other human women on beds who appeared to be still sleeping.

"What's going on?" Talia asked.

The woman's blue eyes glared. "They knocked us out and implanted devices in our bodies." Talia noted the slight English accent.

Crossing her arms and stiffening her shoulders, Talia looked at the Svesti. "What did you do?"

"We decontaminated for viruses, implanted translator and tracking devices, ran in-depth medical checks, inoculated you for standard galactic viruses known to cross species, corrected health deficiencies, removed any contraceptive implants, and genetically altered your DNA to increase longevity to match Svesti lifespans."

"On whose orders?"

"Commander Durek."

Talia gritted her teeth. "Excuse us for a moment. We humans would like to talk privately." The male nodded and moved to another bed.

"Hi. I'm Talia Sullivan. United States Ambassador. I'm with you that this is bullshit, but I think we need to save our energy for the one who ordered it all."

"Rachel Llewellyn. United Kingdom." Rachel unclenched her fists. "Who the hell do they think they are?"

"I don't know what they were thinking, but I have quite a bit to say to the Commander."

"Well, as an ambassador, you can take point, but I'm reserving the right to cause bodily harm."

Both women laughed. "I've been an ambassador of all of a day. Last week I was an author." Talia looked at Rachel, noting her stance. "Military? Law enforcement?"

Rachel's face tightened before she sighed. "MI-6."

"Do you want anyone to know?"

"I'd prefer not just yet."

"Security it is then. I have no problem keeping it under wraps."

"I appreciate it." Rachel ran a hand through her short hair. "This is not what I expected."

"Me neither. Let's keep the other women calm as they wake up and plan how we're going to express our displeasure."

They introduced themselves to the next woman to wake, Natasha Petrov, a doctor from Russia. Natasha's brown eyes narrowed when she heard all that was done to them. "I'll find out more from a medical standpoint." She went to talk to the Svesti.

Ava Taylor was a curvy Canadian woman with green eyes and long, curly red hair. Her lips tightened when she heard the news. "What are we going to do about it?"

"We're going to get a meeting with Commander Durek and give him an earful," Talia said.

"Count me in."

Emmy Norton, an Australian, with butterscotch skin, long brown hair, and sleepy brown eyes, hissed low when she was told the Svesti had implanted a tracker. Then she gave the other women a short, angry nod, "Get me to a computer and I'll see about disabling the trackers."

Last to awaken was Lin Chang, a petite Chinese woman with short, dark hair and dark eyes. "I'm a botanist. I only agreed to this mission to study alien plant life." Her breathing quickened and her face flushed. "What else are they going to do to us?"

"We're going to…" Talia broke off when Natasha came back to their group.

"The doctor, or healer, as they call him, is Ash'n Rivezt. He implanted translator devices behind our ears which also serve as information conduits. Supposedly we all know each other's languages now—Svesti, Galactic Standard, and a couple other ones. He said we needed to be anesthetized because uploading more than three languages at a time can cause severe headaches and disorientation. The trackers are in our left arms. Supposedly it is not safe for females on many worlds and it allows them to find us should we be abducted."

All the women reached for their ears and arms trying to feel for the foreign devices.

"That explains my headache," Talia said, rubbing her forehead.

"Abducted?" Tears filled Lin's eyes.

"Sounds like slavery is commonplace in the universe."

"Oh, this just keeps getting better and better," Ava bit out.

"What about the contraceptive implants?" Rachel asked.

"According to Rivezt, the implants would interfere with the DNA changes they made. It seems we can expect to live an additional fifty to seventy years now. Oh, and most of our scars have been removed."

Talia discreetly lifted her gown. "My pregnancy stretch marks are gone. I'm really not sure how I feel about that."

"What about those of us who use other methods of birth control? Pill? Shot? Do you think it's still effective?" asked Rachel.

"Without doing some research, I don't know the answer to that." Natasha shrugged.

Talia spoke as Rivezt approached. "We'd like to get dressed now and see Commander Durek."

"There are nanosuits for each of you in there." He pointed to an adjoining room. "Once you change, the Commander wishes to meet with you all in the War Room and introduce you to some of the bridge crew."

"We'd like our own clothing."

"I was instructed to give you the nanosuits. They will help keep you safer as you females are fragile."

"Fragile?" Rachel snorted.

"Are you saying we are not safe on this ship?" Talia pursed her lips.

"No, no one on the *Invictus* would dare harm any of you." Rivezt looked affronted, and his blue eyes deepened to cobalt.

"Are we expecting to be in a battle sometime soon? Or boarded by space pirates?"

"No, of course not."

"So these suits are to minimize bruising and the like if we happen to trip over our own feet or walk into a wall?"

"Uhhh..."

"I think we can dress in our own clothing for now. You can give us the nanosuits and we'll take them with us."

Ash'n frowned. "I'm not sure that's what the Commander expects."

"Mr. Rivezt, no offense to you, but right now, none of us care what the Commander expects. Where are our clothes?"

"I'll retrieve them for you." His long, dark ponytail swung as he pivoted.

Talia looked at the group of women. All wore low-heeled, comfortable shoes. *No Jimmy Choos in the mix. Guess we all had the same idea. Who wants to be walking around an unknown spaceship in heels?*

"Did your governments give you any titles or instructions?" asked Talia. "Mine made me an Ambassador, but I have to be honest, I was an author and stay-at-home mom before that."

Natasha shook her head, her blonde French braid brushing her shoulder. "No title, just find out everything I can about the Svesti, focusing on biology."

"I was told to get into their computer systems and try to get schematics of any and all technology. They also wanted star charts and maps," Emmy bit out. "I was threatened with jail time if I bring nothing back. They didn't seem to care what would happen to me if the Svesti caught me."

"They instructed me to try to learn as much as possible," Lin said, head bowed.

Ava chimed in, "It was suggested to me that I make friends and learn anything that might help in case of an invasion."

Rachel said, "I was tasked with finding out military capabilities."

"Me, too," said Talia. "Are you all comfortable with me speaking for our group? If not, then let's hash it out now amongst ourselves so we can show a united front in the meeting." *I'm probably the oldest by a couple years. Not that it matters.*

The women looked at each other, then back at Talia. "We're good with you as our spokesperson," said Rachel. "You've got an official title to back it up, although I'm not sure how much it really means here." The other women nodded.

"Let's go give them hell," Ava said with a feral grin. "Let's show them they shouldn't screw over human women."

The six women, each carrying a folded black nanosuit, followed Rivezt to a large room adjacent to the bridge. "This is the War Room."

"Looks like a conference room to me," whispered Ava. The other women nodded in agreement.

"Let's grab seats, ladies," Talia said.

"Females, welcome aboard the *Invictus*. I am Commander Durek of House Ruxila. We met briefly on your planet. I would like to reintroduce Lieutenant Tolvex of House Vramel, our head of security, and Lieutenant Wurvez of House Binova, our head tactical officer. You have already met Healer Rivezt of House Yula."

Talia nodded. *I wonder what the houses mean? They must be important somehow.* Her eyes traced his biceps, noting the strength of his arms. *Damn, I think they're thicker than my thighs and all muscle. Focus on his words, not his body.* She raised her eyes as he continued speaking.

"You will each be assigned your own quarters with synthesizers that can provide you with food if you choose not to eat in the dining area. Other items can be fabricated as well. I will have someone provide you instruction on how to use them, as well as the comms you will be given.

"We are currently en route to the space station Theron to resupply our stores, then we will continue to Costonia. There you will be presented to the King's court and the Council for your Choosings."

"Choosings?" Talia asked. *This doesn't sound good.*

"Yes, you will meet a number of our nobles and select those of which you may wish to have court you for a troth contract, or if you prefer, a breeding contract."

"What?"

"I didn't agree to that!"

Her body tense, Talia spoke over the exclamations of the other women. "Why would you believe we are interested in either type of contract?"

"I am confused. Did your leaders not inform you of our agreement?"

"What agreement?" Her fists clenched under the table.

"You are the first females to volunteer to become Svesti mates or breeders."

"Oh, hell to the no," Ava shouted.

Talia waved a hand to silence the women's objections.

"Commander Durek, do you have any proof that what you say is the truth?"

"Are you impugning my honor and calling me a liar, female?" Durek's face hardened, his scar prominent and his lavender eyes darkening as he glared at Talia.

I don't care how good you look, you're not going to intimidate me. "Look at it from our point of view. Not one of us has volunteered for marriage or breeding with anyone, nor heard of this agreement. We are on an alien vessel for the first time in our lives and have met none of you before yesterday. Why would we simply believe you? I am just asking if you have proof."

With crossed arms and biceps bulging, Vared growled and dipped his head at Tolvex. Tolvex entered something onto his tablet and holographic videos appeared in the center of the room above the table. He played each video, one from each country, showing the leaders agreeing to give them a woman for a breeding or troth contract. The last one he played was of Rick Newell agreeing with President Furman, looking uncomfortable.

"Our own governments pimped us out," Rachel said, face set in tight lines.

"I can't believe this." Lin's eyes filled with tears. "I fought my parents for years about an arranged marriage and now this happens?"

"When I next see Newell, I'm going to castrate him and feed him his dick." The Svesti all winced. Talia stood and placed her palms flat on the table, leaning forward with locked elbows facing Vared.

"Let me clue you in on our world, Commander. In my country, women only received the right to vote after a century of fighting for it. Women worldwide are routinely paid less than men, even if they are better qualified, educated, or just damn better at their jobs. If we get angry, we're considered too emotional, yet if a man gets angry, people label him passionate.

"We have men that believe women should be nothing more than chattel with no control over their own bodies and are worthless beyond making meals, birthing children, and pandering to male egos, and some of those men like to beat women. Some believe that women should be forced to give birth to children that are products of rape or incest or even if it will endanger the woman's life.

"We have areas on our planet that give our young female children to grown men as child brides, sometimes in trade for livestock. Some cultures believe it is appropriate to mutilate a female's genitalia. All over our world, we deal with human trafficking, and it is mostly women and children who are kidnapped and forced into slavery and prostitution.

"Women in my world have been fighting for their own choices for themselves and their bodies for millennia."

"You tell him, sister."

"Damn straight."

Talia continued, "We each volunteered to come aboard and visit Costonia to learn about your culture and work in our chosen fields. We did not come aboard to revert to what we consider Stone-Age misogynistic thinking and attitudes.

"We believe in informed consent. Yet, we were ported aboard your vessel and our bodies were violated by the Svesti. And now we find out that our own governments, in essence, gave us to the Svesti without our consent."

"Who violated you?" Durek stood and mirrored Talia's position, muscles bunched and tail flicking. His eyes darkened to a deep amethyst and narrowed.

"You did when you ordered Rivezt to implant devices into our bodies and messed with our DNA."

"You were not violated. All of that was necessary."

"Whether or not all of it was necessary is debatable, but we were not given the choice. All you had to do was explain to us what you felt was necessary and why. Some procedures we would've agreed to, but in a different manner."

"Different manner?" asked Rivezt.

Talia turned her head to look at the healer. "Yes. We most likely would've had one or two of us volunteer with the others watching while you explained what you were doing. Then each woman could've made their own choice about what they were willing to do." Turning back to glare at Vared, she said, "But instead, you knocked us out and changed our bodies *without our consent!*"

"Cease your yelling, female," Durek shouted.

"I will when you do. And you can call me Ambassador, Ambassador Sullivan, or Ms. Sullivan, not female. *We. Have. Names!*"

The room went silent except for the accelerated breathing of Durek and Talia as they stared at each other across the table. Durek's eyes dropped briefly to Talia's heaving chest before tapping his comm. "Brauvix, get in here and escort the females to their quarters." He straightened, his scar white on his face.

Through clenched teeth, he said, "This meeting is over. We'll talk later."

Talia nodded. "Something we can agree upon. Ladies, let's go."

Chapter 5

"**T**HAT DID NOT seem like it went well," Karid said as he relaxed in his chair.

Vared ignored his friend. Taking his seat, he asked, "Why were they not wearing their nanosuits?"

"The females did not believe it necessary to wear them at this time." Ash'n grinned. "That ambassador has a way of reframing a topic that has you viewing it in a different way. She basically asked if the suits were to keep them from harm if they might trip over their own feet while on the ship." Everyone but Vared laughed.

"That female is not submissive at all."

"She certainly doesn't give that impression. Listening to her and watching the other females' reactions, I don't think treating them as we would a Svesti female is going to work." Devik's braids brushed his shoulders as he shook his head. "Did you hear some of the things the males on their world do? It's appalling."

"Why wouldn't they want to be pampered and cared for? Especially given how they say they have been treated on their world?" Karid cocked his head to the side. "You would think they would enjoy not having to worry or fight."

"I hate to admit it, but they have a point. We did not inform them in advance, nor ask their permission. From their perspective, we treated them as less than sentient, intelligent beings." Ash'n frowned, his blue eyes thoughtful. "I never considered that. I wouldn't have done the same to any Svesti male unless it was time critical to provide medical care."

His short hair spiked in all directions as Vared ran his hand over his head. "Now that I am calmer, I can empathize with what the females were saying. But the little hellcat didn't have to yell at me. I would've listened." His friends barked out abrupt laughs. "What?"

Devik grinned. "Vared, we have known you since we all began warrior training many solars ago. One reason you have risen in the ranks so fast is that you have a hard head—and not just in battle."

Karid added, "You can be, how shall I say it, a bit attached to your own thinking."

"But you usually come around...eventually." Ash'n smiled.

"Don't you *mentoks* have some work to do? If not, I'm certain I can find something menial and boring for each of you." Vared smiled, then sighed. "Thank you for your honest opinions, my friends. I will make amends to the females later this evening."

After his crew left the War Room, Vared willed his cock to soften. He shifted in his seat, adjusting himself. *Crekkin' thing made itself known while the female was yelling at me. Oh, she was glorious in her anger; brown eyes sparking, cheeks flushed, and chest heaving. The angrier she got, the heavier her scent became. Would she be that passionate while mating?* Vared imagined pressing up against her, subduing her anger with pleasure. The thought of her scent ripening with arousal instead of anger caused his cock to twitch. *Crek! I cannot walk onto the bridge this way.* Vared gritted his teeth and began listing military battles in his head.

"Durek, what is your status?" King Sovex asked.

"All females are onboard the *Invictus* and we are on our way to Theron for our resupply. The *Defiant* is patrolling the sector in our absence. I suggested to its commander that they monitor Earth's abundant communications for any mention of us. He has instructed his comms officer to set up search parameters to filter them, and only those will be reviewed."

"Good. Are the females excited?"

"Excitable would be a better description, sire," Vared said with a sigh.

"Explain yourself, cousin." Traxen's eyes narrowed.

"It appears that Earth's leaders did not inform the females of their true purpose. That, combined with our initial interactions with the females, has angered them considerably." Vared consciously kept his back straight and face impassive.

Traxen leaned forward and stared at Vared. *Crek. Even through the comm, the male is intense.* "I think you need to elaborate, Commander." *Double crek. No more cousin talk; he's not happy.*

Vared took a deep breath. "We ported the females directly to medical bay pods. I instructed our healer to implant translator and tracking devices, as well as scan for contaminants and viruses. The females were given thorough medical scans, health deficiencies corrected, and had their DNA adjusted to increase their lifespans to match the Svesti."

"All of that sounds reasonable. What was the problem?"

"The problem is that the females took exception to all of it...loudly. They were quite vocal about not being informed beforehand or asked for their consent before they undertook any procedure." Vared huffed. "Even more so when they realized their governments had lied to them."

Traxen tilted his head, his expression thoughtful. "The females are unhappy?"

"Yes. Upon reflection of their complaints, I believe they have reason to be." Vared grimaced. "Cousin, the females differ from what we are used to. According to them, the decision to mate and breed is a choice each female makes for themselves, as is the decision to work. As a gender, they have not always been treated well on their planet, with males making choices for them without their input or consent. Unlike Svesti females, they do not trust any male to make decisions for their bodies or life choices. And when I informed them about the Choosing, I was glad they did not have weapons at hand."

"They were that angry?"

"Yes, when we provided proof of their governments agreeing to the females being presented at the Choosing for breeding or troth contracts, one female was as bloodthirsty as any Svesti male." Vared winced in remembrance, then grinned. "It seems though they are small and fragile, they have the hearts of warriors." *Especially that hellcat female.*

Traxen chuckled. "It seems they have made an impression on you. I trust you handled it well and soothed their anger?"

"Remember when you instructed me to not treat them as warriors?"

"Yes."

"With their warrior-like reactions, unfortunately, I did not follow your instructions." Vared bowed his head. "My apologies, sire, I am not an accomplished diplomat. I lost my temper and terminated the meeting."

"Vared," Traxen growled. "You need to fix this. Much depends on the human females."

"I know, sire. My plan is to allow tempers to cool, then apologize to the females, and request a chance to repair their impressions of our race."

"You do that."

"Sire, given their reactions, I am not sure a Choosing ceremony will be productive. I am concerned it will foster resentment and more anger."

With a frown, Traxen said, "I will think on it. It may be best if I meet the females myself before making any other decision."

"I believe that would be wise, cousin. On the other matter we discussed yesterday, I have instructed Wurvez and Tolvex to run long-range scans of XB9428B. We three are the only ones on *Invictus* with access to the intel you sent yesterday. We will forward anything we find, as well as any speculations we may have on the data to you directly."

"Good, Vared, good." Traxen's gaze speared Vared. "No missions to investigate potential labs from the *Invictus*."

Vared clenched his fists below his desk. "I understand, sire."

"I look forward to the scans and analysis. I also expect you to correct the situation with the human females. Regular updates, encrypted only."

"Yes, sire. It will be as you command." Vared bowed his head and ended the transmission.

Crek. How long should I wait before approaching the females? Do they like gifts with their apologies like Svesti females? Vared began searching Earth's data from their public transmissions and internet. He growled as he found conflicting information on apologies and relationship building—the only constant there seemed to be was no one truly understood females. *Perhaps beating on some training bots will relieve my frustration.*

Vared stood in his shower, hanging his head while the hot water pulsed on his bruised skin. *Taking on five bots while distracted was a mistake. I hurt everywhere.*

After he washed the sweat from his body, he tossed the cloth to the side. *I can't stop thinking about her. The mouthy one. I know what I'd like to see that mouth do.* As he imagined Talia's pink lips surrounding his cock, his hand reached down to roll his balls before fisting his member tightly. The three nodes near the head of his cock were sensitive, as was the larger one at its base. Slowly, he dragged his hand up and down his engorged flesh. He pictured her laid out on his bed, her reddish-brown hair splayed over his pillows, legs open to his gaze. All that soft pale flesh for him to kiss and nip and lick slowly so he could discover what touches made her squirm and writhe in pleasure.

Are her nipples brown? Pink? Red? And if I lick where her scent is the strongest, will she taste as good as she smells? Grunting low, he moved his hand faster while he braced himself on the shower wall with his other hand. *Oh, she'd be loud in her pleasure—moaning and sighing. I wonder if I could make her scream.* His muscular legs tensed as he thought of her legs crushing his head to her as he drank from her core. He felt his balls draw up and tighten. Throwing his head back, he stiffened as ropes of milky fluid erupted from him, painting the shower wall before sliding away in the water. Shuddering with the last of his bliss fading, he gasped in the steam surrounding him, muscles now loose. *Crek! No female has ever invaded my thoughts this way.* His head fell forward again. *This is going to be a long trip back to Costonia.*

A Svesti strode across the cargo bay, occasionally glancing between his tablet and the containers. When he was sure he was alone, he sequestered himself in the furthest corner, inserted an earpiece and tapped a small comm. He heard, "I was hoping to hear from you."

"The human females are onboard," he said.

"How many?"

"Six."

"Anything else to report?"

"Rumor is the *Invictus* will be stopping at Theron for a resupply. I do not know when. Most likely within the next couple weeks." His eyes scanned the bay for movement.

"Will the humans be going to the station?"

"Unknown."

"Find out. Encourage it if you can. We need to know when they'll be there. This may be our only chance."

"As you will."

"Much depends on this."

"I am aware, sir."

"Also, encourage the females to dislike Svesti."

"How do you mean?"

"Find ways to make them believe their lives are at risk. Be creative, but be untraceable back to you. And of utmost importance, be careful. We don't want them to die since we need them for the plan to be successful. We need them to return to Earth, sooner rather than later."

"I will do what I can and share more when I know more. You are certain they cannot trace this comm?"

"I am certain. I would not put you at unnecessary risk, Nephew."

"I would not expect you to, uncle. How is Mother?"

“My sister is fine.”

“Please give her greetings from me when next you speak.”

“Of course. Anything else?”

“No.”

“Always Svesti, Nephew.”

“Always Svesti, Uncle.” The male stuffed the earpiece and comm in a pocket. He smiled as he entered the corridor. *Time for the evening meal and an excellent opportunity to find out when we will reach Theron.*

Chapter 6

BRAUVIX LEFT THE women in Talia's quarters after giving them a brief lesson on the synthesizer and comms. Ava said, "I need a drink. Do you think we can get the synthesizer to give us some alcohol?"

"Good idea," said Rachel.

"I could use ice cream. I always eat ice cream when I'm depressed," Lin said.

Talia looked at everyone. "You know, you are right. We need to have a girls' night, regardless of what time of day it is. If we can't get what we need from the synthesizer, I know I have some chocolate packed. I'm willing to share."

Natasha smiled. "I'm Russian. I have vodka in my belongings."

"I have wine," said Emmy.

Everyone laughed. Ava added, "I have to admit I have some cookies in my bag."

"Let's do this. Everyone meet back here in a few minutes with whatever goodies they may have brought," Rachel said.

After several ugly-looking attempts, they figured out how to have the synthesizer make some shot glasses for the vodka.

Making a face after downing a shot, Lin reached for one of Ava's homemade cookies and asked, "What are we going to do? I don't want to mate or breed with anyone, human or Svesti."

"Do you think they'll take us back to Earth?" asked Ava.

"Why would they? They have all the control and our governments will just screw over some other women instead," Natasha said.

"We need to figure out a way to get our control back." Rachel settled on one of the couches in Talia's living area. She patted a cushion. "I like these. They're oversized, like the Svesti."

Talia settled down next to Rachel and raised her glass. "Now you're talking. Does anyone have any ideas? Let's brainstorm." She drank some more vodka.

"Maybe you can be like Mata Hari. Seduce the commander and bring him around to our side," suggested Rachel.

Talia almost spit out her drink. "What?"

"Yeah, the chemistry between you two is off the charts." Natasha laughed as she had another shot before grabbing some chocolate.

"I don't know what you're talking about. We were arguing. Loudly." *Yeah, and you were ogling him before that. You just don't want to admit it.*

"Oh, girl, it looked like foreplay from where I was sitting." Ava waved her hand, fingers waggling. "Hot. Seriously hot."

Lin quietly added, "I didn't know if he was going to hit you or kiss you."

Emmy looked at Lin, "Right? I had the same feeling." She opened a wine bottle, took a swig, and passed it on.

"You ladies are certifiable! Even if I were interested, I am the furthest thing from sexy that there is."

"What are you talking about? You're gorgeous. I'd kill to have your hair," Lin said. She slid down on another couch. "Mine is stick straight and boring."

"I wouldn't know where to begin. I'm sexually boring." Talia frowned and looked into her empty glass. "Damn, I don't think I've ever said that out loud before. I haven't been with a man in years."

"Weren't you married?" Ava asked.

"Yes, but I got pregnant at sixteen. Tim and I were best friends but outcasts in our small town because of our families."

"This sounds like a story. Tell all to Mama Rachel." Rachel poured herself another shot from the bottle making the rounds, before gulping some wine.

Talia looked around at everyone. "I rarely talk about this."

"Talia, as far as we know, we are the only six human women in this region of space. Who else are you going to talk to?" Natasha prodded.

"You've got a point." Talia sighed. "Tim's parents were drug addicts. My mother died when I was five. My dad was a mechanic, but as my sister and I got older, he started drinking heavily. Both families were poor. Tim was geeky, and I was shy. In high school, we became friends and then lovers."

"*You* were shy?" Lin exclaimed.

"Yes, I was." Talia laughed. "I got pregnant within a month of losing my virginity. Tim and I got married because we wanted our child to have a stable home, something neither of us had. Tim worked full time and went to high school; I stayed home with Joshua and got my GED. We spent the next several years doing our best to get Tim a better education so he could get a higher-paying job. I had always written, so Tim suggested I try publishing my work."

"Yeah, but get to the sexually boring part of the story," Rachel said.

"I had a rough pregnancy, which wasn't conducive to intimate relations. Afterwards, both Tim and I were exhausted with work, school, and a newborn. Our sex life was minimal and pretty vanilla. We didn't experiment much, if you know what I mean. When Joshua started school, Tim and I divorced amicably and co-parented. I dated a little, but only slept with one other man, and that wasn't for long. He wanted me to give up my writing and spend less time with my son. Like I said, boring. And it's not like I have a great body or anything. I've never been able to drop those twenty pounds from my pregnancy."

"Wait a minute. Didn't you say you were an author?" Ava looked at her, then recognition spread over her face. "You wrote those shifter romances, didn't you? Those weren't boring."

Talia smiled sheepishly. "I may be sexually boring, but I have an excellent imagination." Everyone laughed.

"You just haven't met anyone who has revved your engine." Rachel smiled. "I think the commander is just the one to do it."

"I'm not looking for a hookup, nor to prostitute myself, even for you girls." Talia stuck her tongue out at Rachel.

"Forget the Mata Hari stuff. Get yourself some hot dick, if that's what you want." Ava's face was flushed. "Who knows what will happen when we reach Costonia. You could end up with another Tim and you can only hope that you become friends. Do you want to give up the chance to experience something other than sexually boring? This might be your only opportunity."

Natasha tilted her head as she looked at Talia, a pensive look on her face. "I think that as confident as you are as a person, you're lacking confidence in your own body and sexuality."

"Body image crap we all deal with," Lin complained.

"Let's fix that." Natasha stood up. "Where's your nanosuit?"

"Uh, right there." Talia pointed.

"Put it on. Let's see what we have to work with."

"Oh, yes, let's do that," Rachel said.

"I think you girls are nuts." Talia shook her head.

"Come on, it's just us. If your ass looks fat, we'll tell you." Ava laughed, then burped. "Oh, excuse me."

"Okay." Talia stripped down to her underwear and picked up the nanosuit. "This looks too big."

"Just try it on," Natasha prompted.

"Alright. Here goes." Talia put on the one-piece jumpsuit. "How does this fasten? I don't see any buttons or zippers."

The women crowded around Talia, trying to help. When Rachel pressed the two ends near Talia's collar together, the suit sealed itself and adjusted to fit Talia's body.

"Oh, that's so cool." Ava grinned. "I just hope you can get out of it again when you need to pee, and you're going to need to pee soon with as much as we've been drinking."

Talia swayed slightly as she made a pirouette. "What do you think?"

"Woman, you look good!" Rachel's blue eyes lit up above her wide smile. "It really emphasizes your attributes."

"What she means is you look curvy and sexy—all woman. Strut and own it." Natasha smiled. "It's obvious that the Svesti don't have body image problems with that self-adjusting feature."

"I'm not sure your sneakers go well with it, though." Lin giggled. "You need leather boots to complete the look."

"Oh, I packed some booties! Let me see if I can find them." Talia opened a suitcase and held up black, ankle-high leather boots.

"I love those," said Emmy.

"Put them on."

Talia slid on the low-heeled boots, then posed with her hands on her hips. "What do you think?"

"Oh, that looks great."

"I love the look."

Talia waved her hand, holding the glass in front of her. "You ladies are good for my ego."

"A toast—To Talia, may you enjoy being a woman and not just a mom." Rachel lifted her glass.

"Hear, hear!" Glasses clinked and everyone drank.

"You do realize we still haven't decided what we're going to do," Talia reminded them. "What are our assets?"

"I'm a chef," said Ava. "I'm not sure how useful that will be unless I can find food that poisons Svesti."

"And I'm a botanist," said Lin. "Maybe I can find a poisonous plant to add to your recipes." Everyone giggled.

"Doctor here," said Natasha.

"Author slash ambassador here. And I know Rachel is in security," Talia said. "What about you, Emmy?"

Emmy hunched her shoulders. "Uh, I work with computers."

Talia said, "Work with computers covers a lot of things. What kind of work?"

Emmy closed her eyes and quietly said, "I'm a hacker."

Talia and Rachel glanced at each other, then back at Emmy. "Well, that just might come in handy." Talia smiled. "Why were you worried about telling us?"

"I'm sort of considered a criminal. I think that's why my government sent me."

"Bully for them," Rachel said. "What did you hack?"

"Maybe the question should be what haven't I hacked," Emmy said. "I've never stolen anything or used any information to harm anyone. Sometimes, if I come across something immoral or illegal, I leave breadcrumbs for the authorities to find it for themselves. For me, hacking something new is like climbing Mount Everest; I do it just because I can."

"Sounds reasonable to me. Hey, does anyone know if we can read Svesti with the translator implant or just speak it?" Rachel asked.

"I think we can read it now. I could understand the stuff on Rivezt's tablet when we were in the medical bay. It just didn't occur to me until now that it was in Svesti," said Natasha.

"Too bad no one is a hairdresser. I'm going to need a trim soon." Ava laughed.

"If we can find some scissors or a razor, I can trim and shorten it, but nothing too complicated," Talia offered.

"You've had training as a hairdresser?"

"No formal training, but I wrote a book once that had a hairdresser as my main character. I spent some time in a hair salon, researching for accuracy. They let me practice on wigs." Talia shrugged. "I know a little about a lot of things because I like to immerse myself in research for my characters."

"That sounds like it could be fun. You get to be someone different on a regular basis." Ava grinned. "Did you ever research how to fly a spaceship?"

Talia smiled. "The closest experience is a few hours in a small plane. Sorry."

"Rachel, can you teach us some moves? I mean, if you're in security, you must know some, right?" Ava asked.

"Sure. I'd be happy to."

"I know I'd like to know how to defend myself, but I'm so small," said Lin.

"Size doesn't matter." Ava giggled, her face flushed. "Well, it depends on what we're talking about."

"Haha. Before we get too drunk to remember, let's get back to our plan. I say we play it by ear for a few days, and get the lay of the land...or spaceship," Rachel said. "We need better intel before we make a plan. Damn, Ava, these cookies are good."

"My own recipe." Ava grinned.

"Okay, Ms. Security Advisor, what kind of intel should we be looking for?" Talia smirked.

"Let's see how they react today. Everyone act normally. We'll see if we can find out more about the Svesti on this ship and at large. Find out their beliefs and customs. Note if any of the Svesti are sympathetic to our plight. Anything we can leverage into something that will help us."

"That actually sounds reasonable," Natasha said. "I'll see if I can find out more about the Svesti medically. It may or may not help us, but maybe there's something to derail their plans."

Talia looked at Emmy. "If you can do it without getting caught, see if you can get into the Svesti systems. See what options we have if we need it. Remember, they're more technologically advanced than us. They may be able to track your activities better than people on Earth."

Emmy nodded, her shoulder-length dark brown hair swinging. "I'll cozy up to someone who looks like they'll answer innocent questions." She widened her brown eyes and spoke in an awed voice. "Oh, you big, strong males must have ways to notice intruders in your computers." The women laughed.

"Don't overplay your hand." Rachel smiled. "I have a feeling the Svesti are not used to women outsmarting them. We need every advantage we can get."

"Hear, hear!"

Chapter 7

VARED STOOD IN front of the door to Talia's quarters, where the trackers showed the females had been all day after the meeting. They'd even missed the evening meal. His tail flicked back and forth in short, jerky movements. He licked his lips and ran his hand over his hair, smoothing it. When he realized what he was doing, he snorted in disgust. *Just apologize and move on. They're females, nothing to be nervous about. You're a commander, for Goddess' sake.* He activated the chime to request entry and waited.

When nothing happened, he tried again. He heard muffled movement and a groan.

"What the hell is that noise? Make it stop," he heard one say. He thought it might be the tall one with the light hair.

"I don't know. Is it a doorbell?" Talia said.

"Well, answer the bloody door then."

"I'm trying. We should've paid more attention to the technology before we got shitfaced. Be quiet; you'll wake up everyone else."

"Let me see it."

Vared grinned at the conversation behind the door.

"I think you have to…"

The door slid open, and he hastily muted his expression. Ladies Talia and Rachel stood there with creases on their flushed faces and hair awry. Vared could see the other females in the living area—three on the couches and the tiny one curled in a fetal position on the floor, all passed out.

"Oh," Lady Talia said. "Commander Durek. What are you doing here?" She ran her fingers through her hair, red highlights catching his attention.

"I came to offer my apologies to all of you. Upon reviewing your complaints, I realized that our treatment of you was less than you deserved." Durek's head dipped slightly. "I ask your forgiveness and request that we begin anew."

"Well, that's a pretty apology." Lady Rachel crossed her arms and cocked her head.

Lady Talia inhaled deeply, then sighed. "I think it's an apology we should accept."

"You're right. Apology accepted, Commander." Lady Rachel nodded her head.

"Commander, I also accept your apology. I do believe that we need to address the cultural differences between our races to foster understanding and to find acceptable compromises. It will help in the future to avoid misunderstandings." Talia smiled.

"I thank you for your kindness. Do you believe I should apologize to the others separately?"

"We can pass it on to the others when they wake up," said Lady Rachel.

"I will follow your lead on this." He looked at Lady Talia. "May I speak with you privately?"

"Uh, I'm not sure this is a good time."

"Please, Ambassador. I won't take up too much of your time."

"Oh, go ahead, Talia. I'll stay here with the others." Lady Rachel pushed Lady Talia towards Vared.

He couldn't see the look in Lady Talia's eyes when she turned back to Lady Rachel, but when he saw Lady Rachel's mischievous grin, he thought it probably held annoyance.

"Very well." Lady Talia walked out the door. "Here in the corridor?"

"If you wouldn't mind a short walk, there is somewhere quieter we can speak."

Her eyes narrowed slightly. "Lead on, Commander."

"This way." He gestured and began walking beside her. "And when we're alone, you may call me Vared or Durek."

"In that case, you may call me Talia. Hey, are the walls a different color?"

"Yes, they begin brightening around the time of the morning meal, are lightest at the midday meal, then darken fully after the evening meal. We can also change the colors if we have the need for unspoken communication."

"Why would you do that?"

"If we lost comms and there was a hull breach and we wanted everyone to evacuate the area. Or in the unlikely event hostiles boarded us, we could adjust based on what would work best for our own stealth yet be detrimental to the enemy."

"Oh, that actually makes sense."

"We need to take the lift to another level." Vared pointed to a door.

Once inside, Talia said, "In my country, we call this an elevator, although others use the word lift as well. I never understood that. Both terms imply you can only go up, not down."

"I never thought of that. We've just always called it a lift." The doors opened, and he led them down another corridor. "In here."

Talia stopped inside the door, taking in the space. "This is amazing. All these plants." Her eyes widened as she saw the orange-barked trees lining the walkway, with rows of various colored plants spread out behind them. There were other plants organized on the walls, filling the space from floor to ceiling. "I never would have expected to see something like this on a space cruiser." Awe filled her hushed voice. Her wonder made his heart skip, and a warm feeling spread in his chest.

"This is our aquiponics area. We grow food and herbs in here. It allows for a healthier diet for our warriors as well as providing fresh oxygen for the vessel." They came to a large open area covered with blue grass. "Some of our warriors like to use this space to meditate or work on their training alone. There's a seating area on the other side where we can rest and talk."

"We must arrange a tour for the other women. Lin, especially, will probably spend all her time in here. She's a botanist—studies plants and their properties."

"Is that the tiny one?"

Talia laughed. "I think she would prefer it if you used the word *petite*, Durek."

Vared smiled. "I will try to remember."

The large bench was soft, and Vared relaxed as he sat next to Talia. "May I ask you a question?"

"Yes, you may."

"Why are you the only female wearing the nanosuit?" In fascination, Vared watched a tinge of pink rise on Talia's pale cheeks.

Talia cleared her throat. "Oh, the other women suggested I try it on so that we could see how they worked. The fastening was new to us, as was the self-adjusting feature. I forgot to change back into my other clothes."

"Why did you forget?"

Talia chuckled sheepishly. "Because we were drunk and angry at all of you. It was a pretty intense bitchfest." As her laughter washed over him, Vared's heart beat faster. He wanted more.

"Bitchfest? I don't know that term."

"Bitch can mean a number of things, but in this instance it means complaining. Fest is a shortened term for festival, party or gala."

"So you had a party complaining about the Svesti." Vared grinned.

"Yep. That's what we did. We also complained about men in general and about our governments. No offense, but it felt fantastic." She laughed again, eyes sparkling. *I see gold flecks glittering in the brown of her expressive eyes. How fascinating.* "I'll be honest, we've been very stressed today."

"I apologize again for my part in that. It seems human females differ greatly from Svesti females."

"Tell me more about Svesti females and your culture, please. Help me understand."

"The virus eliminated over eighty percent of our female population and rendered the survivors infertile. Even those who were breeding at the time and lived, if they had a female youngling, the youngling died within the first year."

"That's horrible."

"Yes. My mother and two sisters died from the virus."

"I'm so sorry, Durek. How old were you when it happened?"

"I was eleven solars." Closing his eyes, he leaned forward with his elbows on his knees, hanging his head. "It felt like all the light left our world. My father and I grieved for many solars." When he felt Talia's hand on his arm, a tingle ran through his body. He looked at her, knowing the sadness was still in his gaze.

Unshed tears glistened in her eyes. "I know there is nothing I can say that will make it better, but please know that if I had the words, I would use them."

His large hand covered her smaller one. He marveled at the smoothness of her skin, her paleness contrasting against his darker complexion.

"Thank you, Talia. I appreciate your kindness."

Talia gifted him with a gentle smile, understanding in her eyes.

Vared continued. "Our Svesti females have always been protected and revered even before the virus. For whatever reason, our birth rates averaged one female birth for every three male births."

"So no Svesti female warriors, huh?"

"Warriors protect and take life when necessary. Females are life-givers. It has always been our way. There have a been a few female warriors, but those were usually the females that were barren or preferred other females as partners."

"I'm glad to hear that the Svesti are accepting of non-traditional couples. It is not always that way on our world," Talia said. "Do your females have occupations?"

"Most have focused on their families. However, we have some who choose to have careers in addition to their families. Many of those become scientists or artists."

"Our cultures are very different." Talia pursed her full lips. Vared had to wrap his tail around his ankle to keep it from reaching for her. "Our male and female birth rates are basically equal. Our women work in just about every profession that men do. Some by choice, other because of financial difficulties."

"You have female warriors?"

"Oh, yes. I'm not saying we still don't have men who think women do not belong in careers such as law enforcement or the military, but women have fought for, and continue to fight for, careers that fulfill them. Some women are happy to stay at home taking care of their families, while others may work and have families at the same time. There are also women who choose never to have a family."

"Females choose not to have younglings? That concept is foreign to me. Our females long for motherhood."

"Maybe. Or maybe your females are the products of their upbringing and culture and have no expectation that they are allowed to want something different."

Vared frowned. "I don't know about that. I've never heard any female complain."

Talia patted his hand. "You may not have. That does not mean that your women haven't felt that way. Enough about that for now. Tell me about Vared Durek."

"What would you like to know? I'm a warrior and commander."

"Is your father still alive? Are you close?"

"Yes. He's a member of the Council on Costonia and manages our family estate."

"Are you married? Do you have children?"

"I have no mate. Most Svesti males my age don't because there just haven't been any females to court. And with no mate, I have no younglings."

"Do you want either?"

"I've spent most of my life believing I would have neither. As a warrior, either would be a point of vulnerability to be used against me. I'm not sure I would be comfortable with that." The warmth of her touch relaxed him even as his heart raced.

"On Earth, many men and women soldiers have spouses and children."

"I am not sure it is the correct choice for me. It hasn't been an issue as I haven't found someone I wished to take as my mate. What about you, Talia?"

She pulled her hand back and rested it on her leg. "Oh, I was married very young, and I have a son."

"You have a mate?" Vared's tail flicked sideways behind him. "And a youngling?"

Talia looked confused. "Didn't my government tell you that when they offered me up as a sacrificial lamb? I'm divorced now. My son is nineteen and in college."

"I do not know these words *divorced* or *college*."

"Oh, divorced means we decided to no longer be married to each other and are free to find another. And college or university means an institution of higher learning."

"So divorce is similar to when our breeding or troth contracts end, then."

"Oh, no. When people marry, the expectation is that it is until death and there may not be any wish for children. However, people change and grow apart or mistook their feelings for love and believe they will be happier apart. That's when divorce usually happens."

"I do not understand why your mate would divorce you. You are everything a female should be—intelligent, caring, passionate and beautiful." Vared's tail gently wrapped around her leg.

"Oh, that's sweet of you to say." Talia's eyelids closed partway, and she sunk lower on the bench, yawning. "Tim and I were best friends, and we made the mistake of experimenting with each other sexually. I got pregnant with Joshua, our son, when I was much too young. It took us a few years, but Tim and I realized we weren't meant to be lifelong partners, just good friends who happened to be co-parenting our son. He remarried a while ago to a delightful woman who loves him like a wife should love him. They're expecting their first child in a couple of months. I'm happy for him." Her mouth stretched again. "I'm sorry I keep yawning. It's not the company. I didn't sleep well last night worrying about traveling with aliens, and I'm still a little drunk. I'm barely awake now."

"Let me return you to your quarters so you can rest." Vared stood and pulled her up gently. He rested his hand against her back as they walked, enjoying her scent. His hard cock made walking uncomfortable. Outside her door, he said, "I enjoyed our conversation. Thank you."

Talia sleepily smiled and patted his cheek. "Your skin looks like fur, but it doesn't feel that way." She drew her hand back quickly. "Oh, that was rude. I apologize."

"No apologies necessary, Talia. You may touch me as you like." *Crek! What was he saying?*

"You know, Durek, I think I could like this version of you. Maybe he should visit more often. He's much less grumpy than the other one I've met."

Vared quietly chuckled. This female's soft and vulnerable side appealed to him just as much as her fiery side. He couldn't resist drawing her to him with his tail at her waist and his hands on her arms. He kissed her forehead, her skin branding his lips with her heat. "I'll keep that in mind. Now go inside and get some sleep. I'll meet with all of you again tomorrow."

"Good night, Durek."

"Vared."

"Huh?"

"Please say 'good night, Vared.'"

"Good night, Vared." *I like hearing my name on her lips.*

The door closed behind her, obstructing his view of her luscious ass in the nanosuit. *Crek. I should've walked behind her more.*

"Good night, *kirani*," Vared whispered as he balled his fists, willing his cock to return to a resting state. He did not want his crew to see him with an erection as he returned to his quarters. *She is not meant to be mine. My mission is to escort her to the Choosing, not bury myself within her wet heat. Control yourself.*

Chapter 8

I N THE MORNING, Brauvix comm'd Talia, stating he would escort the females to the dining area in one hour. She woke the other women with much moaning and groaning on their parts. Hustling them out the door, she went to the bathroom. *Oh, my. Svesti-sized bathrooms would be considered orgy-sized on Earth.* She gazed longingly at the enormous bathtub. *Another time. I wonder if anyone packed bath salts.*

Squaring her shoulders, she turned to the huge shower and played with the controls before finding the right ones to adjust the temperature. *Ahhh, hot water feels so good right now. I should not have had so much to drink last night.*

The women met Brauvix in the hall, and he greeted them with a pleasant smile. All of them had again dressed for comfort; most in jeans and sneakers with casual tops. As the group walked to the dining area, Talia lightly elbowed Ava and said, "You look how I feel."

"I hurt all over. I tried to get the synthesizer to make coffee, but it was awful. How much did we drink?" Dark circles marred the pale skin under Ava's eyes.

"Too much. I brought some coffee, but I haven't figured out how to brew it yet or I'd offer you some."

"Let's just hope that the food doesn't turn my stomach." Ava grimaced. "I really need some caffeine."

"I have some pain relievers in my quarters, if you'd like some. I should've thought to bring them to breakfast," Natasha said.

"Thanks, but I took something already."

"Rachel, don't you look chipper this morning." Talia smiled.

"Ugh. I may look fine, but I'm regretting the vodka." Rachel frowned. "My head hurts. I'm going to need to sweat it out later in a gym or something."

"Maybe we can do some light training after the tour. Emphasis on light. I don't think you need to be throwing us to the mats today or we'll barf on you." Emmy grinned.

"Let's not talk about barfing, please." Lin frowned. "I don't want to give my stomach any ideas."

"How are you feeling, Lin? You're the only one who slept on the floor. I didn't realize it until later, but the bed in my quarters is Svesti-sized. I think all of us could have slept in it if we wanted to." All the women laughed.

"Is your bathroom as huge as mine?" Emmy asked. "If not, you ladies are welcome to use the one in my quarters. The bathtub is to die for."

"I know, right?" Talia said. "I wish I'd had time to use it this morning."

Reaching the dining area on the level below, Brauvix said, "Would you females like to pick your own items or would you prefer to sit and I can bring over an assortment of food for you?"

Natasha said, "I'm good with an assortment. I wouldn't know what to choose." The rest of the women nodded in agreement before finding a table.

"I feel like a child," Lin said as she sat down. "My feet aren't hitting the floor."

"I know what you mean," said Ava. "Everything here is super-sized." Their laughter drew interested gazes from the Svesti males eating their morning meals.

"Females, may I introduce myself? My name is Grulen Jevax of House Midnar." A Svesti male with reddish bronze skin grinned, fangs showing. "Welcome aboard the *Invictus*. Your presence honors our warriors."

"Oh, my," said Emmy. "It's nice to meet you, Mr. Jevax." She pointed and named each of the women at the table.

"Jevax," Brauvix growled as he approached with a large tray of foods. "Do not bother the females."

"Lieutenant Brauvix, I only introduced myself." Jevax widened his brown eyes. "I was unaware that I should not do so."

"Nothing untoward happened, Lieutenant. Mr. Jevax was just being friendly," Talia said.

Brauvix nodded. "There are many nuances to Svesti behavior, Ambassador. It would be best to limit your interactions with the crew until you have been briefed or received an educational pack via the med bay."

"Hmmm," said Rachel. "Interesting. Have we accidentally agreed to something by exchanging names?"

"Hardly, Lady Rachel," Jevax said. "I offer my services to teach any of you whatever you would like to know about Svesti males." He spread his arms, palms open, and grinned widely.

Rachel looked at Talia. "Did he just...?"

"Certainly sounded like it, but then, who knows?" Talia shrugged.

"Jevax, enough! Do you not have duties this morning?" Brauvix stared at the other male.

"I am on my way, Lieutenant. Females, it was a pleasure to meet you." Jevax nodded and left.

"So, Lieutenant, what is this?" Natasha pointed to something that looked like a pale green pastry.

"You all may call me Brauvix. That, Lady Natasha, is *brellia*— a soft sweet pastry filled with *rumik*, which is meat."

"I've noticed that many of you use your last name, rather than your first names. Is that a cultural thing?" Rachel asked.

"We normally reserve our given names for family and friends."

"What about when you have more than one male from a family present? Or females?" Emmy bit into a *brellia* and hummed. "This is good."

"Females are addressed as 'Lady' and their first name, while males would have their title added to their last name. Titles are also used when someone wishes to infer a weight or gravity to their conversation."

"What is this?" Lin's hand hovered over a creamy yellow substance in a cup.

"That is *pertiza*; it is made from the milk of a *maxiem*. *Rumik* also comes from *maxiems*."

Lin smiled as she tried the *pertiza*. "Oh, it's like a sweet yogurt, similar to a pudding."

Brauvix patiently explained each food with the women trying it all. When they had finished, he said, "Would you like a tour of the *Invictus* before your meeting with the Commander?"

"Oh, that sounds wonderful." Talia smiled. "I spent a little time in the aquiponics area last night. Lin, you're going to love it."

"Could we see the kitchen before we go?" Ava asked.

"Of course." Brauvix led them there.

"Who does the cooking? Are there certain times when food isn't available in the dining area?"

"Warriors who enjoy cooking are cycled through the kitchen to help our head cook." Brauvix grinned and gestured to the large male chopping what looked to be a purple vegetable similar to an onion. "Talen Previv, if you have a moment, our guests would like to meet you."

Previv wiped his hands on his apron. "I am honored. I hope you enjoyed your morning meal." He smiled and bowed his head. Brauvix quickly made introductions.

"It was wonderful," Ava said. She began peppering Previv with questions and within minutes, the two had drifted off into their own conversation. Laughing, the women eventually dragged Ava away with Ava promising to come back to talk more with Previv.

Talia took special note of where everything was located on the tour and saw Rachel doing the same. They had to pull Lin away from the aquiponics area, Natasha from the med bay, and Rachel from the training area. Emmy intermittently asked questions about the computers and what they were used for onboard. All the women were in awe of the observation area looking out at space.

"We're really on a spaceship," Lin whispered. "Before seeing all of this, I could pretend it was a dream."

"Yeah, reality is just now hitting me over the head," Ava said.

"It is almost time for your meeting with the Commander. If you will follow me," Brauvix said as he ushered them out of the room.

In the War Room, everyone sat, and Vared apologized to the group.

"I would like to request that you report to the med bay for additional uploads," he said.

"What uploads are these?" Talia asked. *He really does have nice eyes. That color is so unusual.*

"Svesti court customs and rules, Svesti history, and so on. Things that will make it easier for you to become accustomed to our home world."

"Can we obtain uploads on subjects that interest us?" Natasha asked.

"Such as?"

"Well, in my case, medical knowledge, as I am a doctor, or healer, as you call it. I am unfamiliar with Svesti or other alien biology, medications, and treatments. I would like to know more."

"As a botanist, I want to learn about your plant life," Lin added.

"Before we get too involved in what's available, maybe we should ask if there are any adverse side effects to receiving the uploads?" Rachel said.

"Good point," agreed Talia. "And confirm that it is information only, without any personality-changing risks involved."

"Rivezt?" Vared nodded at his healer.

"We did not plan on any uploads other than the ones the Commander has mentioned. However, we can certainly put together any that might interest you; it will just take some time to tailor each one to your specific requests. The greatest risk is uploading too much information all at once. I would have to space out the uploads to ensure you would not suffer from debilitating headaches and pain. There should be no changes to your personality or beliefs from the uploads. I'd like to limit them to one per day per person. The uploads that we have already prepared will take five days to complete. That would also give us some time to work on the additional ones you've requested." Rivezt entered some notes on his tablet.

I guess I should take the lead. I hope I don't regret it. "I'll volunteer for the first upload," said Talia.

Rachel said, "I'd like to observe before I agree."

"As would I," Natasha added.

"I would be interested in learning how you put together the information for the uploads," said Emmy.

"Do you have computer lessons or books on plants that I could use in the meantime?" Lin asked hesitantly.

"I'm just going to hang out with Previv and get some hands-on time with Svesti food and spices." Ava smiled.

"I'm pleased that we're moving forward," said Vared. "Is there anything else you females require from us in the meantime?"

"Do we need to schedule time in the training area, or can we show up whenever we want?" Rachel asked.

"Why would you use the training area?" Vared frowned.

"Oh, Rachel is going to teach us some self-defense moves," Ava explained.

"You have no need for self-defense. That is what our warriors are for."

Talia crossed her arms. "Commander, we do not wish to be more of a burden than we already are, and it is an additional way for us to remain fit."

Vared grumbled. "I dislike it."

"You do not have to like it, but we're going to do it anyway. The question is whether we do it in the training area, the aquiponics area, or in our quarters." Talia knew her smile did not reach her eyes.

"There is a training schedule, but it is rare that the entire area is being used at any given time," Vared said with a frown. "I would ask that you inform Lieutenant Tolvex when you plan to use the area so that we may arrange supervision."

"Supervision?" Rachel said.

"I would like to ensure that our warriors do not bother you females."

Rachel looked at Talia, who nodded. "That's an acceptable compromise."

"It's almost time for the midday meal. Brauvix will escort you to the dining area."

"We'd like to use the training area in two hours, Commander," Talia said.

"I'll inform the Lieutenant," Vared said.

Talia looked at the women as they congregated in the training area on the mats. All of them were wearing some combination of sports bras, T-shirts, leggings, or shorts. Vared and Tolvex were standing at the side of the room, watching them. The Svesti training in other areas kept sneaking peeks at them. Despite all the males being stripped down to shorts and showing off some fine bodies, Talia's eyes kept finding Vared. *Geez. Look at those abs. And those legs, they're like tree trunks.* Involuntarily, she clenched her thighs, then she forced herself to pay attention to the lesson.

Rachel said, "Alright, ladies. Show me a defensive stance." The women looked at each other, then at the men, before standing in a variety of ways. Rachel came up to each woman, tapping them hard with a flat palm on a shoulder. Each woman tottered and fell back. Talia resisted the urge to rub her shoulder. *Damn, Rachel's strong.*

"Can anyone tell me why your stances didn't work?" Rachel asked.

"Uh, you haven't taught us anything yet?" Ava offered with a cheeky grin. The women laughed.

Rachel smiled evilly. "Oh, this is something you should already know. You. Are. Not. Men!"

Confused looks passed amongst the women. Talia said, "I think we need you to elaborate."

"A man's center of gravity is higher, near their sternum. Because you were unsure, you looked at the men in the room to see what they were doing, which will not work for you. Your center of gravity is lower, near your belly button. Your stance has to adjust to account for that."

"Well, that actually makes sense," Emmy said, head tilted.

"Let's try again." Rachel went around to each woman, giving hints and adjusting their bodies. "Really internalize how your body feels right now. If you are in the proper stance for your center of gravity, every offensive move you make will have more power, and you will be quicker with your defensive moves." She went around again, giving hard taps to each woman's shoulder. All remained in position. *Wow! She's right. It is easier to stay in place this way. I hope she stops hitting us, though.*

"This is the basic stance. Your center of gravity will move as you do. I'll eventually teach you some offensive moves, but my intent is that you will primarily learn defense to start."

"You're not going to teach us how to incapacitate an attacker?" Lin asked.

"Not yet. It is highly likely that you will be smaller than anyone who attacks you. Your best bet is to not be where they are expecting you to be. That's what I'm going to teach you."

A Svesti male approached with a cocky grin. "You think I couldn't catch you, female?" His two friends laughed.

Rachel's eyes gleamed, and she smirked. "You think you can take me?"

Talia saw Vared start towards them and Tolvex hold him back with a hand on his arm, speaking softly. She had confidence in Rachel's abilities, but the challenger was bigger than most human males. *I hope she knows what she's doing.*

"Yes, you are puny and defenseless. No match for a Svesti warrior."

"Ladies, move off the mat while I teach this man a lesson." Rachel made a come-here motion and grinned. "Alright, warrior. Let's see what you have."

The male reached for Rachel's arm, but she twisted and spun so that she was behind him. She kicked the back of his knee in a quick, concise movement. He grunted and rotated to face her.

You go, girl. Talia held back a smile.

Rachel continued to talk as she countered each of the male's moves by not being where he attacked. He showed increasing frustration after each unsuccessful attempt. "You see, ladies, a larger opponent is going to underestimate your abilities. Use your smaller size to your advantage. Keep him off balance while maintaining yours."

The male growled loudly and rushed her with arms spread to tackle her. Rachel dropped and slid through his legs, spinning to wrap her arms around his neck as he fell forward onto the mat. She squeezed to cut off his air as he tried to roll back over onto her. "You may want to tap out before you pass out."

A few moments later, the male tapped the mat and Rachel released him, jumping to her feet, facing the women. "You stay safest when you are not where the attack is." Talia's eyes widened as she saw the male get to his feet and attempt to grab Rachel from behind. Rachel maneuvered, pulling on his arm and twisted to toss him over her hip. He hit the mat with a loud thud.

"And always expect an attacker to fight dirty." Rachel grinned, sweat glistening on her face. She looked down at the male. "Had enough?"

Before the male could answer, Tolvex stepped forward and said, "I believe you have taught all of us a valuable lesson. That was impressive to watch. Rovex, Mantoor, and Sproid, get back to your own training."

Rachel nodded at Tolvex. "Thank you." She looked at the women. "Get back in your stances. I'm going to have you do different activities, then when I say 'stop' I want you to go immediately back to your stance."

"Why?" Natasha asked.

"Because you never know what you may be doing when you are attacked. We'll be building your muscle memory by learning to be ready at any time."

Rachel had them run, jog, dance, crawl, crouch, and more. Each time they stopped, she helped the women adjust their stances as needed. Talia noticed Vared and Tolvex talking quietly and occasionally pointing at them. An hour later, they were hot, sweaty, and sore. "That's enough for today. We'll work on it more tomorrow." The women groaned and limped away. Trailing behind everyone, Talia rubbed her shoulder. *My usual yoga routine didn't prepare me for this. I'm feeling muscles I didn't know existed.*

Chapter 9

"**I**S EVERYTHING READY?**" Vared watched Ash'n place equipment near a med bed.

"Yes. I'm just waiting for the females to arrive."

"Are they all getting uploads today?"

Ash'n shook his head, his ponytail swaying. "Only Lady Talia to start. The other females will watch and then determine if they wish to proceed today."

Vared's chest rumbled. "We have told them it is safe."

"This is all new to them. If you look at it from their perspective, they have little reason to trust us."

"I'm not used to my word being questioned," Vared huffed.

Ash'n smiled. "It is good for you, Vared. We cannot rush them nor demand their trust."

"I know you're right, but I don't like it." They turned to watch the females enter the med bay.

"Good morning, ladies." Ash'n dipped his head with a smile. The females smiled back at him as they offered greetings to both males.

"Females. I trust you are well this morning," Vared said.

"We are fine, Commander." Talia pointed at the bed. "Is that where you want me?"

Ash'n nodded. "If you would, Lady Talia. Just lie here and we can begin."

Once situated, Talia asked, "Is there anything I need to do?"

"No. Just rest and I will upload the information."

"What are you uploading?" Lady Rachel asked.

"The first upload is information about the primary houses of Costonia and early history of our race."

"Could you explain more about the process before you start?" Lady Natasha asked.

Ash'n held up a small instrument. "This does nothing more than hold the upload information which I insert like this." He placed a small data device into the instrument. "The translator devices I implanted into you upon your arrival have small ports in them which can receive data from an upload."

"So the uploads are like computer data chips?" Lady Emmy's brows drew together.

"In essence, yes. We transfer the data onto the upload from a special data terminal. When inserted into the port, the data transfers to the brain."

"Do you leave the upload in the brain?" Lady Natasha frowned.

"Not the physical device. Once the transfer is complete, the device flashes green and I remove the upload."

"Do you use the same upload for everyone?" Lady Ava asked.

"If you sanitize it, you can, but I choose to use new ones for every individual."

Lady Lin spoke quietly. "Does it hurt?"

Ash'n smiled at her gently. "The only instances of discomfort or pain is when too much information is uploaded at once. The brain creates pathways to file and retrieve the information, so we limit the amount of data at any one time. We do not wish to create undue stress on a being's brain."

Vared looked at the females as they silenced. They had thoughtful looks on their faces.

Talia looked at the women. "Does anyone have more questions, or should we start?"

Lady Natasha said, "Do you monitor the brain activity during the process?"

"Not usually. We've been conducting this procedure for almost a century. However, I can certainly do so if you would like me to," Ash'n said.

"Yes, I would like to see what happens from a medical standpoint." Lady Natasha crossed her arms.

Ash'n tapped several buttons on the console next to the med bed. A holographic image of Talia's brain appeared above her, with readouts about her pulse, heart rate and other medical monitoring data.

"Oh, that is handy." Lady Natasha grinned.

Vared smiled at her. "We do have some advantages with our technology."

"I'd like to learn more," Lady Emmy said.

"I'll have Tolvex arrange that," Vared said.

"Are we ready?" Ash'n looked at everyone.

"Let's do this," Talia said. "Do I need to close my eyes?"

"Whatever feels most comfortable for you is fine," Ash'n said. "Just turn your head slightly. Yes, like that." He inserted the upload.

Talia closed her eyes. "I don't feel anything."

"You shouldn't. It will only take a few minutes."

"Interesting." Lady Natasha pointed at the hologram. "I can see the neurons firing." She and Ash'n began speaking in medical terms.

Vared heard Lady Ava whisper to Lady Rachel. "That really is some fantastic technology. It reminds me a little of that old movie where they uploaded information to their brains, like how to fly helicopters."

Lady Rachel laughed. "I don't think this is a simulation, though." The females smiled at each other. Vared did not understand the reference.

Ash'n removed the upload. "You can sit up whenever you like, Lady Talia. You may be a little dizzy at first, so use caution."

Talia sat up. "I don't feel any different. Did it work?"

Vared spoke. "How many Houses are there? And how can you tell which House a Svesti belongs to?"

"Twelve." Talia's eyes widened. "And those tattoos on your upper chests, uh..." She frowned slightly as she paused. "clan markings—have your father's House emphasized with your mother's House overlaid in lighter lines."

"Cool," said Lady Ava. "Do they tattoo you at birth?"

"No," said Talia. "They are born with them; something to do with their genetics." She looked thoughtful. "That's so weird how I know all that."

"Guess they have little use for paternity tests," said Lady Rachel. The other females laughed.

"Now that you've seen the process, would any of you other ladies like to proceed with the upload?" Ash'n asked.

"I'll go next." Lady Rachel switched places with Talia.

Vared suppressed a grin as he watched each of the females receive an upload. After they left the med bay, he said, "It may take longer to do it their way, but it's much more peaceful."

Ash'n laughed and slapped Vared's back. "I think we all learned something new today. Changing the way we do things isn't necessarily a bad thing. I believe the females have much to teach us, just as they can learn from us."

Snorting, Vared said, "I have no problems with change."

Ash'n smiled and shook his head. "You have no problems with change you initiate, my friend. You're not as flexible if it's not your own idea—at least not at first."

"Is that how you see me?" Vared's frown pulled at his scar.

"It is not a criticism, Vared. Just an observation. I believe you have reasons for it, even if you may not understand them yet. You usually come around with time."

Vared chuckled. "Perhaps you're right, Ash'n. What is tomorrow's upload?"

"Court customs and protocol."

"The truly boring stuff." Vared grimaced, and both males laughed.

The next morning, a Svesti male entered the med bay with his nose bleeding. Finding no one in the room, he smiled. He entered the Healer's main office, calling Rivezt's name. When he saw the information uploads on the desk in a container, he leaned back on the desk and switched out one upload for the one he had hidden on him.

Shaking his head in mock disgust, he walked back into the main area, grabbed an absorbent cloth for his nose, and left.

I don't think they monitor med bay, but if they do, it should look like nothing more than me seeking medical attention and finding no one to help. The cloth over his face hid his smile.

When Vared entered the med bay, the females were each on a bed, chattering comfortably with each other. He did not see or scent Talia.

"I see you have help today." Vared gestured at the two healers speaking with the females.

"Yes. I asked Healers Markham and Sinoaz to assist to save time and have them become familiar with the females," said Ash'n.

They turned as Talia rushed into the med bay. Slightly out of breath, she said, "I apologize for being late. I lost track of time."

Vared barely heard Ash'n assure her she was not late. Inhaling, Vared enjoyed her unique smell. Her face was pink and her chest rose and fell with deep breaths. His eyes focused on those fleshy mounds and his hands itched to feel their weight.

With a mental shake of his head, he wrapped his tail around his ankle. "Is all well?"

"Oh, yes. I was writing and failed to set an alarm to remind me to be here." She shrugged. "I sometimes get lost in my work and become distracted."

"You could have comm'd Rivezt and taken your time."

Talia's eyes widened, and she licked her lips. "I didn't think of that. I'm still adjusting to the different technology."

Vared smiled. "No harm either way, *kirani*."

Talia's eyes flickered, and she looked away. "I guess I'll have to wait my turn." She turned back to Vared, her brows crinkled.

"Who are the other Svesti?"

Those are Healers Markham and Sinoaz." He pointed to each.

After Ladies Emmy, Rachel, and Natasha were finished, Talia sat on Lady Natasha's med bed for her turn, while Ladies Ava and Lin took the others. She smiled at the Svesti. "Healer Sinoaz, I presume?"

"Yes, Lady Talia. I will be doing your upload today. Have you had any adverse side effects from yesterday's upload?"

"No, I feel fine."

"That's good." Sinoaz smiled. "We can begin whenever you're ready."

As Talia leaned back on the med bed, Vared noticed Ash'n leaning over Lady Lin, speaking quietly and stroking her hand. *He must be calming the skittish female.* Turning his head, Vared watched as Markham began Ava's upload, before his eyes were drawn back to Talia. He admired her curvy body and suppressed a growl at the thought that other males were seeing her reclined and relaxed. Silently chastising himself, he watched as other females eventually sat up.

Vared's head whipped back to Talia when he heard her whimper as if in pain. Her body began to shake. "Rivezt!"

Everyone rushed to Talia. Panic filled Sinoaz' eyes. "It won't slow the data or disengage."

Ash'n engaged the health monitoring system as Talia's nose bled. Then she let out a long scream as her face contorted and her body stiffened, then convulsed. Vared felt his heart race. His tail whipped violently.

Lady Natasha said, "Holy shit! Look at that brain activity. It's like her entire brain is glowing. Her blood pressure is way too high."

Vared growled as he reached for the upload device. "I'll pull it out."

"No!" Ash'n yelled. "If you do, you could cause permanent brain damage." His hands flew across the control panel. "Everyone step back." The sides of the med bed began to rise while wires and monitoring devices began attaching to Talia's body.

"Tolvex. Med bay. Now," Vared said into his comm. He glared at the healer. "What are you doing, Rivezt?"

"I'm putting her into a coma. It's the only way to slow the progression of data into her brain without killing her."

The room was silent except for Talia's labored breathing. Slowly, her body calmed.

"Oh my God," whispered Lady Lin, tears running down her face. "What went wrong?"

"I don't know, but we will find out. This should never have happened," Ash'n growled.

Devik entered the med bay as Sinoaz said, "It's finally disengaging, Healer Rivezt."

"Good. Give it to Tolvex."

"What happened?" Devik's eyes hardened.

"There was something wrong with the upload for the Ambassador," Sinoaz said. "It transferred much too much data and the controls wouldn't work." His hand shaking, he handed the device and upload to Tolvex.

Ash'n tilted his head at Devik. "Use my office."

"I'm coming with you, mate," Lady Emmy said as she followed Devik.

Vared reached out and tenderly stroked Talia's face. "Will..." He cleared his tight throat. "Will she recover?"

His face grave, Ash'n said, "I believe so, but I have never even heard of this happening, Vared. We will have to monitor her brain activity and when it seems closer to normal, I'll try waking her up. Lady Natasha, do you have any insights?"

"No, this is outside my ability. All I can do is help you monitor and use what I know of human physiology to keep her from further harm." She frowned. "I've never seen so much brain activity. I have no idea what long-term effects there may be just from that alone. Fortunately, it seems to be slowing down."

Vared looked around at the other females, taking in their worried faces and tears. "Do all of you feel okay? Nothing unusual?"

The females looked at each other before confirming they were fine. Lady Emmy came out of Rivezt's office. She spoke with Markham, smiled tightly at him as he handed her something, and she rushed back to the office. Vared could see Devik and Lady Emmy's heads lower as they worked.

"Someone hand me a cloth," Vared said. Gently, he wiped the blood from Talia's face.

Ash'n spoke to the females. "You should go rest, ladies. Right now, there is nothing you can do for Lady Talia. I will contact you if there are any changes. Lady Natasha, I would appreciate it if you would remain."

"Of course," Lady Natasha said.

"Come, ladies. Let's go wait somewhere else and not distract the docs," Lady Rachel said. She glanced at Devik and Lady Emmy. "They'll find out what happened and let us know." She glared at Vared with a set face. "You will let us know what went wrong, won't you?"

He nodded. "Yes. There will be no new uploads until we understand what occurred and take steps to ensure it does not happen again."

"That's good." Lady Rachel nodded. "We'll check in later." Her face softening, she looked at Talia one last time before she ushered the other females out of the med bay.

"You should go, too, Commander," Ash'n said quietly. "I'll inform you of any changes in her condition."

Vared barely suppressed his growl and his fingers tightened in Talia's hair. "I don't want her to be alone."

"She's not alone, Vared." Ash'n's understanding smile did nothing to make Vared feel better. "Lady Natasha and I won't leave her. The other healers can handle any other injuries that come in."

Reluctantly, Vared removed his hand from Talia's head, and he stood. "I wish to know immediately about any changes, Ash'n." He walked towards the exit.

"Commander, wait." Vared turned at Lady Natasha's voice. "Look, Rivezt." She gestured to the med monitoring equipment. Ash'n frowned.

"What's wrong?" Vared strode back to the med bed.

"Put your hand on her head again, please," Lady Natasha said.

Vared brushed Talia's hair back from her face. "Like this?"

"See?" She pointed out something to Ash'n.

"That's highly unusual," Ash'n said.

"It's not as unusual for humans as you might think. There have been cases where the presence of someone close to the patient makes all the difference in their recovery. I think he should stay."

"What's going on?" Vared grumbled impatiently.

"It seems Lady Talia's bio signs are more stable when you touch her," Ash'n said.

"Really?"

"For as much as you two argue, I wouldn't have guessed it, but you are calming her." Lady Natasha smiled at him.

"Then I'll stay." Vared sat again, gently stroking Talia's face and hair. "Wurvez can handle the bridge."

"Rivezt, do you have different data sized uploads?" Devik asked as he and Lady Emmy approached.

Ash'n shook his head. "No, I use a standard size for all. They're faster to synthesize and it sets a limit on the amount of data that can be uploaded."

"Who else had access to the uploads?"

"Only the healers." Ash'n's eyes widened, then he clenched his teeth. "But early this morning, I was interrupted before I put them back in the secure area. There was that accident in the cargo bay and I rushed to get there. I left the container of today's uploads on my desk."

"Was anyone here when you returned?" Devik's eyes narrowed.

"No. The other healers didn't come in until after the morning meal and then the females arrived shortly after."

"One of the uploads was switched out," Lady Emmy said, her eyes flashing and her cheeks reddening. "Whoever did it knows enough about tech to try to hide the upload size behind a hidden partition. They also put some programming on there to cause the upload to freeze in the device and override a healer's manual commands to disengage."

"Did you understand what she just said?" Lady Natasha asked.

"I'm not sure," said Ash'n.

Lady Emmy sighed. "It's like this. Pretend Rivezt's office is the normal upload size. A quick check of the upload used on Talia shows that size and nothing particularly unusual. But now pretend there's a hidden door that opens up into the much bigger med bay. The extra programming and data was in that larger area with no one the wiser unless you know to look for a hidden area."

"So this was deliberate?" Vared concentrated on keeping his claws sheathed so he didn't inadvertently scratch Talia. His tail whipped furiously behind him.

"Yes," said Devik. "Were the uploads marked for the individual females?"

"No, there was no need. They were all getting the same information," Ash'n said.

"So it could have been any one of us who received that upload. Talia just happened to be the unlucky one." Lady Emmy's fists clenched. "Someone wants to hurt us."

"Do you know what was on Talia's upload?" Vared asked.

"It looks like Svesti law." Devik shook his head. "I'll have to check deeper to be sure, but it looked like all our laws and cases throughout the centuries."

"Oh, Goddess, no!" Ash'n looked shocked. "That is far too much information at one time. If I were planning to upload something like that for someone, I would have to spread it out over weeks."

"That explains her brain lighting up like a supernova," Lady Natasha said.

"We also have to check and make sure the information in the upload was accurate and not altered even more," Lady Emmy said.

"I had not considered that." Devik looked thoughtful.

"Tolvex, investigate and find who did this," Vared said.

"I would like to request Lady Emmy's assistance," Devik said. "I believe her talents will be useful."

"Lady Emmy requested earlier to learn more about our technology. If she is willing to help, this would be a good start to meeting her request." Vared sent a questioning look at Lady Emmy.

"That works for me, mate."

Devik growled. "Why do you keep calling people mate?"

"I'm from Australia; we call everyone mate. It means buddy or friend. They also use the term where Rachel is from."

"You're among Svesti now. Mate has a much more intimate connotation here. You may find yourself with trouble on your hands if you continue to use the word as you do." Devik gave Lady Emmy an angry look.

Lady Emmy crossed her arms and glared back at him. "I'll take it under advisement. Mate."

Devik huffed. "Come along, female. We have an investigation to conduct."

"Anything you say. Mate." Lady Emmy followed Devik out of the med bay.

"I think he just created a monster." Lady Natasha softly laughed. "Emmy's going to use the word incessantly now, just to irritate him."

The males smiled and shared a look between them.

Ash'n said, "Since you are staying, I would like to go through our archives and research any similar cases and discuss options with Lady Natasha. I may need to consult with a Master Healer on the home world."

Vared nodded. "Before you do that, contact the king on an encrypted channel and let him know what has happened. See if he has a preference for which Master Healer you speak to. He may wish to keep this incident confidential until we know more."

"It will be as you command." Ash'n gestured to Lady Natasha. "If you will come with me, Lady Natasha."

"I keep telling you to call me Natasha. We're going to be working together and there's no need for constant formality." Their voices faded as she and Ash'n walked away.

Alone with Talia, Vared leaned forward to kiss the soft skin of her furrowed brow. "I'm here, *kirani*," he whispered. "Rest now, I'll keep you safe while you heal. Take what time you need, but come back to me, please." He inhaled deeply. *The scent of her fear and pain is less, thank the Goddess.* He shifted in his chair and found a comfortable position and kept a hand on her at all times. "We'll find who did this, *kirani,* and he will pay dearly for causing you harm."

Chapter 10

TALIA HEARD NATASHA speaking softly. "I think she's coming out of it." Soft, indistinct murmurs filled her ears. *Where am I and why does my head hurt so much?* Her shoulders tensed.

"*Kirani,* can you hear me?" Vared's warm breath against her ear and the low rumble of his voice sent tingles down her spine. His hand stroking her hair relaxed her.

"Mmmm," Talia mumbled. She felt the heat of Vared diminish.

"That's it. Open your eyes for us, Talia." Natasha squeezed Talia's hand gently. "Can you feel this?"

Talia nodded her head slowly, grimacing. "Wha...what happened?" She tried to open her eyes, but, damn, it hurt.

"Welcome back, Lady Talia," Rivezt said. She heard the relief in his voice. "Is your head causing you pain?"

"Yesss," Talia hissed.

"That's to be expected."

"Please open your eyes," Vared said.

She finally pried her eyelids open and saw the three of them looking down at her with tired faces and concerned looks. She squinted at the light Natasha had pointed at her. "That's too bright, doc." Natasha turned the penlight off. "Can I have some water?"

Rivezt moved the bed so that Talia could sit upright. Vared held her drink for her while she sipped.

"Could someone explain what's going on?"

"What's the last thing you remember?" asked Rivezt.

Talia closed her eyes and thought back. "I was getting an upload and…" Her eyes opened wide. "Then the pain, so much pain." She shuddered.

Everyone frowned. Vared took her hand. "Somehow your upload was not the same as the ones the other females received. There was an enormous amount of data on it." His tail slapped against the floor.

Natasha said, "Healer Sinoaz was unable to manually stop the upload when he realized there was a problem."

"We put you into an induced coma to slow the data progression and alleviate the worst of the pain," Rivezt added.

"How long was I out?"

"It's been a full day," Natasha said. "Your brain activity returned to normal about an hour ago, so we brought you out of the coma."

"I lost a day?" Talia's shoulders tensed again. Vared's fingers began stroking small circles on her wrist. "What was on the upload?"

"Tolvex said all of Svesti law." Rivezt's normally pleasant countenance turned hard. "Far too much data."

"How did this happen?"

"Tolvex and Lady Emmy have been investigating," Vared said. "All we know is that somehow an upload was replaced that was intended for one of the females." His scar turned white against his face and his eyes looked deadly. "We will find who harmed you and endangered all of you."

She inhaled sharply. *Why does his anger look so damned hot?* "I don't understand why," Talia said.

"Not all Svesti are happy about human females," Vared said, his lips turned down. "There are those that would have the Svesti die out rather than breed with another race."

Talia's teeth clenched. "When I feel better, we need to talk about the use of the word 'breed'. On our planet, we use the word when talking about animals, not humans."

Vared's eyes lit up, and he chuckled. "I look forward to that discussion, *kirani*."

"I'd like to run some tests on Talia, both cognitive and physical, to ensure that she isn't suffering any lasting effects from the upload," Natasha said. "I think you should go get some sleep, Commander."

"Are you certain Lady Talia is okay?"

"I think there is nothing more you can do here, Commander. You should rest."

Vared didn't look happy. "If you need me, please comm me immediately." His body movements weren't as fluid as he left.

"Honestly, he looked like he was going to start stomping." Talia smiled. "Like he was having a tantrum."

"He hasn't left your side, Talia. You rested easier when he was here, so he stayed," Natasha said.

"He did that for me?" Talia wasn't sure how she felt.

"He did. Durek was very concerned about you," Rivezt said. "And he's furious that someone attempted to harm you females."

While they ran their tests, Talia was only paying minimal attention. She kept wondering about Vared's actions.

Personal Journal - Day 6.

Natasha and Rivezt finally cleared me to leave the med bay in time for the evening meal. I can't believe I spent a day in an induced coma. Fortunately, my headache has abated and I don't feel like total crap anymore. In this instance, at least, you can have too much information.

Emmy and Tolvex just left my quarters. Emmy says she's running a program against the law archives on Costonia, the ship's database, and the upload I received to ensure the data is accurate. She also wants to make sure the ship's database itself wasn't tampered with. She says it will take several days to compare all of them, but, so far, everything has matched word for word. I imagine that's a good thing. I'd hate to be using up brain space for garbage.

I can tell Emmy's pleased that she has so much access to the computers now. Tolvex seems to trust her skills, but he is definitely getting pissed that she keeps using the word mate almost every time she speaks to someone. I hope she realizes she's poking the bear. Tolvex might be a little smaller in stature and leaner than many Svesti I've seen, but he's in charge of security. He has to have some mad warrior skills.

Tolvex said they're going to put in some protocols for the uploads. For now, Emmy will observe Rivezt when he puts data on an upload and doublecheck each to ensure there are no hidden partitions or programming. Then they'll be under lock and key until it's time to upload them. Tolvex will check them one last time before the uploads are used. It sounds to me like the crew is taking appropriate precautions. I'd hate for anyone else to go through what I did.

Rivezt doesn't want me to get any more uploads for the rest of the week. I'm okay with that.

Personal Journal - Day 9.

The stress of the last week has started to lessen, and we're getting into a routine. We get up and meet for the morning meal, then head to the med bay so the other women can get their uploads. I'm still medically restricted, so I'll be playing catch up when I can receive them again. Even with the new precautions, I can sense that all of us, including the healers, feel a sense of relief each time an upload occurs without incident. My experience has left a mark on all of us. I admit, I'm nervous about getting more uploads.

Vared shows up for the uploads daily. The male would deny it, I'm sure, but he's just as concerned as the rest of us that something might go wrong. I'm starting to adjust to using the word *male* to describe the men here. I think the fact that all the Svesti impress me as more male than manly helps.

Anyway, after the daily uploads, we each take some time to do what interests us. Ava heads to the kitchen to help Previv with the midday meal. Lin spends her time in the aquiponics area. Natasha stays in the med bay. Rachel works with Wurvez to develop a training program for the Svesti. Emmy and Tolvex are still trying to track the traitor; they're not having much luck there yet.

I come back here to write. It dawned on me yesterday that the main love interest in my latest feline shifter series bears a striking resemblance to Vared.

I feel like the other women are finding their places among the Svesti while I'm in a holding pattern. Compared to the others, I have no special skills. There's nothing unique about me. I have no specialized training and I doubt I have much value as a fiction writer in this environment. Even my experience as a mom doesn't help—there are no children on the ship or even on Costonia.

Back to our routine. After the midday meal, we meet with Vared and other Svesti briefly to ensure we're all on the same page. Then we change, go to the training area, and Rachel works us hard. I know I'm feeling muscles I didn't know I had.

Then after evening meal, we women hang out together for several hours before the day is done. There's a bit of comfort in finding a routine. It gives a sense of normalcy to the whole situation, when there's nothing normal about being on a space cruiser with aliens who view human women as potential saviors of their race. I'm living it, but I still don't believe this is happening to me...to all of us.

In between it all, I'm confused about my attraction to Vared. When we argue, I want him. When he's sweet and caring, I want him. When he's a total moron, I want to dope slap him, then hug him. I'm afraid that if I let him into my heart, even a little, it'll destroy me once he realizes I'm nothing special. I mean, the Svesti have been without females for decades. Any port in a storm, right? But the relationship can go nowhere in the long term because I have every intention of going back to Earth.

I miss talking with my sister. She'd help me get my head on straight. And I miss Joshua. It was hard enough when my baby boy left for college, but now I'm literally light years away from him. I hope he's doing well.

"I don't feel so good," Emmy complained, holding her head with her eyes closed.

"Me neither," said Talia. She swallowed hard and pressed a hand to her stomach. "I'm nauseous and have a headache."

"My vision seems blurry." Emmy squinted as she opened her eyes. "We should go to the med bay." She stumbled towards the door.

"I think you're right." Talia followed her unsteadily.

They held onto each other in the corridor, trying to keep each other upright.

"I'm so shursty," Talia said.

"Shursty?"

"You know, I need to drink shumsting."

"Oh, thirsty."

"Thaz what I zed."

Emmy stopped and stared in disbelief. "You have a purple monkey on your shoulder."

"Huh? Where?" Talia tried to turn her head, but the pain was increasing.

"Now it's a rabbit."

"We need a doctor. Lez go." Talia began stumbling forward.

"Ladies, are you okay?" Jevax approached them with a concerned look.

"No, we need to get to…" Emmy looked at Talia in confusion. "I forgot."

"Doctor." Talia said. "My heart's beating too fasht."

"Your eyes look almost black and your skin is pale and wet." Jevax put an arm around each woman's waist. "Hold on to me. I'll get you to med bay."

Talia and Emmy clumsily wrapped their arms around his neck as he lifted them off the floor and began running to the med bay. Talia's stomach roiled with the movement. "Gonna be shtick," she mumbled.

"Me, too." Emmy's eyes closed and her head bounced as she lost consciousness.

"Oh, Goddess, stay with me, ladies," Jevax said. They met Vared in the corridor.

"What is going on, Jevax?" Vared growled.

"I don't know. I'm trying to get them to the med bay."

Talia's head felt heavy when she tried to lift it. "Vared." She reached for him with leaden arms. *He'll make it better.* "I think Emmy pashed out."

Vared grabbed her gently. "I'll help. Let's go, Jevax."

Her nose buried itself in the crook of his neck. "You're so warm and you smell good."

The males ran into the med bay. "Rivezt!" Talia squeezed her eyes shut as Vared's shout reverberated in her brain.

Rivezt and Natasha rushed from the office. Talia smiled weakly, "Hi. I'm shursty."

Natasha's brow furrowed. "Okay, what else is wrong?" She pointed and began examining Talia as Vared settled her on the bed. Rivezt was doing the same to Emmy when Jevax laid her down.

"Head hurtz. Schtomach. Eyesth." Talia sucked in a breath. "Heart beating fasht."

"When did this start?"

Talia waved weakly. "A little while ago. Both of ush. Where'sh the monkey?"

"Monkey?" Natasha looked confused.

"Or maybe a bunny. Emmy saw it. It wazh purple."

"Ohhh...kay," Natasha replied with concern.

Jevax spoke up. "The ladies were stumbling in the corridor when I found them."

Rivezt and Natasha spoke quietly. Natasha said, "We'll need bloodwork, but it looks like they've been poisoned."

Vared said, "Poisoned? How?" He held Talia's hand, and she closed her eyes.

"I don't know. But from their symptoms and our examinations, they appear to have anticholinergic syndrome. There's a plant on Earth that can induce it. It's called belladonna or nightshade. Maybe there's something onboard that has the same properties. It's rare. I wish I had access to the internet. I would like to look up successful treatment strategies."

Rivezt said, "We do have a copy of Earth's internet from when we left your world."

Natasha's voice rose. "Really? Let me see." Rustling and tapping noises echoed in Talia's brain. "Here. These are the active components and various treatments."

Rivezt said, "Let's start with this one. As soon as we know the females are stable, I can cross check the plant's components against Svesti flora and see if we have something similar."

"How were they poisoned?" Vared asked.

"I don't know," Natasha said. "As hard and as fast as they seem to be experiencing multiple symptoms would suggest they ingested it."

"Jevax. Locate the other females and bring them here. They may have eaten the same thing."

"As you will, Commander." Jevax's words were the last thing Talia heard before she drifted off.

Talia groaned. *My head hurts again.* Slowly opening her eyes, she saw she was in the med bay. *This is getting old.*

"*Kirani*, it's good to see you awake." Vared squeezed her hand gently. "Don't try to get up yet."

"I'm getting tired of waking up on a med bed."

"I'll bet," Natasha said as she and Rivezt approached. "Let me check you out. How do you feel?"

"Thirsty and like I've been run over by a bus." Talia saw the confused looks on the Svesti faces. "It's an Earth expression that means I feel awful."

"That's to be expected. You and Lady Emmy were very ill," Rivezt said.

"How is she? What happened to us?"

"She's still resting. Did you two eat or drink anything before your symptoms started?" Rivezt asked.

Talia scrunched her face as she tried to remember. "Emmy came by my quarters to give me an update and we decided to get a snack. We went to the dining area and grabbed some *pertiza*. We sat at our usual table and there was a bowl of mixed berries. They looked fresh, so we added some to our *pertiza*. We finished, cleaned up after ourselves, and were in the corridor when we started to feel sick. I know we were trying to come here, but I remember little after that."

"Excuse me," said Vared as he stepped away to speak into his comm. Talia heard him talking to Tolvex.

"And it was only you and Emmy?" asked Natasha.

"Yes, the dining area was empty."

"Your throat may be sore, and I'm sure you have another headache. We had to pump your stomachs. You have an IV to rehydrate you and we gave you something to counteract the poison." Natasha smiled gently before a light frown crossed her face. "It sounds like the berries you had were similar to Earth's belladonna."

Talia froze. "Nightshade? That's deadly."

"Yes. You both were very lucky Jevax and Durek came upon you and rushed you to the med bay," said Rivezt. "Please rest while we check on Lady Emmy again."

Talia closed her eyes and prayed for the pounding in her head to stop. She didn't know how much time had passed before she felt Vared's hand touch hers.

"*Kirani?* Are you still awake?"

"Yes." She looked at Vared and saw Tolvex standing beside him. "Is Emmy alright?"

Tolvex said, "She'll make a full recovery, just as you will, Lady Talia." His face hardened. "I questioned those who work in the dining area. No berries of any sort were left out today for anyone. We could not find the bowl either."

"I know there was a bowl on the table," Talia said. "I'm telling the truth."

"We believe you," Tolvex said. "You have no reason to lie or hurt yourselves. It seems the traitor left them for you and removed them after you left."

Talia sat up quickly, her head spinning. Vared reached to steady her. "Do you think it was actually berries from Earth?"

Vared said, "Rivezt will check to see if there are Svesti berries with similar properties, but we should have had nothing onboard that would be harmful to your species."

"I don't understand what the traitor wants. If he wants us dead, why not just kill us without all the subterfuge?"

"I'm not sure he wants you dead," said Tolvex.

"Explain," Vared said through clenched teeth.

"Lady Talia is correct. If he wanted the females dead, it would be fairly easy to do. No offense, milady." Tolvex dipped his chin at Talia.

"None taken."

"I think he wants the females afraid—very afraid. If they have months of constant stress and are fearful of Svesti when they reach Costonia, what kind of impression do you think they'd make at court for a Choosing?"

With a thoughtful look on his face, Vared nodded slowly. "You have a point. The nobles would see timid, fearful females and wonder if their offspring would have those same traits. It could cause the support for an alliance to diminish."

Talia couldn't resist. "So we just have to behave like we're terrified of Svesti and no one would choose us? That's one way to go, I guess." *Not that I'd do that. I'd rather fight to change the system. But maybe it's an option for Lin.*

"It's not in your nature, *kirani*, to behave less than you are," Vared grinned. "Someone would just have to anger you and you would show your true self."

Talia pouted as both males chuckled. *Assholes! I hate that he's right.*

Personal Journal - Day 10.

Another day spent in the med bay, this time for poison. I'm starting to think I should just set up quarters there. Tolvex stayed for a while talking with Emmy, probably going over new ways to find the Svesti who is doing all of this.

Vared and Tolvex think the traitor wants us women scared. We may not admit it to them, but the traitor's plan is working. Of all of us, Rachel is the one most likely to feel prepared for having her life in danger. These surprise attacks, seemingly from nowhere, have me on edge.

At the evening meal where Emmy and I avoided anything that remotely looked like berries, we decided to spend more time learning self-defense from Rachel. Emmy and I didn't do much more than pay attention while sitting on the mat. We were still feeling rough from our time in the med bay.

Hopefully, with enough practice, if the traitor comes for us directly, we'll have a chance of survival.

Chance of survival. What a depressing turn of phrase.

"Ambassador." Talia was just leaving the training area a couple of days later when Vared called out to her. "I would like you to report to the on-call room for a short meeting."

"Could I have a little time to clean up before the meeting?"

"Of course. Will an hour be enough?" *I wonder what he wants. Maybe they've learned something about the traitor.*

"That will be fine." Talia suppressed a moan as she walked away. *Bath, I need a bath. I hurt everywhere.*

Talia sank lower in the bathtub, moaning as the water's heat loosened her sore muscles. *Damn, Rachel didn't have to be so rough throwing us to the mats. I hurt all over.*

She washed her hair, then ran her soapy hands over her body to wash away the sweat. Her breasts felt swollen and tender. She imagined Vared cupping them with his large hands. Plucking her nipples and sliding her other hand downward, she reached between her bent knees. Rubbing her slick clit in slow circles, she relaxed. *What would Vared be like? Would he be tender? Or would he be forceful?* Water splashed as she jerked at the last thought, her moaning barely audible. *Forceful, oh, yes. Hard kisses, confident touches, and taking her hard and fast.* Breathing faster, she felt her orgasm swelling within her and searching for an outlet. *Just a little more. Oh, what would it feel like when he came inside her, hands squeezing her ass?* She shuddered with the pleasure emanating throughout her body as she imagined him pinning her down and growling out his own orgasm. Panting, she came hard. *Hell, if he's half as good as I just imagined, I'm in big trouble.* She stood on shaky legs. *No time for daydreaming, girl. Get dressed.*

Chapter 11

WHEN TALIA ENTERED the on-call room, the Svesti males sniffed the air and their bodies stiffened. Vared's muscles bunched and a low, menacing growl emanated in his chest. He glared at Devik, who smirked and relaxed. When his enraged gaze met Ash'n's eyes, his friend leaned back and spread his palms out in a non-threatening manner. Karid, the naroon, crossed his arms and chuckled. *Crekkin' male takes nothing seriously.*

"Everyone out. Now," Vared ordered.

The males grinned and bowed their heads at Talia as they filed out of the room. Vared stopped her with a hand on her arm when she went to follow them. "Not you, *kirani*." Hitting the lock button on the door controls, he said, "I want to talk with you."

"What is your problem? You call me down here for a meeting then get angry before we've even spoken," Talia said heatedly.

He glowered at her. "You pleasured yourself before you came here."

Her eyes flashed, and her face reddened. "What the fuck? Do you have hidden cameras in our quarters? That's just sick." She slapped at his chest.

"No cameras, *kirani*. I can smell it and so could the other males." Lowering his head, he leaned forward to take a deep breath. "Your scent is enticing, but a distraction for my crew."

A shocked expression crossed her face. "You're telling me that Svesti have an overly developed sense of smell? That would've been handy to know in advance." She crossed her arms and glared at him. "And your crew should have enough self-control to behave themselves if you live with your bloodhound senses all the time."

Vared looked down at her breasts lifted by her crossed arms. He licked his lips as he imagined his mouth suckling on her, marking her. "It's been a long time since any of our warriors have been around females, let alone those who would pleasure themselves without a male."

"Well, where I come from, women take charge of their own needs," Talia spit out.

Vared reached out and slid his hand into her silky hair, loosely pulling her head toward him. "I will be happy to take care of your needs, *kirani*," he growled. Slowly, his mouth moved closer to her plump lips, giving her the opportunity to refuse him. Instead, her eyelids closed, and she remained still as he caressed her lips with his. He started with short, gentle kisses to relax her, then tiny nips with his teeth, taking care with his fangs. He smiled against her lips when she reached her arms up around his neck as her mouth played with his. Licking the seam of her mouth, he drew back slightly. "Open for me, *kirani*. Let me taste you."

Triumph roared through him when her smooth tongue met his. *She tastes better than she smells. Closer, I need to be closer.*

He clutched and kneaded the globes of her ass as he lifted her body higher and deepened their kiss. A rumble sounded low in his chest when she raised her legs around his waist and pressed harder against him. Like a heat-seeking missile, his stiff cock rubbed up against her, prevented from its target by their clothing.

She leaned back and gasped, "Oh, my god. That feels sooo good." Their hips moved in tandem, and he swallowed her moans as he marauded her mouth again.

Talia broke off their kiss to rest her head on his shoulder. He grunted when he felt her open-mouthed kisses on his neck. Turning his head slightly to give her better access, he nipped her earlobe and neck. His tail slid between them to play with her hard nipples. His fangs elongated as he felt her rapid pulse against his tongue. *We can true mate with humans? We didn't know that was possible.*

Controlling himself, he growled in her ear, "That's it—your pleasure is my pleasure. Come for me now, *kirani.*" Raising his head, he watched her face flush and her body shake as her orgasm flowed through her. *Crek! I could watch her come all day long. So damned beautiful.*

Their bodies stilled, his cock hard and uncomfortable in his pants. Pulling her tight against his chest, he moved them to his chair. Sitting on his lap, she caressed his chest softly, head down. His hands now free, he rubbed her back and hair with long strokes. Enjoying the feel of her in his arms and her warmth against his cock, he lightly kissed the top of her head. "Thank you for sharing your pleasure with me, *kirani.* It was beautiful to experience and watch."

She raised her eyes to his, cheeks red. "We shouldn't have done that, Vared."

"Are you embarrassed? There should never be embarrassment between us, Talia." He laid a hand on her cheek, stroking his thumb over her heated skin.

"I don't understand you. One moment you're angry, then you're sweet." She looked down. "You were upset about my scent around your crew, then you give me an orgasm better than any other I've ever had. I still have to walk out of here past them."

Gently, he raised her chin to meet his eyes. "But now my scent is combined with yours. No male will dare to touch you now."

Brown eyes narrowed. "Are you saying you marked me with your scent, like an animal pissing around a territory to warn off others?"

He chuckled at her analogy. "That's one way of looking at it. It's added protection for you."

"Are you planning to give 'added protection' to the other human women?" Her swollen lips thinned.

"No, I have no interest in any other female, *kirani*." Sighing, he rested his forehead against hers. "Truthfully, I shouldn't even have an interest in you. I'm tasked with escorting you safely to your Choosing." Grimacing, he said, "I will have to watch you choose another male." His arms tightened around her.

"I have no intention of choosing any male, Vared. My job is to be an ambassador, not a breeder, no matter what my government promised. My body is my own."

No, it's mine. "King Sovex is aware of the issues and wants to meet all of you before deciding what is to become of you," Vared growled.

"I'm not sure you're hearing me, Commander. No male, human, Svesti or otherwise, is going to decide what I will or will not do with my body and reproductive system." Anger infused Talia's voice and scent, and her body tensed.

"*Kirani*, please, let's just enjoy this moment without discord."

She sighed heavily. "What does *kirani* mean, anyway? You keep calling me that."

Vared's lips curved upward as he laughed. "A *kirani* is a large feline on Costonia. Sleek, beautiful and even-tempered until her pack is threatened. Then she's protective and vicious." His tail wrapped loosely around her waist.

Talia's shoulders relaxed, and a slight smile tipped her lips. "Is that how you see me?"

"Oh, yes, wild and free with a dangerous streak. My beautiful *kirani*." He couldn't help but kiss her again.

"Enough, Vared." She pushed against his chest. "What did you want to speak with me about?"

"You're a cruel taskmaster." He grinned. "We'll be at Theron tomorrow morning. I'd like to request that the females wear their nanosuits, even if it's underneath their regular clothing. We'll take a security team down with us and you females can see the marketplace as we coordinate our resupply."

"Are you expecting problems?"

"No more than usual, but humans are more fragile than many other species and without natural defenses. While the safest option is to have the females remain onboard the *Invictus*, we have a long trip ahead of us. This may be the only opportunity for you to get off the ship until we reach the home world. We'll have some credits available in case any of you find something you need that you forgot to bring from Earth."

"That's surprisingly thoughtful of you, Vared." She gifted him with a wide smile.

"Grrr. Maddening female. I'm not a *naroon*." He nuzzled her nose with his broader one.

"What's a *naroon*?"

"A large bi-pedal mammal with blue fur that tends not to be serious in its family groups. They act like overgrown younglings, tangling and tussling."

Her laughter settled over him. *It's such a joyful sound.* "I'll have to remember that one."

"Do you think the other females will agree to wear the suits?"

"I'll talk to them. It's a reasonable request."

"Thank you. We should reach Theron soon after the morning meal."

"I'll let them know. I should go now."

Vared hugged her before using his hands to lift her by her waist so she could stand.

"We shouldn't do anything like this again, Vared." Talia waved her hand between them. "Our jobs—you delivering us to a Choosing we don't want and my role as Ambassador—are in conflict. Acting like this just confuses the issues."

"Did you not enjoy yourself, *kirani*? You said it was your best orgasm." Vared stiffened.

"I think it was obvious I enjoyed myself immensely. That's not the point. We are adults and should be able to control our actions. It's a distraction we don't need."

Vared considered her words and nodded. "You are correct. It is a distraction."

"I'm glad we understand each other. I'll see you later." Talia's smile looked forced.

Vared unlocked the door and watched her hips sway as she walked away. Licking his lips, he could still taste her. *I want her spread out underneath me, gifting me with all her pleasure. Crek! How do I resist her?*

Shortly after Talia left, Devik entered. Vared sat up and opened his eyes.

"Daydreaming, Vared?" Devik grinned.

"*Crek* you, Devik."

"She's meant for the nobility." Devik's smile dimmed. "Surely you can foresee all the problems if you continue on this path."

Vared ran his hand through his hair. "I know. I know. It just doesn't seem to matter when I'm around her."

"I'm here for you, whatever you decide, Vared. Not that my opinion matters, but I think she is good for you."

"Thank you, old friend. I wish I knew what I was going to do." Vared sighed heavily. "Perhaps focusing on work will help. What do you have for me?"

"First, I would like to ask Lady Rachel to conduct some training classes with our males."

"Teaching what?" Vared's brow furrowed.

"Techniques smaller, more agile opponents may use and how to counter them. She's been working with Karid developing a program. I've been watching her with the females; she has been teaching them well. And she made Rovex look like an oversized *naroon* that first day." Devik's eyes crinkled with humor.

Vared laughed. "She certainly did. It was good for him to learn some humility. I'll talk with Karid about the program. Once there is a plan in place, you can add the additional training to the rosters."

"How many warriors would you like on the security team for Theron?"

"I'm thinking one warrior for each female, while Previv and Volax can go together to arrange for the supplies we need."

"Are you going?"

"Yes."

"Me, you, Karid, Brauvix, and Jevax. Should I assign Ash'n or someone else?" Tolvex tapped on his tablet.

"The females are comfortable with Ash'n. Let's use him," Vared said. "If we can, I'd also like to have a porter lock on the females while we're on Theron. Just in case we need to extract them quickly."

"Okay, that will be taken care of. Now I'd like to show you the initial scans of XB9428B." Devik swiped and a hologram popped up above Vared's desk.

"Karid and I have been scanning for more than ship activity in the area. We modified the scanners to pick up ion and energy signatures. We're running heat signatures on the surface, but we're still too far away for any accurate readings, and we might not get close enough to get any." Devik pointed to a few sections on the hologram. "But if you look here, here, and here, you'll see the remnants of decaying energy signatures. We looked at them closely, and they're from the same vessel. The decay rate indicates that they go past XB9428B weekly, slow down, but don't land."

Vared pursed his lips. "Now why would they slow down, but not land?"

"We have a theory."

"Go on."

"The signature is from a Frezzian engine."

"Frezzians," Vared bit out. "Dishonorable beings who only care for credits." His tail snapped.

"Exactly. And they're averse to personal risk," Devik said. "While the surface of XB9428B is survivable, any water, flora, or fauna is in the mountains, not near where they slow down."

"What are you thinking?"

"Wurvez and I believe the lab may be underground in the desert area and the Frezzians are sending pods with supplies. The Frezzians may not even know who they're working for; it could be arranged without any personal contact."

Vared slowly smiled. "That is a good hypothesis. When is the next delivery scheduled?"

"We estimate in two days." Devik grinned.

"So we may be able to see it happening before we leave the area." Vared clapped Devik on the back. "This could be just what we need."

"Karid and I are now also scanning for that engine signature. We will receive an alert if it shows up anywhere near us."

"Very good work, my friend. Send me an encrypted report and I'll pass it along to King Sovex."

"As you will, Commander." Devik nodded.

"Oh, and ensure that the resupply lists are complete for Previv and Volax. We don't want to miss anything."

"Of course."

"The *Invictus* will be at Theron tomorrow. The females will be going to the station with a security team."

"Do you know what time? Will you be with them?"

"The shuttle will be leaving sometime after the morning meal. No, I will remain onboard."

"Good. Good. I will let our allies know."

"I must go now. Svesti always."

"Svesti always, Nephew."

Chapter 12

PERSONAL JOURNAL - DAY 14.

Oh, my...I'm so confused. How can he make me so damned furious and turned on at the same time? I've only known him two weeks and a future isn't possible. I have to resist him. Regardless of the Choosing (which I have no intention of taking part in), I'll be going back to Earth where my family is.

But with him, I feel like a sexy, wanton woman for the first time in my life. He made me feel better with our clothes on than I've ever felt naked. Can I do what the girls suggested? I'm afraid my heart will get involved. What do I do?

Rivezt began giving me some of the uploads I missed. I'm not sure why Svesti fashion is so important, but at least now I know how to read the command badges on the warriors' uniforms.

Tomorrow we reach the space station, Theron. I wonder how many species of aliens we'll see. I'm alternating between scared and eager.

Hoping to see their approach to Theron, Talia walked onto the observation deck. The viewscreen encompassed most of one wall. With the internal lights dimmed, the vastness of space interspersed with stars drew Talia closer. She tentatively touched the viewscreen, marveling at the texture. While clear, it was not glass or plastic. Smooth like metal, but cool to the touch. *There must be some technology that warms the material. Otherwise, my fingers would freeze and fall off with the vacuum of space on the other side.*

She heard the swoosh of the door behind her.

"It's impressive, isn't it?" Vared asked.

"Yes."

"I sometimes come here when I want to be alone with my thoughts. Should I leave?"

"No, I'm fine. Was there something you wanted? Or did you want to be alone now? I can go." Turning her head to look at him, she found herself captured by his eyes. The lavender had deepened to dark amethyst surrounding his dilated pupils.

"Turn around," he growled.

Slowly, she rotated her body, leaning back against the viewscreen.

"You didn't answer my questions."

He leaned forward and placed his hands on the viewscreen, trapping her head. *Don't touch, Talia. Don't touch his golden bronze perfect body or his luscious dark hair. Keep your hands to yourself.* Clenching her fists, she rested them on her thighs.

Placing his mouth near her ear, he whispered, "Female, you are an agent of chaos."

Shivery heat ran through her body at the feel of his hot breath on her skin. With difficulty, she kept her eyes on his. "I have no idea what you mean, Vared. And my name is Talia, not female."

"You come aboard my ship and almost immediately take me to task in front of my subordinates. You argue with me about almost everything. You make me worry about you dying with uploads and poison. You invade my thoughts until I can't concentrate. And your scent..." He sniffed her neck, causing her skin to tingle. "Your scent is addictive."

Talia shuddered. "We shouldn't do this. We agreed we have jobs to do and this will distract us."

"You are correct. This is a distraction."

He took her hands and pulled them behind her back. His tail moved up and held her wrists lightly, trapping her and pushing her upper body forward. He extended a claw on the forefinger of one hand and used it to separate her nanosuit slowly from her neck to thighs. His claw gently pulled the material aside, framing her cleavage.

Her breasts swelled as she inhaled. He smelled like dark decadence—cinnamon, nutmeg, and chocolate.

"I like this." Outlining the upper lace of her bra, his claw barely touched her skin. "It makes me think of a gift holding a wonderful surprise."

As his claw pulled the lace downward, her breasts pushed upward, nipples hard and seeking his attention. *Oh, geez, he's barely touching me and I think I'm going to have an orgasm. I shouldn't let him do this.*

A gasp escaped her as he tapped the top of an erect nipple with his claw. A searing path of pleasure traveled to her clit, and dampness flooded her panties. Vared closed his eyes and took a deep breath. "Your arousal smells delicious, female."

His tongue traced her areola, never touching her nipple, before he gave the other breast the same attention. Talia tried to move her breasts closer to his mouth, but he drew back.

"You're torturing me, Vared." Her ragged breathing punctuated the silence.

Abruptly he straightened and spun her so her back was to his front, keeping her hands trapped. He pressed his body into hers, forcing her into the viewscreen. When her nipples contacted the cool surface, they became even more engorged. His erection felt like a steel bar in the middle of her back, but her confined hands couldn't touch it. An involuntary moan fell from her lips.

"You've been torturing me with your very presence." His hot breath stirred by her ear. "This is payback, *kirani*." Tremors cascaded down her spine as his chest rumbled against her back.

His mouth and tongue explored her neck, sending quivers spiraling through her. Nipping her earlobe with a fang, he continued his mouth's path along her shoulder.

"Oooh, torture me some more." She leaned into his warm body. *Who is this woman who sounds so seductive? This isn't me. Is it?*

Vared smiled against her skin and his warm, callused hands cupped and lifted her heavy breasts. *Aaah, he must've retracted his claw.* His fingers tugged and pulled on her sensitive nipples.

"Do you like this, *kirani*? Feeling me surround you, strumming your body like a fine instrument so you make beautiful noises?"

"You know what you're doing to me. I'm just not sure why you're doing it. I don't even know if you like me."

"I'm not sure I like you either."

One hand ceased its ministrations and drifted lower—beneath her underwear. His fingers traced the outline of her sex, before one plunged into her while his thumb moved on her clit. Her body jerked toward him and her head fell back onto his shoulder. She couldn't help but move against his hand, wanting more.

"But I do love the sounds you make, especially as you chase your pleasure. You're wet for me, *kirani*, and so tight and hot." He added another finger, curling to stroke her inside and out. "Would you strangle my cock with your cunt? Mmmm...I'd stretch you wide, and you'd take all of me, wouldn't you?"

Gasping at his words, she moaned louder, her vocalizations mixing with the wet sounds he was demanding from her body. His hand pumped a steady rhythm and his mouth continued to kiss and lick her exposed flesh. She pushed against him, wanting more—needing more, chasing her pleasure just as he said. Then her body stiffened momentarily before shaking uncontrollably. She screamed, "Vared!"

Aftershocks shook her body, and he slowed his movements. Withdrawing his hand, he sucked her essence from his wet fingers, groaning. "Taste yourself on me," he ordered. "This is what I do to you."

Her head lazily turned toward him and her mouth reached for his. Their tongues dueled and she could feel the heat rising in her again.

They both froze when Vared's comm chimed. He rested his forehead against hers, and he shuddered. He lightly kissed her before he straightened and walked away to answer. Talia hastily fixed her clothing and rushed past him to exit the observation deck. *Why can't we control ourselves? I can't keep doing this.*

In the cavernous space of the hangar bay, the women looked in awe at the sleek, black spacecraft. Warriors were working on fighters and shuttles. Emmy said, "I just realized that this is the first time I've seen a real spaceship."

"Same here," said Rachel. "They just ported us onboard. I never saw the ship."

Vared said, "We'll take a shuttle to Theron and the *Invictus* will wait for us to return."

Talia asked Vared, "Why are we not porting to Theron?"

"The technology is newer and only reliable for up to three living beings at a time. I would like to ensure we all stay together. You also have to have the ability to scan the area you're porting to, so you don't port into a wall or someone else. Theron maintains a scan-resistant defense within its main areas."

"Oh, I'm glad you didn't port us into a wall. That would've sucked," Ava said.

"Or mix our innards with someone else's," Natasha added. The women grimaced, then laughed.

"Are all of you wearing your nanosuits?" Vared asked.

"Yes," they all said. Lin, Ava, and Emmy were wearing street clothes over their nanosuits.

"Thank you for indulging me," Vared said. "This is our shuttle here." He gestured to the females to enter first.

Onboard the shuttle, he introduced the warriors accompanying them. Ava sat next to Previv and began talking about food, while Natasha sat next to Rivezt, asking about medical supplies on the shuttle. Boots clicking on the metal floor, Talia took an empty seat near Brauvix, but he jumped up when Vared told him to operate the comms in the cockpit. Vared sat in the vacated seat.

"You didn't need to do that," Talia said. She squirmed in her seat.

"He should be in the cockpit with the pilots, not socializing with females," Vared said with a grunt.

"As the commander, shouldn't you be in the cockpit too?"

"No, that's one benefit of being in charge; I can delegate." Vared grinned.

Talia leaned closer to him and quietly said, "I thought we agreed we can't keep doing things like we did on the observation deck."

"Mmmm. I only agreed it was a distraction. I've decided I like some distractions." Vared's eyes gleamed. He reached over to fasten Talia's safety restraint and whispered in her ear, "I can still taste and smell you, *kirani*."

Talia flushed with heat. "Stop it, Vared. Whatever this is between us can go nowhere. I'm not mating or breeding with anyone. I will be returning to Earth to be with my son."

"We can discuss it at another time. This is not the place for it."

Talia growled and raised her voice to a normal level. "Oh, you started it, you *naroon*."

Glancing at Vared, Wurvez chuckled. "Did I just hear the ambassador call you a *naroon*? I didn't realize she knew you so well, Durek." He smiled at Talia. "I see you're learning the choicest insults from our language already. I knew I liked you." Everyone laughed.

"This is like being on a military transport on Earth," Rachel said. "No windows and seats backed up against the walls. Add in the smell of sweaty, dirty socks and it'd feel like home."

Talia grinned at her. "Feeling homesick?"

Rachel crossed her arms. She leaned back with one ankle over the other. "Not in the least. I'm thinking I might take a nap. How long is it going to take us to reach Theron?"

Tolvex said, "One hour."

"Definitely sleepy time for me." Rachel closed her eyes.

Talia closed her eyes as well, trying to relax. The warmth emanating from Vared seeped through her nanosuit and carried his scent. When he spoke to the warriors, his grumbly voice set off echoes in her body. *Damn! What is it about him that is so irresistible to me? I've never wanted any man like I want this alien.* She smirked to herself. *His bad boy appeal is off the charts.* She contained a silent sigh. *But when he's tender, he's amazingly sweet too. The best of both worlds. Too bad we both don't live on the same planet.*

Talia tried not to gawk as they walked to the marketplace from where they'd docked at Theron. The warriors' boots, as well as her own, clunked on the metal grated floors and the sound echoed off the ugly gray metallic walls of the wide corridor. The smell of fuel tickled her nose but faded the closer they got to the marketplace. An array of food odors assaulted her nose—some pleasant and enticing, others not so much.

As they turned the last corner, Ava said, "Oh, my god."

As a unit, the women stopped and took their first look at the marketplace. Stalls lined the walls as far as the eye could see, with storefronts interspersed between them. There were an additional four levels of walkways, stalls, and stores extending upward. It was a riot of color between foods, fabrics, and aliens. So many aliens. *Holy shit! I understood there were other species out here, but the sheer number is mind-boggling. And to think all of them space travel and this is traveling to the market for them.*

"I think I'm going into sensory overload," said Emmy.

"Is there any organization to this place or are we going to have to walk the entire thing?" Lin said.

"This is like the biggest mall combined with a flea market that I've ever seen," Talia breathed. "How many credits do we have to spend?"

The other women laughed. "Retail therapy day," Natasha said. "And we have big muscular males to carry our packages." The warriors looked at them in askance and the women giggled.

"Oh, this is going to be fun," said Talia. "What's first?"

"I'd like to see a weapons shop," Rachel said.

"Clothes." Natasha and Lin said together. Lin added, "And plants."

"Spices and food," Ava said.

"Tech," Emmy piped up.

"I think I'd like to see some jewelry and clothes. I wonder if they have souvenir shops like on Earth. I could get Joshua something." Talia smiled.

Tolvex looked up from his tablet. "There are shops on this lower level that have all that you've mentioned. The higher the level, the more expensive the goods."

"Lead on, warriors." Rachel smiled. "While we have lots of experience shopping, you have more experience navigating a space station."

Volax said to Vared, "With your permission, I will take my leave now and arrange for the resupply of the non-food items."

Vared nodded. "Let me know when you've finished and when the first deliveries are expected at the shuttle so we can return to help."

"As you command." Volax turned and entered a nearby lift.

At the weapons shop, Rachel made a beeline for the knives on display. Talia almost laughed out loud at the warriors. They were alert for danger but casting covetous glances at some weapons. The shop owner, a gray insectoid being about six feet tall, watched Rachel as she tested the weight and balance of various knives and daggers. Talia suppressed a shiver. *At least he doesn't look like a cockroach; those are truly creepy.*

She turned to say something to Vared when a hair comb in a display caught her attention. After Jevax helped Rachel haggle with the owner for two daggers and sheaths, Talia asked the owner about the comb. Out of the corner of her eye, she saw Rachel ask Wurvez a question before they left the shop ahead of the group.

"It is lovely, isn't it?" The owner pulled it out with a three-fingered hand to show her.

"Yes, but I'm curious why you have it," Talia said.

The owner smiled and said, "Look." He pressed the largest jewel and a short ice pick popped out of one comb's tooth. "This can be coated with a poison. It is popular with female aristocrats and assassins."

"You should get it," Rachel said. Talia hadn't seen her return.

Talia crinkled her nose. "I'm neither an aristocrat nor an assassin."

"Doesn't matter. It's pretty and even if you never use a poison, you can always use it as a lock pick if needed. We're not on our planet anymore. You never know."

"She's right," Vared said from behind her. "It would suit you as an adornment."

Looking up at him over her shoulder, Talia said, "I don't know that I need it."

"When you are at court, you will have many opportunities to wear it," Vared said.

"It really is beautiful," Talia wavered.

"Go on. Buy it," Ava encouraged.

Talia nodded, and Vared made the purchase for her. He handed it to her. "Try it on. I'd like to see it on you."

She grinned and inserted the comb into her hair. Laughing, she posed. "How do I look?"

"Beautiful, as always." His eyes heated. "Keep it on while we're here."

"I can always stab anyone who gets handsy."

"Now you're talking," said Rachel with a grin.

Their next stop was a spice shop. The owner was a purple humanoid with four arms. Talia felt a giggle rise. *Four arms! I could've used those when Joshua was a toddler.* Ava and Previv made a number of purchases, which Previv arranged to have delivered to the shuttle.

All the women got excited when they entered a fabric shop, immediately rushing to fondle some of the cloth. The shop's owner, a short birdlike creature with colorful plumage on its head, approached with a smile. "Hello, I am called Trillia. How may I help you females?"

"We're browsing right now," Natasha said. "Where we're from, fabric is sold in yards and bolts. I'm uncertain what measurements you may use." She and Trillia conversed with Trillia showing Natasha various accessories. Each of the women chose materials and Natasha added scissors, pins, needles, and threads.

"Can you deliver this to our shuttle?" Tolvex asked. Plumage waving, Trillia nodded and made the arrangements.

Talia grinned to herself. *I still can't decide if Trillia is a male or a female. I can't see any mammary glands or breasts, but birds don't have them anyway.*

In the tech shop, Wurvez and Tolvex explained various items to Emmy. Talia wasn't sure what Emmy had purchased, but Emmy's grin showed she was pleased.

"Can we browse the stalls a little?" Lin asked quietly. The women all nodded.

Seeing some jewelry, Talia stopped at one stall and admired a necklace with a starburst pendant studded with lavender stones. Across the way, Natasha, Lin, and Emmy were looking at some more fabric. To Talia's right, Rachel and Ava were at a food stall debating whether to try some fried confection.

"That necklace would look good on you," Vared said.

Talia smiled. "Thanks, but I'm just window shopping."

Vared's brow crinkled. "I do not see any windows for sale."

Smiling, Talia said, "It's an Earth expression. It means I'm looking, but not buying."

Vared smiled. "Oh, I understand now."

"I think I'm going to join Rachel and Ava and try whatever it is they're buying, though. I could use a snack." Talia walked toward the other women, but she never got there. A large orange alien with three bulbous black eyes picked her up, threw her over his shoulder, and began walking briskly.

"Let me go!" Talia screamed and pounded on his back with her fists. She heard Vared howl in anger but couldn't see him. She craned her neck to look up and saw five more of the orange aliens following them.

"Quiet, female," one hissed at her.

"No!"

He grabbed her hair and backhanded her. "I said be quiet!"

Talia's face throbbed, and the pain radiated from her cheek to her head. "NO! LET ME GO!"

"Give her a shot. We need to get out of here fast," one of his companions said.

The alien who hit her grabbed her hair again and injected her neck. Talia's world went black.

Chapter 13

WHEN TALIA WALKED away to join Rachel and Ava, Vared nodded to the jewelry stall owner. "I'll take that necklace."

As the owner handed him the wrapped package, Vared heard Talia scream, "Let me go!"

He saw a Durelian carrying Talia over his shoulder, with five more following. Vared's anger erupted in a loud howl. He scanned for the other women. Ladies Rachel and Ava were with Brauvix and Karid fighting off more Durelians. Jevax, Ash'n, and Devik surrounded Ladies Emmy, Lin, and Natasha. Previv was running to join Devik and Karid.

Vared tapped his comm, yelling into it as he ran to catch the Durelians who had Talia. "Port all the females as soon as you can. Track female one; I'm going after her. If you can get a good porter lock on her, transport her. Durelian mercenaries have her. Wurvez and Tolvex, get the females back to the shuttle as soon as possible if they can't be ported."

He saw a Durelian hit Talia. *Someone will die for that.* Enraged, he ran faster. She continued to yell and fight against her captor, then he saw her being injected and go limp. *No!* Once

Talia was unconscious, the Durelians increased their fast walk to a run toward the docks.

Vared unsheathed his claws and attacked one from behind, reaching around to slice his throat. All of them turned to face Vared except the one carrying Talia, who just said over his shoulder, "I'll get her to the ship. Take care of him."

The Durelians rushed Vared. He drew a knife from his harness, and he slashed at them, killing one immediately. One mercenary jumped on his back, wrapping an arm around his neck. Vared reversed his knife and stabbed overhead behind him. He heard one of the Durelian's eyes pop and a high-pitched scream. The Durelian's arm dropped. Fangs exposed, Vared spun to stab the Durelian in the stomach and pulled upward to disembowel his opponent. He turned back to the two remaining Durelians who were bleeding from the numerous cuts he'd inflicted. He slashed one across the chest with his claws and watched the mercenary drop.

Grabbing the last one by the throat, his claws piercing the Durelian's neck, Vared growled, "Where are you taking her?"

"I don't know," the Durelian wheezed.

"Why did you take her?"

"We were supposed to get all the humans if we could."

"What does your employer want with the females?"

"I don't know."

"Who hired you?"

"I don't know. Grolo handles the negotiations. I'm just muscle."

"Then you're of no use to me." Vared squeezed until he heard the mercenary's neck crack, then let the body fall to the floor. He saw the Durelian carrying Talia disappear into the airlock for Dock 269A. He howled in rage.

"Looks like Grolo will be hiring again." Vared turned to face a Jalaxian with dreadlocks near the airlock of Dock 267A who was speaking to another.

"Not sure why mercs keep hiring on with him. He has an unacceptable turnover rate." The second blue alien was cleaning under his fingernail with a knife.

Vared looked harder at the two as he approached them. "Are you the mercenaries with the Wing Raiders?" *I hope so. Your captain has an excellent reputation.*

The one with dreadlocks smiled. "Depends on who's asking."

"I am. If you are and your ship is nearby, how much to follow the ship leaving Dock 269A and get me onboard?"

"I don't know if we want the job."

Growling, Vared approached the Jalaxians. "How much?"

Nail Cleaner looked at Dreadlocks. "Oh, come on. You know you'd love to take on Grolo and steal his prize. Besides, she didn't look like she was consenting to go with him."

Dreadlocks tilted his head. "You've got a point." The Jalaxian started into the airlock of Dock 267A and motioned to Vared. "Well, move then, if you're coming."

They entered the *Fortitude*, the Wing Raiders' ship. Dreadlocks said, "I'm Yaz; that's Lezon." He yelled toward the bridge, "Let's go, Rain! Get out of the docking clamps and covertly follow Grolo."

A female voice yelled back, "Strap in, boys. I've been tracking them."

Yaz, Lezon, and Vared stepped onto the bridge. Lezon gestured to Vared to take a seat. Yaz took the chair next to the pilot, while Lezon sat next to Vared. They all engaged the safety harnesses.

Rain, a human female with light hair and green eyes, sat in the pilot's chair. "I'm going to head away from them until we're behind the station, then engage the cloaking and reverse direction to catch up. What's the plan after that?"

"I need to get on that ship and rescue my female," Vared said.

"You're human?"

"Yes."

"I imagine there's a story there."

"You betcha, Svesti. The woman we're rescuing, she's human too?"

"Yes."

Vared looked at the other occupant of the bridge. "I'm assuming you're Makai."

The large male nodded, his dark braids swaying. He had two white braids on the left side of his head. "I am. Why does a Svesti commander need the assistance of the Wing Raiders? You have a space cruiser in orbit."

"Vared Durek. Well met. And my cruiser is too unwieldy and too far away. I don't want Talia in the Durelians' hands any longer than necessary." Vared's tail whipped in hard, short flicks.

"Why do you have humans on your space cruiser?" Makai asked with a hard face.

"They are representatives from their respective governments traveling to Costonia." Vared kept the information about the Choosing to himself.

"They're with you by choice?" Yaz's voice could cut stone.

Vared sighed. "Did they look like they were under duress on Theron?"

Yaz and Lezon glanced at each other. "No."

"Then why would you assume they weren't with us willingly?"

"Because it is unheard of for human females to be in our part of the galaxy by choice."

"Are you here willingly, Rain?" Vared asked.

"Now I am. I wasn't when the Frezzians took me."

Another Jalaxian with part of his head shaved and braids, accompanied by a pink-haired human female, joined them on the bridge. "What's the plan for rescuing the female?"

"You were going to rescue her before I asked?" Vared said.

"Of course we were," Lezon said. "We saw her being abducted and had already communicated with Makai. We got a little distracted watching you eviscerate those Durelians." He smiled, fangs showing.

"It was beautiful to watch. A little messy, but beautiful." Yaz turned in his chair and agreed with a grin.

Vared could feel a growl rising in his chest. "And what were you planning to do with her?"

Makai stared at him with his arms crossed. "Give her a choice to return to the Svesti, remain with us, or join a settlement. We do not harm human females."

Vared's chest settled. "Thank you. It pleases me to know that if something had happened to me, there was aid going to her immediately." He directed a respectful nod to the group.

Rain interrupted. "If you're all done with the testosterone thing, Grolo's ship is ahead. It looks like he's headed for XB9428B."

Vared's head snapped to the viewscreen. Eyes narrowing, Makai asked, "What does that mean to you, Durek?"

Silent for a long moment before squaring his shoulders, Vared said, "I think there may be a Zuvgran lab on XB9428B." *Traxen isn't going to like me sharing the information, but the Wing Raiders are known to be honorable.*

"Shit," the pink-haired female said. "That's not good." She hurried to a console. "I'm scanning for signs of any Zuvgran."

Makai nodded. "Thanks, Kara. Crax, weapons on standby, just in case." The Jalaxian with the shaved head moved to another console.

"What do they want with human females?" Yaz growled.

"Can't be anything good," Rain said.

Makai's green eyes turned cold. "The experiments they do on all species are atrocious. I would like to destroy their labs."

"So would I. Right after I downloaded their data. The Svesti still haven't found a cure for the virus the Zuvgran unleashed on us."

"Do we rescue the female before Grolo reaches XB9428B or wait until they land?" Yaz asked.

"As much as I want the lab, Talia's safety and well-being comes first," Vared said.

"Goddamnit!" Rain exclaimed.

Everyone looked at the viewscreen. Two Zuvgran fighters appeared flanking Grolo's ship. "They must've been cloaked."

"We cannot board Grolo's ship covertly with those fighters there," Makai said.

"*Crek,*" Vared said.

Kara said, "I'm not seeing any more Zuvgran ships between here and XB9428B, but they could be cloaked."

"Rain, continue to follow at a safe distance. Kara, keep scanning. Check the surface for activity. Find out where they're headed on the planet. Yaz, I want a spot to land where we won't be kicking up sand and giving away our position. We'll need a stealthy way to approach wherever they end up," Makai ordered.

"I'd like to contact the *Invictus* on a secure channel," Vared said.

"Lezon, make it happen," Makai ordered.

"Do you need privacy?" Lezon asked.

"No, here is fine." Vared waited impatiently for the communication request to be acknowledged by the *Invictus*. They patched him through to the shuttle.

"Status," he said when he saw Karid's face.

"All females except the ambassador are onboard the shuttle with minimal injury to Ladies Rachel and Emmy. Mostly bruising. Lady Emmy had a few cuts. Rivezt has already healed them." Anger radiated from Karid. "Where are you, Commander?"

"I am with the Wing Raiders following the Durelian ship. It looks like they may be heading to XB9428B."

"We show the Durelian ship and two Zuvgran fighters. Are you cloaked?"

"Yes. We were going to board Grolo's ship until the fighters showed up. Now we are making plans for a ground rescue." Vared ground his teeth. "When I last saw Lady Talia, she was unconscious from an injection." He heard growls from behind Karid.

"Your orders?"

"When you are out of range of the planet or any Zuvgran craft, cloak and make your way to orbit XB9428B. Prepare a shuttle and a team for possible landing on the planet. See if you can get a porter lock on the female. If you can, port her directly to the med bay and let me know. If not, standby for further orders. I will coordinate more when the Wing Raiders and I have decided on a plan. Is her tracker still working?"

"As you command. We lost her tracker on Theron as expected, but never regained it as she left the station. The Durelians must have a dampening field." Karid frowned. "Are you planning to investigate the other matter while you are on the planet?"

"If we have to enter a facility to rescue the ambassador, yes. Otherwise, my only priority is the female." Vared felt an overwhelming need to reach Talia and ensure her safety, lab be damned. *I'm coming, kirani. Stay strong.*

"I can have an insertion team ready to go once she is safe." Karid's eyes gleamed in anticipation.

Vared shook his head. "No, Karid, if anyone is going to anger the king, it will only be me."

Karid's mouth drew taut. "Commander, I can solicit volunteers only. I dislike you being there without support."

"I appreciate it, Karid, but no. As much as I'd like to give Svesti a chance to take out Zuvgran, the *Invictus* crew is backup only. I will have the Wing Raiders for support. From the looks of them, they can hold their own." Vared looked around the bridge to see the Jalaxians nod in agreement.

"I dislike this," Karid grumbled.

"Your objection is noted. I will contact you again when we know more. Durek, out."

After Karid disconnected from the transmission, Vared sat in silence, trying to remain calm. Worry and rage consumed him. *Breathe. You'll do her no good if you do not think clearly.* His hands clenched and unclenched repeatedly. The voices of the Wing Raiders faded to the background as he willed himself to relax and find the cold, unemotional warrior inside him. *Crek. It's never been so difficult to push the emotions down before.*

"They're descending towards the planet," Rain said.

"Don't lose them. We need to see where they take her," Makai said. "Kara, do you see a facility of any type? Security?"

"No, not yet."

They watched as Grolo's ship landed on the desert surface. Sand blew around an enormous area, then a large hangar door opened up in the ground. A hoverdisk with six Zuvgran ascended to the surface. Four Durelians exited the ship with the still unconscious Talia carried over the shoulder of one. She was handed off to a Zuvgran. Vared's tail began flicking uncontrollably again. He wanted to growl as his claws extended.

"Mark that location, Kara," Makai said.

"Well, duh," said Kara, making a face at Makai.

"Just once, I'd like some respect from my crew." Makai sighed as another Jalaxian joined them.

"We respect you, oh great one." Yaz smirked. "We just like to keep you humble."

The Durelians returned to their ship while the Zuvgran and Talia descended back into the facility.

"Ideas on how to infiltrate?" Makai said.

"I don't think we'll be able to land anywhere in the desert without detection," said the newcomer.

"Tren's right. We'll be too exposed and their sensors will pick us up before we get there," said Lezon.

"And there's the question of how to open the door covertly," Yaz added.

"We have to assume that once we open the door, they'll know right away," Tren said.

"Kara, have you been able to get any scans from below the surface?"

"Minimal—there appears to be some sort of rock that interferes with my scans. But it looks like where they entered is a ship hangar and there's been little to no activity since the Zuvgran went back in with our girl. I can't tell the layout, but the heat signatures indicate they've taken her here." Kara tapped her console and a hologram of her scan appeared before her. She pointed to a spot a click north. "There are a lot of other heat signatures in that area, three that are stationary." Her face hardened. "There may be other abductees there already." Hisses and growls filled the bridge.

"If we get close enough, can you disable their security and open that door?" Makai asked.

"Absolutely." Kara nodded.

"I have a new toy I've been working on," Tren said.

"Tren is our engineer," Lezon explained to Vared.

"What is it?"

"It's a mini-jetpack/hoverdisk combination that works in atmosphere. I call it a hover jetpack. Kara could do her thing, while Rain gets us right over the hangar and we jump in with my toys. We could also travel distances quicker than running."

Yaz shuddered. "Have you even tested it? I'm not a big fan of slamming into the ground."

"Some. It's still a little jerky switching directions, but it should work."

"Famous last words," said Rain with a smile.

"Do you have enough for all the males?" Makai asked.

"Yes."

"Go get them. Meet us in the cargo bay so you can train us on the units. I'll make a final decision on whether we use them after I see how it works." Makai crossed his arms and glared. "I hope it works better than your weapon spinner. We almost lost Lezon to that one."

"It will. Trust me." Tren grinned. Everyone groaned.

Chapter 14

T HE THROBBING IN Talia's head and her dry mouth were the first things she noticed as she woke. *Did I drink too much again?* Unfamiliar voices in the background slowly filtered into her consciousness. Cautiously, she opened her eyes, squinting in the bright light. She tried to turn her head and realized she couldn't move because there were restraints over her ankles, wrists, stomach, and neck. She closed her eyes and concentrated on her breathing. *This is so not good! Don't hyperventilate. Stay calm. Figure out what's going on before you react. Be smart.*

Long moments passed while she worked to control the panic raging through her system. *What happened? The last thing I remember is...Theron. That's right, I was walking to get some food when those orange aliens grabbed me.* Her cheek echoed in pain as she remembered the backhand. *Bastard! Then he stuck me with something. I must've been drugged.* Her breathing sped up. *Breathe, Talia. You're alive; that's something.*

She opened her eyes again, keeping her lashes low. It felt like she was on a metal table. *Damn! It's cold in here. What the hell am I wearing? It feels like I'm naked under tissue paper.*

Adjusting her head, saw two gray beings in black jackets, but couldn't make out much from the harsh angle.

"I think this combination will work," a gruff voice said.

"Are you sure this is the one? We've had so many failures." The second voice sounded younger than the first.

"Yes, I adjusted for each failure. I can't test it on any of the other females because they're too weak from previous tests. Humans are so fragile."

"We must run tests on this female after we inject her to be sure."

"Of course. Then we'll drop her off somewhere where the Svesti can find her and wait for the virus to spread."

"They won't even realize there's something wrong until both Svesti and humans are rendered infertile. Unlike the last virus, there will be no illness or death, just lack of young. It's foolproof."

Oh, shit! Talia sucked in a breath.

"I think she's waking up." Talia closed her eyes and lay still. She heard heavy footsteps approach.

"The female is still asleep."

"Are you certain? We don't want her to have any memories of us."

She felt an icy finger poke at her arm and didn't react.

"She's still unconscious. You know human females always cry or scream when they wake."

"Yes, they are annoying. It is convenient that they are the only species capable of bearing Svesti young. We can wipe out two bothersome races at the same time."

"The humans will be a large pool of new slaves for us. How long do you think it will be before our Emperor will allow us to subjugate their planet?"

"I will not begin to presume to know what the Emperor's plan is. Neither should you." The gruff voice sounded irritated.

"As you say," said the younger one, chastised. "Is it ready?"

"Yes." Talia almost jerked when she felt a pinch in her arm.

"Heal the injection site. We want nothing to raise suspicions when the female is found."

Talia heard noises, then felt a warmth over her arm.

"Done."

"We will need to wait several hours before we can test her. Come, let us have something to eat while we wait."

Talia heard their footsteps fade and a door swish closed.

Fuck...Now what do I do? Talia opened her eyes and tested her restraints. Desperate, she wanted to pull and tug at whatever was holding her down, but she was afraid to leave marks for her captors to see. She didn't want them to know she was awake and drug her again.

The Svesti put a tracker in me. They'll come for me, but it sounds like I'm a danger to both our species now. Shit! Shit! Shit! What do I do?

Talia lay there, spinning scenarios in her head. *Will this virus still be infectious after I'm dead? I have to leave a note or something so they know. If I committed suicide, would the Zuvgran just take another woman and do the same to her? What if I escape and find somewhere uninhabited to live out my days? No matter what happens, I still have to warn both humans and Svesti. How do I do that?*

Her dread increased. *I'll never see Joshua or my sister again. I'll never find out where this thing with me and Vared could go.*

She felt tears welling up. *No crying. You can't wipe your face. Your captors will know you're awake.* With a strength of will she didn't know she possessed, she locked down her emotions and let her mind race, searching for a solution.

Talia didn't know how much time had passed before she heard the swish of the door and then new voices.

"What are you doing?"

"I want to see the human." Loud footsteps and the voice moved closer.

"We're not supposed to be in here. This one is protected." The second voice sounded like it hadn't moved.

"What a waste." Talia jerked slightly when she felt a large cold hand on her calf. She called on every reserve she had to keep from reacting further.

"You should not be touching her."

"I bet this female's cunt is hot and tight. Too bad she's asleep. I like to see the fear in their eyes when they fight." The hand moved higher. *Oh, god, no.* Talia felt as if her skin was crawling, trying to get away from that hand.

"If they find you in here, you know will happen."

"What are you doing in here?" The gruff voice from before was angry. The hand on her body squeezed her, then lifted.

"Just checking on the human." Arrogance laced that voice.

"That is not your job. You are prohibited from being in here. Get out."

"You scientists think you're better than warriors," the arrogant voice grumbled.

"We scientists are following the Emperor's orders, which are you warriors are not to interact with this human. If you disagree with the Emperor, state your objections to him."

"I'm going now, scientist." Heavy footsteps moved away, and the door swished.

"Damn warriors always thinking with their genitals," the older voice said. "At least it looks like he didn't wake her."

"Should we start the tests now?"

"Yes. Harvest several of the female's eggs and obtain some blood."

Through sheer force of will, Talia remained still when a needle pierced her abdomen and another pinched her arm. She felt the healing warmth again at both injection sites.

"Here," the younger voice said.

Unidentifiable noises pierced the long silence. The older voice said, "Look."

Rustling movements, then the younger voice said, "It looks like the eggs are dying."

"Exactly. It's working." Self-satisfaction laced the older voice. "Human females are born with all their eggs instead of growing new ones periodically like other species. This means we can kill all their eggs at once."

"And the Svesti males?"

"Let's look at the blood."

"The virus is in the female's blood and multiplying."

"Good. It is airborne, so if any human or Svesti breathes around her, she will infect them, and they will spread it as well."

"The Emperor may give you special recognition for this accomplishment." The younger voice sounded awed.

"I do not do this for the recognition, but for the advancement of the Zuvgran race." *Self-righteous evil prick.*

"Very noble."

"Even better, this female is to be presented to the Svesti court for a Choosing. We'll be able to infect all the Svesti leaders at the same time."

"Wasn't it a Svesti noble who informed us the human females would be on Theron?" *There's another Svesti traitor?*

"Yes, he thinks we are only rendering the females infertile. He does not know we've added to the virus to include the Svesti males."

"Ahhh, is that wise, if he's helping us?"

"If he's foolish enough to believe we would leave the Svesti alone, that is on him. We have made no promises."

"I see. How long do you think the virus will remain infectious in the female?"

"At least six months. That's what the testing on the other females indicates. Now that we know it works, this window of opportunity is too valuable to waste with more testing." *Other women have been here and experimented on for six months? They have to be rescued, too.*

"What do we do now?"

"Now, give more sedative to the female, and I'll arrange for Grolo to pick her back up. We'll disable his dampening field on a time-delay so the Svesti can find her with him. They'll kill him and his crew, rescue the female, and no one will know about our involvement."

"You have thought of everything."

"It is not difficult to out-think those weaklings."

Talia felt another injection in her neck and heard no more.

Chapter 15

A FTER TRAINING IN the cargo bay with the hover jetpacks, which involved all of them hitting walls or other surfaces hard until they figured out the sensitivity of the controls, Vared and the Jalaxians finalized the plan to rescue Talia. Rain would get the ship close enough for Kara to disable their security and open the hangar door. The Jalaxians and Vared would execute a high-altitude jump from the Fortitude using the hover jetpacks. They would remain together until they found Talia, then the Jalaxians would look for other prisoners. Rain would land the Wing Raiders' ship to collect them once they met on the surface. In orbit, the *Invictus* would be on standby.

"Come," said Makai. "Let's grab some weapons." The Jalaxians led Vared to their weapons storage. Makai tossed each of them a nanosuit. "We'll need these to counteract the cold of the jump." The males stripped to put the suits on under their clothes.

Tren passed out helmets. "For oxygen while we're jumping. I upgraded them with an internal display to show the location of the other helmets and heat signatures." He handed them bunches of small, circular discs. "Explosive charges to plant around the base to ensure everything goes boom when it's time."

"Nice," said Vared as he picked out some plasma grenades and tucked them into his weapons harness.

Kara walked up and handed them some comm devices. "For your ears. The comms will be on one of our encrypted frequencies." She showed Vared how to use it. "You'll be able to communicate with each other and us here on the ship."

"Thank you."

"Everyone, grab some of these." Kara handed out computer storage devices. "Plug these into any computer you find. I'll be able to download the data directly with no more action from you. When I'm done with each one, I'll set the self-destruct mechanism on it. It won't take out their computers completely, but it will keep them from discovering who took their info. Anything we get, I'll encrypt and send it to the *Invictus,* too."

"Once we're all clear, we'll destroy the base," Makai said. "Let us know when we're good to jump." Kara headed back to the bridge while the males went to the cargo bay to wait.

It was the middle of the night on XB9428B when Vared and the Jalaxians made the jump. Vared kept a firm rein on his emotions as the cold air whipped at him. Tren led the way and when he activated his hover jetpack to slow down, Vared did the same. Using gentle touches on the controls, they maneuvered over the bay door until Kara opened it.

"I'm not showing anyone in the cargo bay," Kara said in the comms. "I've taken control of the security feed. I'm running a loop now."

As the males dropped into the cargo bay with weapons drawn, they separated and planted some explosive charges before regrouping near a large doorway.

Kara said, "You're good to go down the hall. I'm searching the feeds for any humans now."

"Thanks, Kara," said Makai. He gestured to Vared. "Lead the way, Svesti."

Vared began running down the corridor. The Jalaxians kept pace with him.

"I'm showing no movement until the eighth door on the right. There are four heat signatures in that room. I think it's their security monitoring area," Kara said.

"Lezon and I will take that room," said Yaz with an eager grin.

"Quietly," said Makai. "No need to let anyone know we're here just yet."

"On it," said Lezon. He and Yaz slowed at the door, planting explosives, while the others kept going. As Vared ran, he ignored the muffled grunts and groans behind him.

"I show heat signatures in every room, left and right, but no movement. I think they're asleep. The rooms we originally thought might hold humans are still occupied. Keep going until I tell you to stop," Kara's voice said softly in all their comms.

"Kara, security room secured. We're plugging into the computers now," said Lezon.

"Data is coming in, guys." Vared could hear the smile in Kara's voice.

The males intermittently planted the explosives as they continued silently down the corridor. The end was in sight when Kara spoke again. "The next door on the left shows two heat signatures. It's the one I think your girl is in."

Vared retracted his helmet, sniffed and slowed at the door. "She's in here."

Makai nodded to Vared. "Do you want backup?"

"No, see if you can find other humans," Vared said.

The door slid open noiselessly, and he could barely suppress an angry howl when he saw Talia restrained on a metal table. A Zuvgran scientist with his back to the door was entering data on a computer screen. Wrapping his arm around the scientist's neck, Vared growled into the male's ear, "What did you do to her?"

The Zuvgran grabbed Vared's forearm, trying to loosen the pressure on his neck. He wheezed, "My finest work."

"What does that mean?"

"It means the end of the Svesti and human races."

"Be more specific, Zuvgran."

"No." The scientist grimaced. "Your timing is atrocious, but the plan will still work."

Vared used his other hand for leverage and snapped the Zuvgran's neck. As he let the body slide to the floor, he inserted a storage device into the computer in front of him. "Kara, I just inserted one of your devices into a lab computer. I've found Talia. She's unconscious."

"I've got the data coming in. Check on your girl."

Vared had already turned to remove the restraints binding Talia. He brushed her hair back from her forehead as he whispered in her ear. "*Kirani*, wake up. We need to get out of here." If her chest hadn't been rising and lowering slightly, her stillness would have made him think she was dead. His tail flicked rapidly. Her skin was cold as he rubbed his hands along her arms to warm her. "Talia, can you hear me?"

Her eyes slowly opened, and she smiled at him. She threw her arms around his neck. "Vared, you're here." *Thank the Goddess, she woke up.* They hugged tightly, then she began crying and pushing him away, "No! No! No! You shouldn't be here. Oh shit, you touched me."

Confused, Vared reached for her again, but she tried to slide away from him, almost falling off the table. He held his hands up. "*Kirani*, please be careful. I don't want you to get hurt. Let's get you to the *Invictus* and have our healer make sure you're okay."

Talia swung her legs down and put the table between them as she used it for support to stand. "No. We can't go to the *Invictus*. They're using me as a Typhoid Mary. And now you're infected."

Frowning, Vared said, "I do not know what they did to you, but you are not making sense. We must get you out of here and have Rivezt heal you."

"Listen to me! We can not go to the *Invictus*." Talia clenched her fists and stared at him with wide eyes. "They injected me with a virus that kills human and Svesti fertility. They planned to have someone come back and take me somewhere where you could find me so I could infect both our races. They said it was airborne, so you are probably infected now, too. We can't go near anyone."

Vared stilled and sucked in a harsh breath. "*Crek!*" He thought for a moment. "What about the other human women? Are they infectious, too?"

Talia shook her head, her hair comb winking in the light. "I don't think so. Whatever experiments they did on them did not work and they said the women were too weak to try this strain on."

Vared tapped his comm to the *Invictus*. "Wurvez, change of plans. Have someone bring the *Intrepid* to the surface while cloaked and port the pilot back to *Invictus*. The Ambassador and I will use the *Intrepid* to rendezvous with the *Invictus* so you can tow us. We have been infected with a virus and cannot risk contact with any human or Svesti until we know more. We will quarantine aboard the *Intrepid*."

Vared then spoke on the *Fortitude*'s comms while looking into Talia's eyes. "Kara, whatever you get from this lab needs to get to the *Invictus*. Talia and I have been infected with a virus and will quarantine aboard another ship the *Invictus* will send. If you find any other humans, Talia says it's unlikely they're infected, but it may be a concern. Makai, if you are unwilling to take them aboard the *Fortitude*, Talia and I will take them with us. I do not know what the effects may be on Jalaxians or if you can transmit it, but Talia informs me it makes humans and Svesti infertile."

"Who are Kara and Makai?" Talia asked.

Vared held up his hand to silence her as he listened to the comms.

Kara said, "Already encrypting the information and transmitting."

Makai grunted. "We found three human women, but two are already dead. The other says the scientists were angry that whatever they injected her with didn't work. Let me ask her what she wants to do."

Vared gently smiled at Talia. "We'll figure this out, *kirani*. Trust me."

"I do trust you, Vared."

"Well then, if I'm already infected, let me hold you for a moment." He opened his arms wide. *I need to touch you. Please let me take care of you.*

Talia's face scrunched, and she shuffled to him. They hugged tightly. She sniffled.

He stepped away and reached over his shoulders to grab his shirt by the back. He lifted it off, sliding it through his weapons harness. He tugged the shirt over Talia's head to cover her. "There. That should keep you a little warmer, *kirani*."

Talia beamed at him as she ripped the tissue gown off from underneath. "Thank you. This is much more comfortable and covers a hell of a lot more than what they had me in."

Makai said, "Durek, the human wishes to go with us for now."

Kara broke in. "I'm showing Grolo's ship just entering our scanning range. He appears to be headed this way."

"Grolo?" said Vared. "Why is he coming back?"

Talia said, "I heard the Zuvgran say that they were going to have Grolo come back and transport me. Something about disabling his dampening field when he was away from here so you could track and rescue me."

"Any way we can take Grolo's ship and make some credits on this adventure?" Yaz asked.

"Rain, hover close enough for us to get to you with the jetpacks. Wing Raiders, meet back at our ship. Durek, let me know when you're clear of the planet. Kara, has Grolo attempted contact with the base yet?" Makai said.

"No."

"Check for previous exchanges between the two. I have a plan, but everyone needs to be out of here first."

Vared lifted Talia into his arms and began running back towards the cargo bay.

"I can run," she said.

"I don't know what the effects of the drugs they gave you are and I can run faster," he said.

She snuggled into his chest. "Okay. I'll let you have this one."

He chuckled and nuzzled her hair. "Thank you."

"Wurvez, where's the *Intrepid*?"

"Just landing now, Commander. A half click south of the opening in the surface."

"I'll let you know when I'm there."

"As you command, sir."

Vared said, "Tren, can this hover jetpack carry two people?"

"It should, but I haven't tested it yet." Durek heard everyone from the Wing Raiders groan into the comms.

"I guess I'll find out."

"Who are you talking to?" Talia asked.

"I had a little help reaching you, *kirani*. I'll explain everything later."

When they entered the cargo bay, Vared said, "Hold on tighter." He pressed the controls for the hover jetpack, and Talia squealed as they rose. Instead of touching down on the surface, he maneuvered them with the jetpack to cover the ground quickly. "Wurvez, I'm approaching the *Intrepid*. Has the pilot ported back yet?"

"Yes. Activating the ramp remotely for you," Karid said.

Vared aimed them at the opening and touched them down slowly. "We're in." As the door closed behind him, he ran to the cockpit and set Talia in a chair. "Buckle in. We need to go." He strapped into the pilot's seat and set the *Intrepid* on course. When the shuttle left the atmosphere, he unbuckled and knelt before Talia. "I'm sorry you were taken. I should have stayed by your side."

She lightly pressed a hand to his scarred cheek. "It wasn't your fault, Vared. I'm just glad you found me before their plan could succeed."

He kissed her palm. "Did they hurt you, *kirani*?"

"Not really, but I was terrified they would realize I was awake and knew their plan." She shivered. "I don't know what they would have done to me then."

Vared wrapped his arms around her and rested his head on her lap. He whispered, "I imagined horrible things happening to you."

Running her hands through his hair, she softly said, "So was I. Thank you for coming for me."

He raised his head. "I'll always come for you." Vared tenderly kissed her. At first, the kiss felt bittersweet as their fears intermingled, but the heat between them burned it away, leaving only joy and passion. His hands cupped her head as he deepened the kiss, their tongues dueling. They broke apart, gasping. "Oh, *kirani*, the things you do to me."

Vared's comm interrupted them. With a sigh, he tapped the console and returned to the pilot's seat. "*Intrepid*."

Karid said, "The *Fortitude* is asking for a secure comm to speak with you."

"I'd like you, Tolvex, and Rivezt in the War Room on the comm with us," Vared said.

"Give us a moment."

Soon, a holographic image of the War Room's occupants appeared in the cockpit. "We're patching in the *Fortitude* now, Commander." Another hologram of Makai appeared.

"Captain Makai. I'd like to introduce you to some of my crew." Vared made the introductions. "And this is Lady Talia Sullivan of Earth."

Makai nodded. "Lady Talia, I am glad to see you safe."

Before Talia could answer, Devik said, "Commander, King Sovex is requesting to speak with you."

Vared snorted. "The male has impeccable timing. No time like the present to admit I didn't follow his orders. He might as well join us."

When the hologram of the king appeared, all the Svesti thumped their chests with their fists and bowed their heads. "Sire."

Traxen narrowed his eyes. "I see I have interrupted something, Commander."

Vared said, "King Sovex, may I introduce Lady Talia Sullivan of Earth, United States Ambassador of Planetary Affairs and Captain Makai of the *Fortitude*. Lady Talia, Captain Makai, may I introduce King Traxen Sovex of House Davelk, His Royal Majesty of Costonia."

After exchanging short pleasantries, Traxen said, "Report, Commander."

"We had an incident, Sire. We were just about to debrief and plan our next course of action." Vared's back was straight, and he looked the king in the eye.

"I see. Go ahead, then."

Vared explained briefly all that had happened. Then Talia told her story. When she got to the part about the Zuvgran warrior touching her, Vared's tail wrapped around her ankle with a gentle squeeze and he held her hand. All the Svesti growled loudly when she said that a Svesti noble had worked with the Zuvgran. He heard Kara's voice behind Makai. "Oh, wow, they're growling in stereo."

Makai informed them that before leaving the base, Tren had released a gas into the ventilation system to ensure that any remaining Zuvgran stayed asleep for several more hours. "We have a plan to take Grolo's ship and blow up the base, but we need your help to do so."

"What do you need?" Vared asked.

"Kara sent Grolo a message from the Zuvgran base stating that there has been a change of plans and they need to take four human women, not just one. The plan is that Grolo's people will be needed in the base to help transport stasis pods. She is breaking into Grolo's computers as we speak so that we can determine how many mercs he will have left on his ship once the majority of them descend into the base. My question is can you port three of us directly into Grolo's ship once Kara has the dampening field down?" Makai said.

Devik said, "We'd need to have trackers on your people."

Vared heard Tren say, "I can have those ready to go with the frequencies for you."

"Then all we'd need is the specific location you want to port to on Grolo's ship," Devik said.

"Once we have Grolo's ship out of the way, we can blow up the base," Makai said.

"I'd like the *Invictus* to take the shot," Karid said with a tight grin.

"Your Majesty? I know we weren't supposed to get involved with this base. However, I had no choice when they kidnapped Lady Talia. The Wing Raiders and I downloaded everything we could from the Zuvgran computers already. I would like your permission to destroy the base," Vared said. He held himself still as he waited for his cousin to answer.

"Commander, we will speak more about all of this later. However, in the meantime, proceed as you think best. Captain Makai, I thank you and your crew for all your assistance. Lady Talia, I am glad you are with us again. Our scientists will do their best to find a cure or vaccine against the virus. Contact me when the base is destroyed with an update on the search for the traitors." Traxen terminated his connection.

"Okay, since the king is gone, can I go all fangirl for a minute?" said Kara. He saw her pink hair, then her face appear behind Makai's bicep. "You're her, aren't you? Talia Sullivan? You wrote that dragon shifter series. I loved it!"

Talia smiled. "Yes, that's me. It's nice to see another human so far from home. I'm glad you enjoyed the books."

"How'd you end up out here as an ambassador?"

"That's a long story. I'd be happy to share it at another time."

Makai cleared his throat. "Kara, we really need control of Grolo's systems."

Kara blushed. "On it, big guy. Bye, Talia." She waved her fingers.

Laughing, Talia said, "Bye, Kara."

Makai said, "We'll contact you when we have more information."

Chapter 16

ONCE IT WAS just the *Invictus* and *Intrepid* on the connection, Rivezt said, "How are you both feeling? Any fevers, nausea, anything unusual?"

Vared and Talia shook their heads. "Beyond my face and jaw being sore from when the orange guy hit me, I feel fine," said Talia.

"There should be a small med unit on the shuttle that the Commander can use to heal it. I will also need blood samples from both of you."

"Have you received the info from the base?" Vared asked.

Tolvex nodded. "All the medical information has been given to Rivezt. We'll encrypt it all and send it to King Sovex. If there's a traitor, we can't let the crew know we're aware of the virus. How are we going to explain you and Lady Talia on the *Intrepid*?"

"Use me," Talia said, to her surprise.

"What do you mean?" Wurvez asked.

"Make it sound like I'm traumatized from my experiences with the Durelians and terrified to be around others. Durek was the one who saved me and he's the only one who can get near me without me freaking out."

"That might work," Tolvex said, his eyes thoughtful. "But why not bring the *Intrepid* into the hangar bay?"

"I panic at the thought that others could enter the ship without my knowledge."

"It makes you sound weaker than you are," said Vared with a frown.

"No one really knows me yet. And among humans, Post-Traumatic Stress Disorder or PTSD isn't considered as shameful as it used to be. A couple of the women might question it, but really, who among the Svesti would know any better how I might react? Isn't it to our advantage if they underestimate me?" Talia shrugged.

"She has a point," said Rivezt. "I can say that as a healer, for now it is best to allow her time to emotionally heal from the trauma as she wishes."

"The human females will want to speak with you," Tolvex said.

"We can do it via voice only. I don't want anyone to see me. It will allow people to imagine what might have occurred but offer no proof one way or another." Talia grimaced. "I dislike misleading the women, but I see no other choice until you've identified the traitor or traitors."

"I would like to consult with Lady Natasha about the virus. Her knowledge of human medicine is greater than mine," said Rivezt.

Talia nodded. "We should be fine if she knows the truth. She's used to maintaining patient privacy. And Rachel might be an asset for flushing out a traitor and can keep it under wraps. Emmy could help with tech stuff, but I'm not sure how well she could keep it all a secret. I just don't know her well enough yet to judge."

"I think it would be a good idea to have Lady Emmy help us. She is becoming very proficient with our technology and looks beyond the obvious," Tolvex said.

Talia shrugged. "I'm good with it if you feel comfortable. Vared?"

"If you think it's best, Tolvex, brief Lady Emmy at the same time as Ladies Natasha and Rachel," Vared said. "Impress upon them the need for secrecy."

"What do you need on the *Intrepid*? We can port some stuff over for the two of you," said Tolvex.

"Food and clothes," said Vared.

"If you could send over some of my toiletries and a few notebooks and pens from my quarters, I would appreciate it," Talia said.

"I will arrange for your supplies." Tolvex jotted notes on his tablet.

"Commander, the *Fortitude* is contacting us," said Wurvez. "I'm bringing them up now."

Makai appeared again. "*Invictus*, Durek, we're transmitting the tracker information now."

"Got it," said Tolvex.

"Kara's into Grolo's systems. There are only ten Durelians onboard his ship. We've sent a message that the Zuvgran require eight of them for transporting the humans. As soon as the Durelians descend into the base, you will port us inside the ship to take control. Once Grolo's ship is out of range, the *Invictus* can target the base and destroy it."

"Are you sure there are no humans left on the base?" Talia asked.

"Yes, milady. The only other human survivor is onboard the *Fortitude*. Our medic is treating her now."

"How far out is Grolo?" Vared asked.

"He's entering the atmosphere now," said Wurvez.

"We still haven't discussed payment for your aid in rescuing Lady Talia," said Vared.

"Your help in taking Grolo's ship is payment enough." Makai smiled. "And it never hurts to make new friends." Everyone laughed. "Ambassador, if you should require the assistance of the Wing Raiders in the future, we will do whatever we can to help you."

Talia dipped her head and felt her eyes tear up. "Thank you and your crew for all your help. It means a lot."

"It's showtime," Kara said. "I'm opening the bay doors now and lifting hoverdisks."

"I show eight Durelians leaving Grolo's ship," said Tolvex.

"Coordinates for the port?" Wurvez asked.

"Sent," said Kara.

"Good hunting," Vared said.

"Porting now," said Wurvez. There was a short pause before he said, "I show the Jalaxians onboard the ship."

They all watched as the Durelians descended into the bay and Kara closed the bay doors.

"We just dumped Grolo and his pilot on the planet's surface and are taking off now." Talia heard an unfamiliar voice say in the *Fortitude's* background.

"We see you," said Kara.

Several minutes passed before Talia heard, "We're clear. Have *Invictus* do their thing."

"Wurvez, destroy the base," Vared ordered.

"With pleasure, Commander."

Talia saw a streak of white light, then a large explosion on the surface. A gigantic cloud of sand and dust rose from the planet. When it cleared, she could see an enormous crater where the base had been.

"Direct hit, Commander. The base is gone." Wurvez grinned. "That felt good."

"Excellent. Makai, do you require anything else of us before we continue on?" Vared asked.

Makai grinned, fangs showing. "No, Durek, we're good here. We wish you well."

Transmissions completed, Talia's body shuddered. Drawing a deep breath, she unbuckled the safety restraints. "Where are my quarters? I'd like to take a shower." She turned her head away, hiding her face from Vared.

"I'll show you," he said, placing a warm hand on her back. They walked without speaking through the corridor and into a set of living quarters. "The sanitary facilities are in there." He gestured at a door inside the bedroom.

"Thank you," she whispered, head and shoulders drooping and hair covering her face.

"*Kirani*, what is wrong?" Vared gently lifted her chin.

She sniffled. "I don't want you to see me like this."

"Like what?"

Hot tears tracked down her face. "Small. Weak."

"You are not weak. Small in stature, maybe, but a giant in courage." He wiped the tears from her face with his thumbs.

"I'm not brave. They terrified me." She slapped his chest, then balled her fists and beat on his hard pecs. "They! Touched! Me!" She fought against his arms as he tried to hold her. "They injected me with something that could end both our races. And now you're infected, too."

"Shhh, *kirani*. You're safe now. I have you." Vared's powerful arms held her tight as she sobbed. His tail rubbed her back in soothing motions. When she was calmer, he led her to the shower. She zoned out as he started the water, took off his boots, removed his weapons from his harness, and dropped his harness in the refresher. Even as he undressed her, she felt disengaged from the world around her.

He took her hand and entered the shower, the hot water drenching her and running off his nanosuit-covered chest. Green blood dripped from his pants and swirled in the water. He turned her so her back was to his chest and washed her hair. She closed her eyes as his gentle fingers massaged her scalp. As he used a cloth to soap her body with care, his touch wasn't clinical, but also didn't feel sexual. More tears leaked from her eyes as his tender ministrations eroded the fog in her brain little by little.

She remained motionless when his hands left her, feeling the water wash away the shampoo and soap. She heard squishy splashes before he dispensed more soap and felt his movements as he cleaned himself briskly. He carried her to the drying tube where warm air surrounded them, ridding them of moisture.

"Arms up, Talia." Vared drew a clean shirt over her head. At the feel of the silky material caressing her skin, she opened her eyes. He was wearing royal blue lounge pants, crotch bulging. "Rest while I go check what the *Invictus* sent us. You should eat."

She nodded and admired his taut ass as he left the bedroom. She stared at the large bed for a moment before turning to enter the main living area. She curled into a corner of the large couch, noting the quarters looked similar to her own on the *Invictus*, but with only one sofa and a chair. Chaotic thoughts and worries tumbled in her mind while she waited for him. *Will we find a cure for the virus? If not, I may never be able to hug Joshua or my sister again. Where will I live? How do I live?*

Her thoughts quieted with Vared's return. He pulled her suitcase and two boxes off a maglev unit in the corridor and placed them inside the door. "All the non-food items," he said. "I'll go prepare some food."

She unpacked in his absence. She smiled faintly when she found her notebooks and pens, placing one of each on a table.

When he returned with a tray with two bowls of steaming yellow soup and a variety of finger foods, they sat opposite each other. The spicy soup's aroma tickled her nose, and she sighed when she took her first spoonful. "This is good. What is it?"

"*Shurlix* broth. *Shurlix* is a vegetable on Costonia."

"It tastes similar to Earth's tomatoes."

"I am glad it appeals to you."

While they ate, he explained each of the foods to her. Stomach full, she leaned back and said, "Thank you. I haven't eaten since yesterday's breakfast. I really needed that."

He frowned. "They didn't feed you?"

"I was drugged or pretending to be drugged the entire time."

Growling, he said, "They died too quickly."

She laughed softly. "I'm just glad to no longer be there." Taking a deep breath, she asked, "What do we do now?"

"I have to send our blood samples to Ash'n, then you rest."

She looked at him, seeing his concern on his face. "That's not what I meant, Vared."

"One step at a time, *kirani*. We don't have to decide it all right now. You're safe. We're quarantined, so the ship's complement is not at risk. We will find the traitors."

Talia rubbed her arms. "So, how do we take the blood samples?"

"It's easy." He found the instrument and looked at the writing on a vial. "This is for your sample." He inserted the vial into the cylinder and took her arm. "You center the tip over a vein and press the button."

She felt a small pinch, and a light turned green. "I'm assuming the light means it's done?"

"Yes." He changed out the vial and took his own blood sample. "I'll put the vials in a container and arrange for them to be ported."

While he was gone, Talia put their dirty dishes in the recycler and a wave of exhaustion hit her. She crawled into the bed but couldn't sleep. She felt Vared lift the covers and lay next to her, warmth emanating from his body and his unique scent filling her nostrils. Resting her hand on his chest and lifting her head, she said, "Thank you again for rescuing me and taking care of me, Vared."

He smiled and tucked her hair behind her ear. "It was my pleasure and honor, *kirani*."

She shivered at his touch. Leaning forward, she kissed him. The kiss began tenderly but quickly turned passionate. *Maybe I'm not so tired*. His hands caressed her back as their mouths and tongues explored each other. She reached down to squeeze his erection, and he broke off the kiss.

"No," he said, immobilizing her hand.

"No?" *What the fuck?*

"You need rest."

"It can wait."

His face tightened. "No, Talia. We're not doing this."

She stared at him in disbelief. "Fine," she huffed. "I certainly don't want you to do anything you don't want to do."

She rolled away from him onto her side, thumping her pillow. *He's been all over me for days and when I'm finally ready to give in, he says no.*

His hand hovered momentarily over her hip, before gently pulling her closer to his chest. His hard cock rested at the small of her back and his tail wrapped around her ankle. Her pillow absorbed her silent tears of confusion. *How can I be so angry at him, yet feel protected?* The rhythm of his breathing lulled her to sleep before she could find an answer.

Personal Journal - Day 17.

I've got a lot to process. The Theron space station was enormous and the variety of aliens was immense. Tall, short, thin, fat, humanoid, insectoid, birdlike, reptilian, mammalian, and more. Different colors and textures of skins, furs, scales, and feathers. I could go on, but suffice it to say, if you can imagine it, it probably exists somewhere in the universe.

All kinds of stuff for sale on Theron. Fabrics, foods, weapons, trinkets, technology. You name it, it's there.

If only that was all I had to process. Durelians kidnapped me on Theron and took me to a Zuvgran base where scientists injected me with a virus that is killing my eggs. I could probably handle that since I'm thirty-six and wasn't expecting to have another child, anyway. Although it should have been my choice. I am so angry that my choice was taken from me. But the virus is highly infectious and renders all humans and Svesti infertile. I overheard the Zuvgran talking about invading Earth and taking humans as slaves.

Vared and a group of Jalaxians, hot blue aliens called the Wing Raiders, rescued me. It seems the Wing Raiders have some human women in their crew. I'd like to hear their stories.

But now Vared is infected, too. He and I are quarantining on a shuttle right now, hoping there's a cure or vaccine that will allow us to rejoin the collective, so to speak. I have so many questions and concerns about the future, especially if they don't find a solution for the virus before we reach Costonia. I mean, it's not like we can be in the general population.

Vared confuses me, angers me, and turns me on like I've never felt before. He was so gentle and caring when I spaced out after my rescue. But when I tried to initiate sex, he turned me down flat. It seems, even out here in space, I'm still not good enough. My emotional baggage just keeps tagging along.

No matter how hard we tried, Krista and I weren't good enough to keep our father sober. I wasn't enough to keep Tim. Most men I dated didn't want me the way I am or with a child. I mean, it's not like I don't try to be a good person and do for others. But now that I'm damaged by this virus, it looks like Vared no longer wants me either.

So now I'm stuck in quarantine for an indeterminate amount of time with a male I desire, but who doesn't want me. I'm afraid to ask what else could go wrong.

Hell, who knew you could be horny and depressed at the same time?

Chapter 17

VARED WOKE BEFORE Talia. Eyes closed, he savored the feel of her warm, supple body pressed against him. His morning erection hardened as he inhaled her scent. Reluctantly, he slowly unwrapped his tail from her leg. Maneuvering so as not to wake her, he got out of bed, dressed after his morning absolutions, and headed to the cockpit to comm Karid.

"Report."

"All is well here. The supplies made it onboard, and we're en route to Costonia. Tolvex and I informed Ladies Rachel, Emmy, and Natasha of what is going on. Lady Natasha and Ash'n are working on understanding this new virus. How are you and Lady Talia?"

"We're fine." Vared frowned. "Have you had any luck finding out how the Durelians knew the females would be on Theron?"

"Not yet. Devik and Lady Emmy are investigating." Karid crossed his arms, his gray eyes somber. "We must have a traitor or traitors on the ship communicating with the home world if a noble is involved."

"I agree." Vared sighed. "I will contact the king after the morning meal, so if there is any more information that I can give him, let me know before then."

"As you will." Karid nodded, then grinned. "How will you spend your hours, Vared, alone on the shuttle with a female and little work to do?"

Vared's shoulders tightened and he gritted his teeth. "Enough, Karid. The female has just had a traumatic experience."

"Yes, and she will move beyond it with help. And you will be together for the foreseeable future. According to Lady Natasha, even if we neutralize the virus, Lady Talia's eggs are irreparably damaged, and it would be inadvisable for her to have young. It is unlikely that the nobles would want a barren female."

A growl rose in Vared's chest. "She is more than her womb."

"I agree. And we may not find a cure for your fertility either." Karid's expression reflected his concern. "It is quite obvious to those who know you that you are already attracted to her. Why not find happiness together?"

Shaking his head, Vared said, "I am a warrior and any female with me is at risk."

"Before the first virus, warriors had mates and young. Why is now any different?"

"I don't know." Vared huffed and clenched his fists. "It just feels different."

"Hmmm." Karid leaned forward. "Have you considered she is already at risk and will continue to be at risk simply because she is a human female? Is the risk of being with a warrior any more or less risk than she is in now?"

"Enough, Karid. I do not wish to discuss it anymore." Vared felt his eyes narrow. "Leave it."

"For now, my friend." Karid inclined his chin. "I will contact you when we have more information."

After disconnecting the comm, Vared sat back in his chair. Karid had no idea how difficult it had been not to take what Talia had offered last night. Despite every cell in Vared's body wanting her, he had behaved with honor and not taken advantage of her vulnerable state. He lowered his head in his hands, elbows resting on his knees. *What do I do? She makes me feel more alive than I have in solars, but I'm not sure that being together is safest for her. Even if she is no longer part of the Choosing, she wants to go back to Earth. I'm afraid that if I take what I want, I will never be able to let her go.* Drawing a ragged breath, he stood. *Maybe some exercise will clear my head.*

Breathing heavily, Vared walked towards his quarters, wiping the sweat from his face and chest. His muscles were limber after running through his training forms and punching a bag. He noticed Talia was not in the bed as he headed to the shower, although her scent lingered, making him smile. As he washed and dressed, he thought of what foods she might like for the morning meal.

Talia had just finished eating when he arrived in the dining area. She was wearing a loose T-shirt over black leggings.

Frowning, he said, "I had planned to feed you."

"It was no problem to make something for myself." She dropped the remnants of her meal in the recycler. "Thank you again for rescuing me yesterday, as well as caring for me when I went into shock. I appreciate it." Her eyes were dim as she talked. Looking away, she said, "I moved my belongings to other living quarters. I should be fine now."

Vared suppressed an angry rumble and his tail flicked. "You did not need to move."

She glanced at him sideways. "I think it's best. We may be stuck together on this ship until we reach Costonia. We should respect each other's privacy."

Vared grunted unhappily, his tail now snapping. "Is this really what you want, *kirani*?"

She flashed him a tight smile. "As I've said, I think it's best."

"As you wish."

"I haven't explored much yet, but this shuttle seems very different from the one we took to Theron."

Vared spoke as he gathered his own morning meal. "This is the commander's shuttle and used for official travel. We host nobles or visiting dignitaries, so it is less utilitarian than the combat shuttles."

"That makes sense." She sighed. "Is there anything I can do aboard the ship to help? There are a lot of hours to fill."

"Right now, not much. I do not know what Rivezt and Lady Natasha might require from us, but I cannot imagine it would be much more than providing various samples for them."

She frowned. "I can do some exploring and writing today, but I will need more things to keep busy. I'm not used to a lot of free time."

"Neither am I. We'll figure it out." *I know what I'd like to do.* He reached out to hold her hand, but she pulled away.

"I'll leave you to your meal." She hurried away before he could speak.

Confused, he finished his meal. *Females are perplexing.*

"Vared, how are you and the female feeling?" Traxen's eyes darkened as he looked at his cousin.

"Neither one of us is showing any ill effects from the virus. Rivezt and Lady Natasha have the data from the lab and are working to find a cure or vaccine."

"How is she doing?"

"As well as can be expected." Vared crossed his arms. "We are not telling the crew about this new virus. Wurvez and Tolvex have informed the crew and the other females that Talia is extremely fearful after her ordeal and only trusts me to be near her. It explains why we are on the shuttle being towed while we search for the traitors and a cure."

"Good. I have only informed those who need to know here, as well as your father. His connections may be useful for rooting out the traitors. Rivezt and Lady Natasha have sent their initial findings. They will be focusing on a vaccine to protect Svesti and humans from contracting the virus, so that you and Lady Talia can rejoin the *Invictus*." Traxen frowned. "They are not sure if a vaccine will return your fertility or if there will be problems with your future seed."

Vared grimaced, his scar pulling his skin tight. "We must come up with a plan in the event they do not succeed before we reach Costonia. We cannot take the chance that we might infect the home world."

"We are looking at options now. But we need to understand this new virus better before we can plan." Traxen clenched his jaw. "Cousin, I hate that this has happened to you."

Vared nodded. "I thank you, Traxen. But it is what it is."

"When our scientists find an answer, I hope to be able to return Lady Talia to Earth. Unfortunately, she will be unsuitable for a Choosing."

Vared flinched. "I see."

Traxen's eyes narrowed. "What is it?"

"Nothing."

"No, it is not nothing. What do I not know?"

After a long sigh, Vared said, "I have strong feelings for Lady Talia."

Traxen tilted his head. "Is it an effect of the virus?"

Vared chuckled ruefully. "Hardly. I have been drawn to her since I met her."

"Why have you not said anything before now?"

"What was I supposed to say, cousin? You can't have her in the Choosing because I want her? That my desires come before that of our race?" Vared's tail flicked rapidly. "Besides, she did not want to partake in the Choosing at all. She wishes to negotiate terms for future Earth females and return home to her son."

"She has a child? I was unaware of that." Traxen frowned.

"He is an adult in school."

"How does she feel about you?"

"We are like magnets, pulling and pushing at each other." Vared shrugged. "She keeps telling me we cannot get involved with each other. And I have been hesitant because of the dangers to her being with a warrior. She deserves better than me."

"There are few males better than you, Vared." Traxen nodded slowly. "You've given me much to ponder. I had not considered that the females might become attracted to anyone before a Choosing. That was shortsighted of me."

"If I understand correctly, there are some cultures on Earth who still arrange pairings, but it is not as common as you may have hoped." Vared paused, then added, "You should also know that my fangs have been elongating."

Traxen's face held surprise. "You think we can true mate with humans?"

Vared nodded. "I think it is a distinct possibility, cousin."

Traxen was silent as he thought. "That's surprising information." He nodded. "Inform Lady Talia that I would like to hear her ideas on how we should proceed to entice females to breed with our Svesti males."

"It will give her something to do while we wait in quarantine."

"Perhaps you could work with her on her proposals."

"We have already established that I am not a diplomat, Traxen." Vared grunted.

"No matter. You are an intelligent male, and you have time to discuss the whys and wherefores with her."

"As you will, sire." Vared dipped his head.

"Is there any progress on the traitors onboard the *Invictus*?" Traxen's lips thinned.

"I know Tolvex is working with Ladies Rachel and Emmy, but I have not spoken with them yet today."

"Svesti working with Zuvgran to release another virus. These are dark times, Vared." The king's braids swayed as he shook his head. "It doesn't matter whether the traitors knew about it affecting Svesti fertility. After everything we have gone through, to know that Svesti would willingly be part of doing to another race what was done to ours is discouraging. I thought we were better than this."

"*We* are, Traxen. Others are not. And they have put all of us in danger," Vared growled. "We will root them out."

Vared found Talia in her quarters. "The females would like to speak with you."

Talia asked, "Can I do it from in here?"

"Yes." He tapped his tablet. "Do you still wish voice only?"

Talia nodded. "It is better for now."

He handed her the tablet and pointed. "Just press there when you are ready." He stepped back and leaned against a wall.

"Talia? Can you hear us?" Ava said.

"Yes, I can."

"There must be something wrong with the connection; we can't see you," Ava said.

"There's nothing wrong. I would prefer voice only," Talia said quietly.

"Oh," Lin said in a low voice. "Are you okay?"

"Just have a lot to process." Talia's voice hitched. Vared's tail began to sway.

"Oh, sweetie. We're here for you. Whatever you need," Ava said.

"I appreciate that. I think I need some time, though. I'm not ready to talk about it."

"Status."

"The female is onboard the *Intrepid* with the Commander. The Zuvgran lab on XB9428B has been destroyed."

"This is not what was planned." Displeasure laced the voice.

"I am aware. The Commander followed the female after the Durelians kidnapped her. He enlisted some aid from the Wing Raiders and rescued her."

"Is she infected?"

"Unknown. What little I have heard is that she is traumatized by her kidnapping and only allowing the Commander in her presence, which is why she is on the shuttle. The other females have expressed grave concerns about her emotional state."

There was a long silence before the reply came. "It is possible they suspect she was infected with something and that is why she is sequestered."

"That may be, Uncle."

"You must get her onboard the *Invictus*. If the Zuvgran were successful before her rescue, she must infect the other females before they reach here."

"I do not have that ability."

"Find a way." An angry growl filled the comm link. "We have worked too hard to have our plan fail now."

The male shook his head. "How do you suggest I do this? I am not high enough in the command structure to argue the point."

"Figure it out. Always Svesti."

The Svesti onboard the *Invictus* grumbled as the link was disconnected. *How does he expect me to follow his orders without exposing myself?*

Chapter 18

PERSONAL JOURNAL - DAY 22.

I've been in a surreal holding pattern since my abduction. After that first morning, Vared was pretty insistent that we share meals together. Conversation was stilted between us for the first couple of days. I know a lot of that was me and my hurt feelings. Surprisingly, he hasn't pushed me to talk beyond asking me what I'd like to eat and telling me that the king has requested I come up with some ideas about what an agreement between our two peoples might look like. Vared said the king would like us to work together on it when I'm ready. All that Svesti law in my brain may actually come in handy.

So the new routine is morning meal, then Vared goes off to do commandery things while I exercise and think about the ways humans can aid the Svesti without giving up our autonomy. Then I shower, jot down those ideas and highlight questions that need answered before our midday meal. Usually after that, the girls comm to check on me and Vared does some physical training. I try to avoid him when he's working out. I'm afraid I'll jump his bones if I see him when he's half-naked, working those muscles.

Anyway, I get some writing in before the evening meal and then we have a check in with the group that knows about the virus. Sometimes, we have to do more tests for Rivezt and Natasha. They say they think they're making progress on a vaccine. So far, though, they have had no luck finding the traitor.

I'm not sleeping well and I think it's starting to show. I swear I've got a set of luggage taking up residence below my eyes. Being in limbo—not knowing if I'll have to quarantine for the rest of my life and, if so, where—and worrying about the traitors and what they might do to the other women is stressing me out. I keep waiting for the other shoe to drop. I don't think I've felt this level of anxiety since I was sixteen and pregnant. Honestly, it might be worse now. At least back then, I had Krista and Tim for emotional support. Right now, I just feel very alone.

My instincts tell me if I reach out to Vared, I'll feel better, but my head tells me I'm only going to end up with a broken heart. I admit it. I'm drawn to the male. It's like there's this invisible tether pulling me towards him. It feels like the sensations of home, safety, and excitement are all wrapped up together in his direction. It makes no sense.

Rereading what I just wrote makes me wonder if the virus is also affecting my mind. Even if it is, I'm not sharing the info with Natasha and Rivezt. It's too embarrassing.

If I try to lean on Vared now, would I just be using him, since he no longer wants me? I just know that underneath all that gruffness, he has a big heart. Now that I may not be able to return to Earth, is there any reason for me to keep resisting?

Either way, I can't keep avoiding him. We may be together for a very long time. We were friendly before my abduction. We can at least be friends, right?

I really, really need a hug.

"What would you like for the midday meal?"

Talia looked up from her notebook at Vared carrying a box into the dining area. "Whatever you want is fine. I've liked every food so far."

"Well, let's see what they ported over for us." He started unpacking the box. He held up a loaf of bread. "What is this?"

Talia hopped up and took it. She inhaled deeply. "Oh, it's freshly baked bread. Ava must've made it."

"Bread?"

Was his nose crinkling? How oddly endearing.

"Svesti don't have bread? Oh, you're missing out." Talia looked at some of the other items. "It looks like she sent over the makings for sandwiches."

"Sandwiches?" Vared looked confused.

Talia laughed at the look on his face. "Yes, you place meat, cheese, and vegetables on a slice of bread. Spread condiments on another slice and then put it altogether. Let me show you." She bumped his hip with hers. "Move. Give me space to work."

He held up his hands and stepped back. "Enlighten me, female." A wide smile filled his face.

Talia picked up a yellow vegetable. "Is this *shurlix* before it's made into a soup?"

"Yes." He leaned back against the counter and watched her.

She swallowed her sigh at how sexy he looked. *Focus, girl.* She sliced the bread and the *shurlix* before she pulled some leaves off something that looked like blue lettuce. As she worked her way through the other items, she realized Ava had sent them food that was comparable to Earth's for sandwich fixings. There were even some condiments that looked like mayo and mustard. "Is there any food here that you know you don't like? If so, I won't put it on your sandwich."

"No, I'm sure I'll like all of it."

She took another look in the box and grinned as she pulled out the last container. "Oh, if this is what I think it is, Ava is a genius." She hummed tunelessly as she made them lunch. *Hmm, I think two sandwiches to start for him. He's a big boy.* Suppressing a giggle, she opened the container to find something that looked like flat potato chips. Dumping some on their plates, she said, "Okay, they're ready. Just grab us something to drink, please."

At the table, Vared looked at his plate, then at her. "Do we need utensils?"

Talia smiled and took a bite of her sandwich. "Mmmm, no. Oh, this is good."

His eyes widened as he took his first bite. "This is delicious."

"Don't sound so surprised." She laughed. "Try a chip."

After a few more bites, he said, "You seem more like yourself today, *kirani*. Are you feeling better?"

Stifling a sigh, she said, "I know I've been standoffish, Vared, and I'm sorry if I've made you uncomfortable. I'm still processing everything."

He cocked his head at her. "I've been concerned, not uncomfortable. I wasn't sure what you needed from me."

"You gave me time to work through some of it on my own. That's what I think I needed."

He frowned at her. "You don't look like you've been sleeping."

"Honestly, I haven't been, at least not well. Too much to worry about." She shrugged and gave him a half-hearted smile.

"We can ask Ash'n for a sleep inducer."

"I'd rather not take any medication I don't have to."

"Hmmm, we'll see how it goes." He waved at her empty plate. "I'm going to make another sandwich. Would you like one as well?"

She smiled. "No, thanks."

"What were you working on when I came in?" He piled food onto his bread.

"I was writing questions to ask you."

"About?"

"Svesti views on things like surrogacy and in vitro fertilization."

"Perhaps you should explain what those terms mean to humans so that we are certain we are talking about the same things," he said as he sat down.

"Good point. I sometimes forget that we might not use the same words even with the translators." Talia explained the terms as she watched him down another huge sandwich and more chips.

An awestruck expression crossed his face. "You have females who will offer their womb to carry another female's child? That is not something that has ever been done on Costonia."

Talia nodded. "Oh, yes. Some might do it for a family member who can't carry their own child for medical reasons; others do it to help couples who can't do it themselves." She bit her lip. "Although, I'll be honest, there are probably some who do it for the money."

"I'm not sure surrogacy would be something we would need, since our remaining females are infertile."

She gestured excitedly. "What I was thinking is there may be human women who might be willing to carry a Svesti child, but not by having sex, while there may be other women who would be willing to donate some of their eggs, but not carry a child. For many women, it is difficult to give up a child you've conceived. And in this case, we're talking about that child remaining on another planet, which would make it even more difficult."

"Females would be willing to donate their eggs? We have tried fertilization outside a womb with other species, but have not been able to sustain growth of an embryo."

"Well, if you weren't compatible with the other species, that might be part of the problem. On Earth, we have sperm banks where men donate for women who wish to conceive without a man, and I know there are frozen eggs too."

Vared had a strange expression on his face as he stared at her. "Do you think it is something that might work?"

Talia shrugged. "Right now, medically? I don't know. But if we put it in as an option in the initial agreement, we've covered it if it will or ever does work."

"What made you think of this?" Vared's tail wrapped around her ankle.

"I don't think you'll find a lot of human women that would be willing to enter a breeding contract with a Svesti. Oh, and I was thinking we need to change the name to birthing contract. It's accurate and less offensive to humans."

"Some of our older Svesti might grumble about it, but I think birthing is an acceptable term." Vared's grin turned into a frown, stretching at his scar. "You don't think human women will want Svesti males?"

Talia sighed heavily. "It's not about wanting Svesti males, Vared. If we put out photos and videos of your males, I can guarantee there will be a lot of human women who would want to have sex with a Svesti male. But having a child with one and not be a part of raising it? I don't think we'll find enough willing women to make a significant difference for your race. Raising and nurturing your child is a strong drive in our DNA." She blinked at the sudden tears in her eyes. "Just look at me. My son is technically an adult, and it's killing me to know that I may never get to hug him again. I know I couldn't walk away from a baby."

Vared's tail made soothing motions against her calf, and he took her hand in his. "*Kirani*, the healers will find an answer. You'll see your son again."

Talia scoffed. "Vared, the healers haven't found an answer to the original virus, let alone this one. I need to be realistic."

"It hasn't even been a week. We need to be patient. You know it's a high priority for both our races to find an answer."

She looked down to where his thumb rubbed small circles over her knuckles. "I know you're right, but it's hard, Vared. Especially since there is nothing I can do but wait."

"I understand, *kirani*. It's not easy for me either, wondering what I will do if I cannot be a warrior with and for my people." He grimaced. "It is what I know, who I am. So who am I if I am not a warrior?"

She hunched her shoulders. "I've been selfish, worrying about me. I never even considered how your life will change if they can't find an answer." His face was blurry through her watery eyes. "And all because you saved me. I'm so sorry, Vared."

"Don't be, *kirani*. I would do it again without regret." His gentle smile didn't ease her guilt.

"But…"

"No, Talia." His fingers tightened on hers. "Don't blame yourself. You did not create the virus." His eyes glinted over his thinned lips. "The Zuvgran have much to answer for, as do the traitors who helped them."

"We'll find them, won't we? I'm worried they'll do something to the other women."

"Yes, *kirani*, we will. And they will pay for what they've done." The harshness was gone from his voice when he said, "Go change into your workout clothes. I think you need to train."

"With you?" She mentally cursed when she heard the squeak in her voice.

"Yes. The physical activity will be good for you and we don't want your progress to stall." He jerked his head toward the door as she stood. "Go. I'll clean up here and change before meeting you in the training room."

She walked quickly to the door. Her breathing stopped for a moment as she looked at him leaning over to grab the dirty plates. She felt her panties dampen when she saw how his pants outlined his firm buttocks. *I'm not sure training together is a good idea.* She rushed off.

"Again."

Sweat dripped into her eyes and she raised her arm to rub her face on her T-shirt sleeve. *I'll have to wear a sweatband if he's going to train me regularly.* Her arms felt like limp noodles. *Not sure what I was so worried about. Right now, I just want to hit him. Hard.*

"I think I'd like to take a break," she wheezed.

"You've barely started, Talia. We want these movements to be instinctive. And the only way to get there is repetition." Hard, rhythmic thunks accompanied his words as he continued to punch the hanging weight bag next to her.

"Bullshit. I've been hitting this wood on the bag for over an hour." The staff fell to the mat as she put her hands on her hips. "I'm tired and my muscles hurt. I need a break."

Frowning, he straightened and walked toward her. "Are you okay?"

"Yes, but I need a break. You need to remember my work isn't physical. I didn't work out this hard on Earth. And I swear that staff is fifty pounds heavier now than when I started. Do you have technology that increases the weight?"

Lavender eyes widened, then a full-throated belly laugh resounded in the room. His grin showed off his fangs as he clasped his hands to his stomach. She tried not to lick her lips as she watched his abs contract.

"Are you laughing at me?" She felt a smile tugging at her lips. *I've never seen him so relaxed and happy.*

"Wa...ter," he gasped as he tried to catch his breath.

She tossed him a water pouch while opening one for herself. Her eyes traced the long line of his throat as he tipped his head back and swallowed. *Oh, my.* She gulped down some water hoping to cool her ardor.

"Thank you, *kirani*." Humor laced his voice. "I needed that."

Pretending to be upset, she said, "You laughed at me." She added a pout for good measure.

"No. Well, yes, I guess I was laughing at your words." His mirthful eyes met hers. "When you complained about the weight of the staff, it reminded me of my early warrior training. I can remember thinking someone must've filled my rucksack with boulders after some runs." He grinned. "And the idea of using technology to make it heavier the longer it's used struck me as hilarious."

"I'm glad you find my words so amusing," she said without heat.

"And I admit, some of the laughter was relief." His eyes softened. "Having you push back against what you felt was wrong felt normal." A frown tugged at his lips. In a low tone, he said, "I've missed normal, Talia."

Damn this male, being all sweet. His eyes dropped to her chest as she drew in a deep, steadying breath.

"I don't know what normal is anymore, Vared. But I'm glad you're feeling better." When he raised his eyes to hers, the heat in them froze her in place. Silently, they stared at each other for a long moment. She abruptly shook her head to break the spell, her sweaty hair cold against her neck. She shivered. "I think I'm going to wash up and change."

He slowly nodded. "Good idea." His fangs flashed. "Afterwards, we can see how much blood Ash'n and Lady Natasha want from us today."

She laughed as she walked away.

Chapter 19

THROUGHOUT HIS SHOWER and getting dressed, Vared couldn't help smiling. Talia was healing and returning to herself. Even though they'd been on the same ship, he'd missed her fire and laughter.

He frowned slightly. *She's still not sleeping. I was hoping to exhaust her with training, so her body had no choice but to rest.*

He didn't know why he'd told her about his worries about not being a warrior. It wasn't like him to share his private inner thoughts like that. *Crek! What kind of male am I? Whining to a female like a youngling that I am uncertain about my future does not inspire confidence.* His scar tugged at his facial muscles as his frown deepened. *But she didn't seem to judge me. She seemed concerned for me, not worried about me being a weak male.*

He abruptly shook his head. *This is accomplishing nothing. It is done. I'll deal with what comes like I always do.* He sighed. *I just wish I knew what to do about my desire for her.* He adjusted his stiffening cock in his pants before leaving his quarters.

"What do you want us to do with this?" In the dining area, Talia held up the handheld medical scanner that had been ported to the *Intrepid*. The holographic images of Ash'n and Lady Natasha smiled at them.

"We need detailed scans of both of you. We want to know if the virus is affecting any other parts of your bodies—down to the cellular level," Ash'n said.

"Emmy and Tolvex modified that scanner for us to record the data we need and send it directly to our workstations," Lady Natasha said. "We'll need you to scan each other slowly."

"We didn't want to send a complete medical bed to the *Intrepid*. And we didn't want to enlarge the handheld scanner and make it too heavy to hold. So as you scan, the computer will patch it all together as if you'd been scanned in a med bed," Ash'n explained.

"Tell us what to do," said Vared.

"Commander, I'd like you to scan Talia. Talia, stand with your feet shoulder-width apart and your arms out."

"Like this?" Talia said as she followed Lady Natasha's instructions.

"Yes. Commander, start at her head and keep the scanner close to her body, but not touching it. Scan down one side and, in essence, outline her body with the scanner. Then we'll have you fill in the other areas."

Vared took the scanner from Talia's outstretched hand. Standing behind her, he started the scan on the right side of her head, over her shoulder, over and under her extended arm before moving down. He crouched to scan her leg.

"A little slower, Durek," Ash'n said. "There's a lot of information being gathered and we want to ensure we don't miss anything."

Vared slowed his movements as he scanned Talia's legs. As he moved the instrument upwards to scan her inner thighs, he tried to ignore her plump ass in front of his face. He sucked in a sharp breath when the scent of her essence hit him. *So close, yet so far. I could lean forward and...*

"Commander? Is there a problem? You seem to have stopped," Lady Natasha said.

Crek! "No, just adjusting my stance to continue," he lied.

He continued the scan slowly. When Vared reached where he had begun, Ash'n said, "Good. Now, scan the back of her head to her right foot. Then start again to do the left. After that, you can do the center of her back."

Vared followed the healer's instructions. He moved Talia's hair out of the way and felt her shiver. He committed the dips and curves of her body to memory as he scanned, wishing he was using his hands instead. They both let out a long breath as he finished the scan of her back.

"That's good, Commander. Now we need you to scan the front of her body. Talia, you can put your arms down now," Lady Natasha said.

Vared was close enough to feel the tension emanating from Talia. He leaned forward and whispered, "Relax, *kirani*. It'll be over soon." Louder, he said, "Turn towards me, Talia."

She spun to face him, her cheeks pink. He looked over her shoulder at the healers. "Just the three scans?"

Rivezt nodded. "Yes, that should be enough."

As he started scanning, Vared stared down into her brown eyes for a long moment before directing his attention to conducting the scan properly. His hand shook slightly as he ran the scanner over each breast and the hard nipples straining at her shirt. Both times he needed to crouch to scan her legs, he suppressed the growl in his chest as he scented her growing arousal. He ended the last scan at the apex of her thighs and swore he could feel the heat emanating from her core.

"Emmy and Tolvex did a fantastic job programming the scanner," Lady Natasha said absentmindedly while looking at a screen he couldn't see. "It's almost as seamless as a med bed scan."

"Lady Talia, it is time to scan the Commander," Ash'n said.

Vared handed her the scanner and stood with outstretched arms, facing the healers. Talia placed a hand on his shoulder blade and her body stretched against his. Her nipples were hard points dragging across his back.

"Sorry," she said, sounding out of breath. "You're tall, and I need to reach the top of your head."

"It's fine. Do what you need to." *Crek! I hope my cock doesn't bust my pants open before the scans are done.*

Her hand drifted lower as she rested against him for support while she scanned. Her touch felt languid. *Is that her breath I feel near my ass?* He clenched his butt cheeks involuntarily and heard her gasp softly.

"Do I need to scan his tail?" Talia asked.

Ash'n and Lady Natasha looked at each other, then back at her. "Yes, please."

Vared tried to remain impassive and motionless, but he jerked slightly when he felt her gentle exploratory touch at the base of his tail.

"You can face me now," Talia said.

He relaxed his arms and turned. Her face was flushed, and she averted her eyes. She stretched to reach the top of his head and wobbled. He took the hand without the scanner and placed it on his chest. "Use me." He inhaled deeply. "For support."

Her fingers fisted in his shirt and his nipples hardened. Her scent enveloped him and he closed his eyes to keep from reaching for her as she continued to scan. He felt her hand drift to his thigh as she worked her way down, before switching sides. He opened his eyes during the last pass. She bit her lip as she squatted in front of him, running the scanner over his cock and balls. Her fingernails bit into his thigh.

"Is that everything you need?" Vared asked without turning to look at the healers.

"It should be, for now," Ash'n said.

"Then we'll speak with you tomorrow," Vared said as he disconnected the comm. "*Kirani?*" He reached a hand down to her. "Let me help you up."

She placed her hand in his and raised unfocused eyes. The desire in them struck him in his heart, and he growled. "Come, *kirani.*"

Her body shivered, and her eyelids lowered. Her long dark eyelashes contrasted against the pink of her skin. Her short, ragged breaths seemed to echo in his cock as she stood unsteadily. She withdrew her hand from his and stepped back. "I'm sorry, Vared. I'll go to my quarters and leave you be."

"Sorry for what?" He could hear his confusion in his voice.

She waved a hand between them. "For my reaction to something that should've been clinical. I know you don't want this." Talia turned and hurriedly rushed away.

Shocked, it took him a moment to register he wasn't following her. *Move, you naroon!* He caught up with her in the hall. "Talia, stop."

She froze but didn't turn to face him. "This is embarrassing enough, Vared."

"I don't understand what you mean."

"I know you no longer want me since I can't give you children."

"What in the Goddess' name are you talking about?" His raised voice echoed in the hall.

She spun to face him. "Don't yell at me. Don't deny it. I am not good enough anymore now that I'm damaged."

He slowly and deliberately approached and crowded closer to her when her back touched the wall. Placing his hands on the wall on either side of her head, he pressed his aroused body to hers.

He whispered in her ear. "Does this feel like I don't want you? I want you all the time. Everywhere. I want to slide into your hot, wet cunt and feel you come on my cock. I want to taste you, pleasure you, make you scream in ecstasy." He shook his head. "I shouldn't want you, but I do."

"Because I'm damaged," she whimpered, shaking her head in denial.

"NO! Because you want to go back to Earth. Because I'm a warrior and danger is part of my life, which means danger would be part of yours. You should be safe and protected." His fingers played with her silky hair. He growled low. "Because I'm afraid if I take you, I won't let you go, no matter what you want. You bring out my basest instincts, *kirani*, making me forget that I'm supposed to be a civilized male."

"What about me being damaged? I know you want children."

"*Kirani*, before I met you, I had already resigned myself to the fact that I wouldn't have younglings."

"But now there's a chance," she argued. "You could find a fertile human woman and continue your line." She grimaced. "You deserve that. You're a good male."

He rested his forehead on hers, sharing her breath, his voice low. "What you aren't understanding, *kirani*, is that I don't want any other female, just you. I'd rather have you."

Hope shone from her eyes, then dimmed. "Then why did you reject me?"

He frowned. "When did I reject you?" His thumb rubbed the soft skin of her cheek.

"The first night here."

"You had just been kidnapped and were traumatized. It would have been dishonorable of me to take what you were offering then."

"I knew what I wanted and needed."

"We're still learning about each other, *kirani*. You were in a vulnerable state. So I said no, as much as it hurt to do so."

"So it wasn't because I'm damaged?"

"Will you stop saying that you're damaged? You. Are. Not. Damaged," he said through clenched teeth. "There is nothing wrong with you. You are not your womb."

Wonder shone from her eyes as she raised a hand to caress his cheek. "You really believe that."

"Of course I do. What can I say or do to prove it to you?"

She smiled and leaned forward to whisper against his lips. "Take me, Vared. Do all the things you've been wanting to do and make me think of nothing but you and the pleasure you give me."

He shuddered as he whispered back, "But what about the rest of it? Earth. Warrior. Danger." *Crek! She's got me so horny, I can't even speak in complete sentences anymore.*

"They may never find a cure or they could find one tomorrow. We'll deal with it when we know. I'd rather take something for ourselves now and worry about the rest later." She sighed. "I've never felt this way before, Vared. I don't know what to do with it all. I don't have all the answers, but I feel like I will regret not trusting that it will somehow work out for the best—for both of us."

He stared into her eyes for a long moment, searching for something; he didn't know what. Growling, he dipped his head to give her a hard kiss. Desire ignited and their mouths and hands stoked the flames higher. He couldn't get enough of her.

"Not. Here," he said between kisses. "First. Time. Bed."

She nodded as he picked her up and strode to his living quarters. Her core rubbed against his abdomen, and the scent of her arousal became heavier. Their tongues dueled before gentling and exploring. Her soft hands were hot on his skin. Sighs, whimpers, and growls were like an erotic song in his ears, making him harder and his stride falter.

Kneeling when he finally reached the bed, he sat her on the edge. He ended the kiss and held her head between his palms. "Are you sure, *kirani*? I do not want you to have regrets."

Heavy-lidded brown eyes slowly opened to gaze at him with lust and warmth shining from them. Her lips were red and swollen. She placed her hands on his face and pulled him closer. "If you stop now," she growled, "I will gut you."

A surprised laugh erupted from him, and he hugged her close. "My female is bloodthirsty."

"Your female is hungry for you. Do something about it."

Her hands left him and she grabbed the hem of her shirt to pull it over her head. Some lacy concoction encased her full breasts, and he sucked in a breath when she cupped them. Vared stared and tried to memorize the moment.

"You are so beautiful, *kirani,* but you are overdressed."

He released the front catch and her breasts spilled free, nipples beckoning him. *Tan, her nipples are tan.* He bent forward to lick one, and it hardened further, the areola puckering. She gasped when he blew a gentle breath over it. He wanted to know what made her crazy. Licking and sucking and noting her reactions, he smiled in satisfaction when she whimpered, "Oh my god." He gently ran a fang over her nipple again and her hips bucked.

Bringing his tail up to play with it, he gave his attention to her other breast. Licking its plump underside to the nipple, he hovered and touched it lightly with his tongue. Her hands pulled on his hair to bring him closer, and they fell back onto the mattress. Resting his weight on his elbows, he worshipped her nipple as she silently demanded. Fingernails dug into his biceps and her hips moved restlessly against him. *More, I want to taste more of her.* He drew hard on her nipple and it extended before it left his mouth with a wet pop.

Vared looked at the pretty picture she made against his sheets. Skin flushed, chest heaving, nipples reddened and hard, and her hair splayed out just as he'd imagined. *Crek, she is wondrous.* Tugging on her pants, he paused when she opened hazy, lust-filled eyes.

She smiled and said, "I think you're overdressed too."

Keeping his eyes on hers, he stood and reached to pull his shirt off from his back. As he revealed more of his body, her pleased hum made him glad he trained regularly. He knelt again to remove her pants. Licking his lips, he gazed at her glistening pussy. Spreading her legs so he could see her better, he lightly traced her opening with a lone finger. Her moan encouraged him to explore further. The human internet had mentioned a female pleasure center called a clit. He knew he'd felt it on the observation deck. *Where is it? Ah, there it is.* Watching her closely, he played with it, touching, rubbing, and rolling it. He experimented for a bit with different pressures and motions to see what she liked best, but her scent called to him and he had to taste her.

Slowly, he licked her from her opening to her clit with one long swipe. Her hips bucked upwards.

"More," she said breathlessly.

"Like this?" He did it again. Her drawn-out groan made him smile.

"Stop teasing me," Talia chuffed impatiently.

He growled against her core and sucked hard on her clit. Her thighs clenched against his ears to keep him in place. Everything he'd done with his fingers, he repeated with his tongue, relishing the increase of her arousal. He looked up at her as her moans became higher pitched. She twisted restlessly, but he kept her in place. Stopping, he waited. She opened her eyes to look down at him. He smiled against her before running a fang sideways across her clit, growling simultaneously. Eyes widening, her body stiffened and then she shook uncontrollably as her orgasm broke over her. Her eyelids squeezed shut, and she yelled his name, "Vared!"

He licked at the cream flowing from her core. She tasted even sweeter and spicier than she had on the observation deck, and he was voracious. Movements slowing, her body occasionally jerked as another spike of pleasure took her by surprise. Deeply, he inhaled, wanting her scent to settle inside him and never leave. He lifted his head to see her breathing heavily, fingers plucking at her nipples.

Grinning in satisfaction and feeling her wetness on his face and chin, he rose to remove his pants. She opened her eyes just as his cock sprang free. She licked her lips and languidly sat up to reach for him. "My turn."

He hissed as her soft fingers wrapped around his cock. When she began exploring his nodes, he grabbed her hand before squeezing the base of his cock. "No, *kirani*. I want to come inside you and I'm too close to the edge right now. You are glorious in your pleasure."

His tail came up between her legs to caress her opening before dipping inside her slowly. Her lids fell to look at his tail, and she spread her legs further to give him better access. When she undulated on it, he had to squeeze his cock harder to keep from erupting all over her chest. *Crek! She is so sensual.*

A wicked smile crossed her lips. She leaned forward and licked the pre-cum on the head of his cock. Squeezing so hard, he thought he'd lost blood flow, he rasped, "You naughty female. Maybe you should be spanked."

She tilted her head and looked up at him, a siren's call in her eyes, then pulled the head of his member into her mouth. He was large, so she licked and sucked what she could, her hips pumping against his tail. When her tongue started to explore his nodes, it took everything he had to pull away from her. The suction noise of her wetness as he slid his tail from her was loud enough to be heard over their heavy breathing. She pouted.

"Lie back, Talia. I have something better than my tail for you."

"Promise?" Her eyes glinted with humor.

"Oh, I promise you'll enjoy it."

He grinned as he swiped his cock in her wetness before pushing slowly into her. She moaned as his head nodes rippled the interior of her cunt. His head dropped forward, and he grunted as her insides gripped and sucked at his cock. *Tight. So crekkin' tight. So good.* Stopping when he was buried deep inside her, he felt the node at the base of his cock rest on her clit. *I'm not sure if that will feel better for her or me.* He leaned forward and kissed her, their tastes mingling together.

She pulled away to gasp, "I need…" Her body twisted, but his weight kept her in place.

"What do you need?"

"You. More. Move," she panted.

"Eyes, Talia. Look at me."

She stared at him. He leaned back and caressed her legs as he hooked them over his forearms.

"Give me your hands."

She raised her arms, and he held her hands in his. Palm to palm, fingers entwined, he slowly withdrew his cock most of the way, his head nodes sensitive to the suction of her pussy. He pumped into her with long, slow strokes, rotating his hips when his balls slapped her ass to slide his base node against her clit. Her eyelids fluttered.

"Keep your eyes on me, *kirani.* I want to see you receive your pleasure this time."

He kept the slow pace for as long as he could, but he could feel the pressure building at the base of his spine. He wanted, no, he needed to feel her come on his cock. "Can you take more, *kirani*?"

She nodded enthusiastically. "Take me…however…you need, Vared," she said as her hips moved in tandem with his.

He slammed into her, bottoming out and balls slapping her ass.

"Yes! More, Vared. More!"

As Vared kept fucking her hard and fast, his tail came up to rub her clit when he drew back. His node and her pleasure center met on each downstroke. Her breathing sped up, and her scent was heavier in the air. Her wetness grew even slicker, and the friction against his cock was almost unbearably good.

"Come, *kirani*, come on my cock now." He released one of her hands and pinched her clit. Her screaming wail accompanied the shudders of her orgasm. The contractions of her cunt against his cock sent him over the edge. He howled as he emptied himself inside her, and the edges of his vision turned black.

Panting, he released her other hand and let her legs slide down. He bent and grasped her ass in his hands and lifted her up.

Confusion in her eyes, she breathed, "What are you doing, Vared?"

"Need to lie down with you, but don't want to leave your cunt. Just moving us up further on the bed."

He sat on the side, scooted back, and turned to lean back against the headboard. Occasional quivers of her cunt on his flaccid cock as he maneuvered made him groan.

Their bodies slick with sweat cooled them as their breathing returned closer to normal. His hands and tail caressed every part of her he could reach. Gently pushing her hair from her face, he kissed her long and deep. Resting his forehead on hers, he said, "Thank you, *kirani*. You are even more spectacular than I imagined."

Chapter 20

M IND OFFICIALLY BLOWN.

Talia traced the lines of Vared's face with gentle fingers. When she ran them over his lips, his tongue licked her fingers and she shivered. She watched in fascination as the deep amethyst of his eyes lightened to lavender.

"Was it everything you imagined?" she asked. His chuckle made his cock twitch in her pussy and her nipples scrape his chest. *Oh! I like that.*

"It was better, *kirani*. I'm very interested in seeing how reality compares with the other things I've imagined doing with you." He nipped at her fingers. "And I admit, the human clit is worth investigating more." Her pussy clenched at his words, and he groaned.

"Svesti women don't have one?"

"No, but I've never been with a Svesti woman. We have very few left."

"Don't take this the wrong way, but you seem very knowledgeable about the female form." *I don't sound jealous, do I?*

"I admit I have spent some time on pleasure planets, although it's been a couple solars since my last visit. But that was just physical release. There was only one female who I cared for early in my warrior training who I spent time with." He looked sad.

"Did you love her?"

"I thought we'd sign a troth contract, perhaps even true mate, and spend our lives together. But it wasn't meant to be."

"What happened?" Her fingers outlined his slightly pointed ear. *How can an ear be sexy?*

"Shazeen wanted me to discontinue warrior training and become a farmer on her family's estate or a merchant. Something less dangerous for us both."

Her fingers stilled.

"And what did you want?"

"I had always planned on becoming a warrior. After losing my mother and sisters to the virus, I couldn't turn away from that path."

Her hands gripped his shoulders. "She was wrong to want you to change so much." They locked eyes.

He said, "She was right, though, about the dangers."

"You know, on my planet, people say things like 'You could slip in the bathtub' or 'You could get hit by a bus tomorrow.'" Talia paused at his quizzical look and caressed his chest. "It means that there is danger in everyday life, too, and you can't let fear of *what if*s stop you from exploring what could be."

Chewing on her lip, she said, "I admit I don't always remember that. And I'm discovering the universe has more dangers than I was prepared for. But that won't stop me from doing what I think is best. I just may be more cautious about some things than others." She met his searching gaze and watched his eyes darken.

"Would you consider sharing your life with a warrior?"

Laughing, she said, "Uh, I'm pretty sure I have a warrior inside me right now. Can't get much more shareable than that." Her laugh trailed off when he didn't join her.

"That's not what I meant, *kirani*. I think you know that."

A heavy sigh left her. "I know, Vared. Honestly, the biggest reservations I have now have nothing to do with your profession. If we were on Earth and you were human, I would be very open to something permanent between us. But we are literally from two different worlds. I don't know how to merge the two to meet all my needs."

He kissed her tenderly. Drawing his head back, he said with a grin, "Speaking of your needs, did you imagine us together like this?"

Her cheeks were hot. "Not exactly like this."

"What did you imagine?" Extending a claw, he circled a nipple. *Traitorous thing, hardening so quickly.*

"I'm not really comfortable discussing it, Vared. I've never behaved so wantonly before. I'm a little embarrassed." She averted her eyes.

Hand on her cheek, he said, "I've told you before—there is no room for embarrassment between us. What you perceive to be wanton, I interpret as a strong, confident, sensual female taking what she needs. It excites me." When she looked at him, he said, "*You* excite me like no other female. I can't count the number of times I've masturbated to thoughts of you over these past weeks."

Fangs flashing, he said, "Please don't make me go back to that. The reality is so much more satisfying."

She giggled nervously, "You've been thinking of me as you rub one out?"

"Rub one out?"

"Humans have many euphemisms for sexual parts and activities. Rubbing one out is another way of saying masturbating."

"I look forward to learning all these different sayings eventually, but what I want to know now is what you imagined when you were rubbing one out." His boyish grin drew her in.

She leaned forward to nip at his earlobe. "Reality was a thousand times better than my imagination. But one thing I'd like to experience that you didn't do…"

Turning his head, his breath was hot in her ear. Shivers ran through her body and she felt her clit swell. "What was that, *kirani*?"

She whispered, "I really want to feel your hands squeezing my ass as you pound into me." She gasped as she felt him instantly harden inside her.

"Ride me, Talia." His hands grasped her ass. Her hips bucked. She leaned back with her hands on his thighs. Raising and lowering her hips slowly in a figure-eight motion, they both drew in harsh breaths when he was buried deep. He looked down to where they were joined. "I love seeing and feeling your pretty pussy suck at my cock."

She watched his member disappearing into her as she lowered herself again and moaned. He looked at her, his eyes almost black with desire. *He makes me feel beautiful. I can't remember ever feeling like this before.* Wanting him deeper and harder, she leaned forward to support herself with her hands on his shoulders. His hands kneaded her ass cheeks as she slammed down on his cock as hard as she could.

"Give me your breast, *kirani*," he rasped. She used one hand to lift her breast to his mouth.

On one of her downward motions, he sucked hard just as her clit hit his node, sending even more sensation to her core. "Oh!" He looked up at her exclamation and she could see his pleasure at her reaction. She smiled at him. His dark, decadent scent surrounded her. "More," she gasped. "I need more."

He released her nipple and swung them sideways, while flipping her onto her back. "What my female wants, my female gets." She locked her ankles behind his back as he pounded into her hard. She felt him squeeze her ass in his large, hot hands. When his claws pricked at her skin, she couldn't hold back her orgasm. Throwing her head back, she screamed his name.

His movements became unsteady as her rippling pussy squeezed his cock. A deep rumble from his chest set off a round of aftershocks through her. With her eyes and hands, she admired the long stretch of his chest and neck as he came, head thrown back and his face contorted in pleasure as he grunted her name.

Moving his arms up, his hands framed her face as he rested his weight on his elbows. They shared long, deep kisses as their bodies relaxed. She caressed his sweat-slicked back, arms, and chest.

When she could speak again, she said, "Reality. Better."

His chuckle rumbled throughout her body. *Damn, I really like that.* They both groaned as he lifted himself from her. She drew in a deep breath as she watched his ass flex when he headed to the bathroom. *He has no bad side.*

Suddenly exhausted, she closed her eyes. She barely registered when he returned with a warm cloth and cleaned the wetness between her legs. She felt him wrap his arms and tail around her. She smiled sleepily when she heard him say, "Rest, *kirani.* I'll watch over you."

Personal Journal - Day 27.

These past several days have been the best of my life. I've discovered a part of myself I never knew existed. Vared is a generous and inventive lover. I'm blushing and squirming in my chair, just thinking of some of the things we've done.

I've used the expression *climb him like a tree* in a lot of my books, but until Vared, I didn't truly understand the urge. I get it now. And I want more of it.

We spend as much time together as we can. If I'm writing and he has ship duties to attend to that won't distract me, he'll do them in the same place I am, usually with his tail wrapped around my ankle. I wouldn't have believed it, but I'm actually more productive with him sitting there quietly than I am alone. That's a new experience for me.

He's still training me, but his training differs from Rachel's. Rachel focused on how to avoid and escape. Vared focuses on how to disable first, then escape. He even has me practicing the best places to stab an opponent with the hair comb he bought me on Theron. I now know where the sensitive parts are on a Svesti, Durelian, Frezzian, and a number of other species. I hope I never need to use that knowledge.

If they ever find a vaccine or cure, we're going to have to figure out how to end a training session without sex, though. He's insatiable after we've hit the training room—something about my scent overwhelming him after I've exerted myself. We've yet to make it to our quarters before our clothes come off. That could be a problem around other people. Thank goodness for cleaning bots.

I've never been a big fan of drama in my personal life. Not after experiencing my father's drunken ramblings and rages. But somehow it's different with Vared.

No doubt about it—the male can be pigheaded. We don't really argue about anything personal between us, but more about how best to handle different situations in birthing and troth contracts. Sometimes we'll end up shouting at each other, then he'll get frustrated and we end up fucking. Hard. Then we have a much calmer discussion and find a compromise that works for both of us.

I know some might see it as him trying to use sex to control me or get his way, but I see it as fucking some sense into the male. It's like once we've been intimate, his stubbornness evaporates.

Most times he comes up with a better resolution than I had originally started with. Either way, you can't argue with results.

But, here's the kicker—arguing passionately with him doesn't make me want to cringe and hide, nor do I want to avoid it altogether. There's this underlying degree of trust that he will never intentionally hurt me, be it with words or fists. It's liberating for me. For the first time in my life, I feel like I don't have to hide any part of me.

I'd bet that most wouldn't believe me, but Vared is the sweetest, most caring male I've ever met. It's not just about the times we have tender, loving sex (it's not always carnal), but how he sees to my comfort. Little things like ensuring I eat first, how he believes in me and bolsters my confidence, and not only wants to hear my innermost thoughts, but shares his as well. And he touches me like I'm precious—even during our most primal moments—it's addicting.

I'm sleeping again. I don't know whether it's the training and sex wearing me out or Vared wrapped around me at night that's doing it for me, but my mind is finally letting me rest.

A very large part of me secretly wishes they don't find a cure or vaccine and Vared and I have to sequester ourselves in some distant part of the galaxy to keep our races safe. Then the guilt overwhelms me that I'm thinking that way at all. What kind of mother does that make me? I miss Joshua. I want to see him grow, get married, have a family. Being his mom is the most important part of my life, a privilege I don't deserve but find so much love and pride in. I don't want to give up that role—not even for what I'm building with Vared. And I don't want Vared's choices taken from him either.

Where's a fairy godmother when you need one?

During the evening meal, Talia said, "I've been meaning to ask you. What is the difference between a troth contract and a true mating?"

Vared's face turned solemn. "A true mating is a biological need to mark your mate. Once you are true mated, then a troth contract becomes almost meaningless. You have chosen to remain together for the rest of your lives."

"So Svesti start with troth contracts, then decide whether or not to true mate?" She felt her brows furrow.

"Sometimes. Sometimes they true mate without a contract."

"How does this marking happen?"

"Our fangs elongate and we bite each other's neck during intimate relations."

"So it's unlikely that there will be true matings between Svesti and humans, since we don't have fangs." Talia frowned and moved some food around on her plate.

"I don't know about that. I know I have felt the urge to true mate with you, but I would never mark you without your agreement." He placed his hand over hers. "We used to have fated mates as well."

"Fated mates?"

"A fated mate is the one person who is meant for you in all of the universe. If a couple who true mated were fated mates, then their clan markings would also change color. There hasn't been a recorded instance of fated mates in a hundred years. It was thought the Goddess blessed the fated mates when they found each other." He smiled. "My parents were true mates from the start."

"You've wanted to true mate with me, huh?" She felt her face flush.

His lavender eyes met hers. "I believe we are meant to be together, *kirani*. But it is something you must agree to. I cannot and will not choose for you."

"I appreciate that, Vared, more than you realize." She leaned over, kissed his lips softly, and whispered, "You are a good male."

Vared's eyes bored into hers. "Be sure, *kirani*. If we ever true mate, I won't be able to let you go."

She stared back at him. "If I ever make that decision, you won't have to."

"Head down, *kirani*."

Talia shivered as Vared gently ran his claws along her back before pushing lightly on her shoulders. On her knees, she placed her cheek on the bed, the scent of them emanating from the sheets. She inhaled deeply and her nipples slid on the cool, silky surface. She squirmed to find some relief from the heat building in her body. Warm hands tugged at her hips to raise her butt higher.

"Goddess, I love your ass, Talia." She trembled as he explored her curves.

His tail languidly played with her clit as he pushed his cock slowly into her pussy. *He feels so much bigger in this position—and his nodes—they'll be the death of me.* She jerked when she felt his finger trace her anus.

"One day, *kirani*, I'm going to take you here with my cock." Extending a claw, he lightly traced again.

Turning her head as far as she could to look at him, she said, "I'm not so sure about that."

A slow, wicked smile exposing his fangs broke over his face. He leaned forward on his hands, encasing her body with his. Nipping at her ear, he simultaneously pumped short strokes into her.

Hot breath stirred her hair as he said, "Oh, I think so, *kirani*. I'll stuff you with my cock, and my tail will fuck your cunt at the same time. You'll be so wet and full and tight, squeezing so hard that we won't know where each of us begins or ends."

Her pussy clenched at his words, and she felt his indrawn breath. He straightened, grasped her hips, and pulled them back as he slammed forward, his base node hitting her perineum.

"Yes! Vared! More!" His tail sped up as his hips did. She tried to find purchase on the sheets to push back to meet him. His hand tangled in her hair and tugged to hold her in position. The slap of flesh meeting flesh and their moans filled the air. It felt like there were low volts of electricity running through her veins, searing her from the inside out.

The pressure kept building. Then his tail slapped her clit, and his thick finger breached that forbidden place simultaneously. The world turned white, and she screamed as the electric pleasure exploded within her body, pussy spasming uncontrollably as he fucked her through her orgasm. As he shot his hot seed into her, she came again, panting as she fell forward when he released her hair.

He fell to the bed beside her, pulling her into his arms. The movement of his chest under her cheek let her know his breathing was as ragged as hers. Callused hands soothed her body. The tip of his tail gently poked at her anus.

She grasped his tail and tugged. "Knock that off." His rumble of laughter shook against her cheek as she stroked his tail.

"You never disappoint, *kirani*."

She raised herself on her elbows to look at him. *That is one satisfied male.* She grinned.

"Neither do you, babe. I'm not sure I'll be able to walk anytime soon."

He smacked a quick kiss on her lips. "Unfortunately, I have to meet with the king soon. As much as I hate to leave you alone in our bed, I should get cleaned up and presentable."

She waved a hand. "Go. Do what you need to. I'll just lay here waiting for my parts to function again. Then you can feed me." She twirled her hair with a finger and shot him a look from under her lashes. "For some reason, I seem to have worked up an appetite."

He swatted her ass playfully. "You are always hungry." He slid out from under her. "Should I get you a snack before my meeting?" She licked her lips as she took in his naked body. "And don't look at me that way. The king might not forgive my lateness." He lazily stroked his cock as he gazed down at her.

She flipped onto her back and threw her forearm over her eyes. "Go. Take all that delicious Svesti maleness out of my vicinity. I don't want you to be late for the king."

"Snack?"

"No. I'd rather wait until we can eat together. Maybe I'll just take a nap." She felt him pull up the sheet to cover her cooling body as she yawned.

"Rest, then, beautiful one." His lips brushed her forehead. "I'll be back when I can."

"Mmmm, okay," she mumbled before exhaustion overtook her.

The Svesti male worked at the console at the edge of the cargo bay. Ever since Theron, he hadn't been able to do anything else to scare the human females. They were more cautious and rarely alone.

He didn't know why the Commander and the kidnapped human female hadn't rejoined the *Invictus*. His uncle was insistent that if there was even a remote chance the Zuvgran infected the female before her rescue, she needed to infect the other females. He'd thought long and hard about how to make that happen.

He typed the last few lines of code into the console. *That should do it.* He whistled tunelessly under his breath as he walked away. *Now, to ensure my alibi.*

Chapter 21

"YOU LOOK...RELAXED, cousin," Traxen said with a smile.

Vared grinned. "I am."

"I would have thought you would be exploding with unused energy by now in quarantine."

"I am occupying my time." Vared knew his face had to be showing his happiness.

Traxen's smile grew, his lavender eyes glinting with humor. "So you and Lady Talia are getting along better."

"Yes."

"So she will be staying when we have a vaccine."

Vared's smile fell. "I don't know. The future is uncertain for both of us. We are, as humans say, playing it by ear."

"What a curious expression." Traxen's countenance turned thoughtful. "What will you do if she returns to Earth?"

Vared couldn't stop the growl or his clenching fists. "I don't know, cousin."

Concerned, Traxen leaned forward. "Are you sure this is the best path for you?"

"I only know that her happiness and well-being mean more to me than my own."

"I see. I am here for you, cousin, whatever happens."

Vared dipped his head. "I appreciate your support, Traxen."

"How goes the search for the traitor?"

"Not as well as I would like." Vared felt his scar tug at his cheek when he frowned. "He is covering his tracks well. Tolvex and Lady Emmy have been reviewing security recordings and working to figure out how the traitor is communicating from the ship, while Wurvez and Lady Rachel have attempted to set some traps to lure the traitor out. So far, nothing."

"I want him found." It surprised Vared that Traxen's growl did not shake his desk.

"As do I, cousin. He put the females in danger multiple times."

"Any progress on a potential agreement with Earth?"

"I think you will be pleased with it when we are finished. Talia has had a number of interesting ideas. Did you know that on Earth, there are females that will agree to what they call surrogacy? A fertilized egg is implanted in their womb and they will carry the young until birth."

Traxen's surprise was evident. "Is that truth?"

"I looked it up on the human internet we downloaded and, yes, it does happen."

"What an interesting concept. Hmmm."

"There is one thing, though, that I need your guidance on, sire."

"What is that?"

"Talia has suggested that to integrate our races more, we should not only consider birthing and troth contracts, but allow limited emigration from Earth without that specific intent or expectation. If it works well, we can expand the program."

"Elaborate."

"Earth has many problems. One is overpopulation and another is there are females who are abused by their mates. Talia suggests we allow some of those females and their young to emigrate to Costonia. She believes if we provide the females with aid—housing, financial, and emotional support—and allow them time to heal and experience true safety, we will help their race. Their young would grow up familiar with Svesti culture. Some females may ultimately choose Svesti males, but should not feel pressured to do so, especially after their treatment by human males."

"And should it only be those with female young?"

"No. Talia believes, and I agree with her, the genders of the young should not be a factor."

"Interesting." Traxen tapped a claw on his desk. "She has other ideas like this?"

"Yes. Talia believes a multi-pronged approach to integrate our races where pairings primarily occur naturally, rather than by contract, would yield the best results for both races in the long-term. Although she agrees contracts will aid in the short-term."

"The humans may not realize it, but even though they lied to her about the Choosing, they chose a worthy ambassador."

Vared smiled. "They did. She's intelligent, and she cares about what is best for both races. She's also cautious. She would like to integrate in a measured approach rather than, as she says, opening the floodgates. With some of her ideas, she would like Svesti to be stationed on Earth, perhaps rotating through details, so that pairings might occur naturally there as well."

"I look forward to seeing what the two of you come up with."

"We're still working out some of it, but it is going very well."

"Good. My reports from the healers are they may have a vaccine for you soon. The research you extracted from XB9428B had everything for this latest virus. Unfortunately, there was nothing on the one that infected our Svesti females."

"That is promising news for both races." Vared gritted his teeth.

"But not so promising for you," Traxen said gently, his eyes darkening.

"I admit I am conflicted, cousin. I haven't been this happy and content since before the first virus. But I cannot put my happiness above our race or Talia's." Vared's tail flicked rapidly.

"Perhaps we can make it a condition of the agreement that Lady Talia is to remain on Costonia as the ambassador."

"No. Not if she does not wish it, cousin."

"I have crews building additional relay stations to enhance communications with her world. Once they are operational, she could speak with her son and family regularly."

"I'm not sure that will be enough for her."

"It is something in favor of staying, Vared. And don't discount your dubious charms, either." Traxen grinned.

Vared laughed before he turned serious again. "No matter what happens, I cannot regret this time with her, Traxen."

"You deserve to be happy, Vared. May the Goddess guide you." Traxen bowed his head briefly.

"And you as well, cousin. Until tomorrow." Vared disconnected the comm. He sighed heavily as his comm chimed immediately. "*Intrepid*," he said.

"Commander, incoming private transmission from your father. Should I patch it through?" Brauvix asked.

"Yes, thank you."

Vared activated the holographic feature on the comm.

"Father, it is good to see you." He noted some silver interspersed in his father's dark braids. *He's starting to show his years, just a little.*

"Vared, my son. You look well." Twinkling brown eyes and a hearty voice mirrored the affection that he felt for the male.

"I feel well."

"No adverse effects from the virus?" The twinkle dimmed.

"Beyond my fertility loss, none. Have you news on rooting out the traitors?"

"Unfortunately, not yet. They are being cautious." His father's face hardened. "We will find them and they will answer for their crimes."

"From your lips to the Goddess' ears." Vared sat back. "Is all well with you?"

"Fine, fine." His father waved impatiently. "I am not the one to be concerned about."

Vared grinned. "So you continue to be a hearty male and hope to entice a human female to a troth contract?" He bit the inside of his cheek to keep from laughing at his father's outraged look.

"I can still take you in the sparring ring, you insolent male." His father glared for a moment before chuckling. "Why do you deliberately rile me so?"

"Because I can and you expect it." Vared's smile widened. "I've missed you."

"And I you, although sometimes I don't understand why," his father grumbled affectionately. "How is the human female?"

"Her name is Talia, and she's fine." Vared attempted to keep his happiness from showing.

Narrowing his eyes, his father said, "What is it you are not telling me, son?"

"Nothing." *Crek!*

"There's something..." His father stopped speaking when he heard Talia's voice.

"Vared? I thought I'd bring you a snack instead." Talia halted when she saw his father. "I'm sorry; I didn't realize you were busy. I'll just leave the tray here and talk to you later."

"Vared, introduce us."

Vared swallowed his sigh and made the introductions. Despite his best efforts, his mind wandered as his father asked Talia to call him Canaan and they exchanged small talk. They spoke about the virus and the Choosing. Vared imagined himself with Talia on his lap, sharing time at his family's estate with his father. A small smile graced his lips at his musings.

"Vared? Are you even listening?" Talia's small hand slapped his bicep. He shook his head.

"I apologize. Did I miss something important?"

Talia huffed and tapped her foot impatiently. He couldn't help but notice how her crossed arms pushed up her breasts and made them look fuller.

"Eyes up here." She swatted his nose. He raised his eyes to hers and grinned. "I'll leave you to finish your conversation with your father." She turned, and he barely refrained from licking his lips. He loved how her pants outlined her ample ass.

"Thank you, *kirani*, for the snack." Without looking back, she waved in acknowledgment as she left the room.

"I recognize that look. I don't know whether to congratulate you or worry," his father said.

Vared looked at the most important male in his life. "What look?"

"The same one I used to give your mother." Canaan smiled sadly in remembrance. "The one that said *I will cherish and protect you and how soon can I get you naked* all at the same time."

"Father!"

"What? How do you think you and your sisters came to be?" Canaan grinned.

"I do *not* want to hear about Mother naked." Vared shivered in horror.

His father laughed before his eyes turned serious. "She can no longer have young, Vared."

Vared growled. "I don't care."

"So the continuation of our line is not important to you?"

"It is, but not as important as Talia." Vared held his breath, waiting for his father's disapproval. His father's face remained impassive and his voice calm.

"I see. How does she feel?"

"She is conflicted. She has a son and sister on Earth and cannot imagine not seeing them again."

"And you?"

"I am conflicted, too. As a warrior's mate, her life would be exposed to danger, and I want her safe. Also, I wish her to be happy, even if it's not with me."

"And how are you together?"

Vared couldn't help the joy spreading across his face. "Better than I ever could have dreamed, Father."

"What if you were to relocate to Earth?"

Vared tilted his head. "We hadn't considered that." He thought for a moment. "I'm not sure that would work. I don't know how humans would react to a single Svesti living among them without a treaty—or even with a treaty. Would they target her in ignorance, putting her in danger?"

"A valid concern." His father drew in a breath. "One last question, my son. Who are you with her?"

"I'm not sure I understand what you are asking." Vared knew his confusion must show on his face.

"Are you Commander Durek? Or someone else?"

Vared closed his eyes. "I'm me. Just Vared. Sometimes a warrior, sometimes a commander, sometimes an idiot or a fool, but I do not feel I have to be anyone but who I am in that moment.

I feel like a better male when I am with her." He opened his eyes and looked at his father. "Does that make sense?"

"Yes, it does."

"Are you disappointed in me?"

"My son, you are the last of our direct line. I admit when I learned of the human females, I had hoped you might find one to breed with. Not just to continue our line, but so you could have young as I did to bring you joy. And that young would bring me joy as well." Vared's tail flicked rapidly as his father spoke. "However, given a choice between continuing our line or my only son's happiness, I will choose your happiness every time."

Canaan smiled and Vared's tail stilled. "While I am angry that the Zuvgran shortened our time together, I am grateful beyond measure I had what time with your mother that we did. Her love did make me a better male. And she was quite willing to let me know when I was being an idiot or fool." They both chuckled. "If being with Lady Talia brings you even half the happiness I had with your mother, then I am elated for you."

"I still don't know what to do. Even if she were to choose to stay with me, I am still a warrior."

"Do not let one female's fears become yours, son. Does Talia fear you being a warrior?"

"Not that she's mentioned."

"Did you tell her about Shazeen?"

"Yes."

"And what did Talia say?"

"She said Shazeen was wrong to try to change me."

His father grinned happily. "It sounds like she accepts you as you are and you are the one worried."

"That is accurate."

"And do you feel there is anyone who would protect her better than you?"

Vared couldn't stop the low growl from rising in his chest. "No one could. I would kill and die to protect her."

"Then it seems to me that the safest place for her is by your side." His father's level look froze Vared in place. "Don't give up a chance at happiness for something that may never happen, my son. Even before the virus, not all males had the chance to experience the love of a good female. Don't waste yours."

Vared blew out a breath. "How did you get to be so wise?"

"I had no choice with a son like you constantly testing me." Canaan chuckled.

Vared grinned. "I know I don't say it enough, but I am glad you are my father. I am who I am because of your love and guidance."

"I am glad you are my son, Vared. You may not believe this, but I am also a better male because of you. Unconditional love has that effect on you. You keep striving to be worthy of it."

Unconditional love has that effect on you. You keep striving to be worthy of it. His father's words bounced in Vared's thoughts as he searched for Talia. *Even today, I was worried he would be*

disappointed in me. I am glad he is not like Karid's sire, who almost disowned him for becoming a warrior.

Vared frowned when he didn't find Talia in their quarters or in the dining area. *Where is she?* He sniffed, testing for her scent, but he could not find a recent trail. Becoming worried, he used his tablet to locate her tracker. *Crek! How did she get there?*

"Tolvex," he growled through his comm. "Talia is no longer on the *Intrepid*. I show her on the *Invictus*. How did this happen?"

"*Crek!* I'm on my way to her now."

"Did you port her?" Vared's shoulders tightened, and his tail was whipping wildly behind him.

"Of course not."

"Port me to her."

"Negative, Commander. We can't risk it."

"If she's already there, what difference does it make?" Vared's voice felt like gravel in his throat.

"Emmy had a plan in place, in case something like this were to happen. Hopefully, it worked as designed."

"What plan and why wasn't I informed?"

"She just told me about it this morning, Vared. I haven't even had time to check her programming. Let me check and see what's going on here and get back to you."

Vared growled louder. "Protect her and send her back here as soon as possible."

"As you command."

Metal crunched as Vared punched the wall. *Kirani, what happened?*

Chapter 22

I'M GLAD *I took a shower and got dressed before barging in on them.* Talia shook her head, smiling as she headed to the dining area. *Can't believe he was checking out my boobs in front of his father. Men are the same everywhere.*

She saw a whitish-blue light. Before she could yell for Vared, she was ported from the *Intrepid*. When it was done, she was in what looked like a small med bay. *Where the hell am I and who's messing with me now?*

While examining her surroundings, she came up against an invisible obstruction, keeping her from half of the room. Using her hands, she tried to see if there was a way through, but she couldn't find one. When she heard running footsteps, she looked for something to use as a weapon and moved back.

Emmy skidded to a stop on the other side of the room and pumped her arm. "Yes! It worked!" Ava and Lin ran in behind her.

"Talia, it's so good to see you." Ava tried to approach, but ran into the barrier. "What the hell?" She rubbed her nose.

"Emmy, why the hell am I here?" Talia demanded.

"I set up…" Emmy broke off her words and tilted her head towards Ava and Lin.

Talia sighed. "We might as well tell them."

"Tell us what?" Lin asked quietly.

Tolvex rushed in and locked the door behind him. "Lady Talia, are you okay?"

"Yes, Tolvex, but I'm confused."

"Devik, was anyone in the brig?" Emmy asked.

"No, no one is there."

"Damn, damn, damn. Let me see what happened." Emmy tapped on her tablet.

Ava crossed her arms. "Would someone tell us what the hell is going on?"

Talia nodded at Tolvex. He said, "This is confidential information, ladies. When Lady Talia was with the Zuvgran, she was injected with an airborne virus that kills human and Svesti fertility."

"What? Are you okay?" Ava asked Talia.

"Yes, but that's why Vared and I have been on the *Intrepid*. We're hoping they'll develop a vaccine to keep everyone safe. But I don't know if you're all infected now."

"No, we shouldn't be," said Emmy. "When we spoke a few days ago, you mentioned being worried about the traitor using you to infect the *Invictus*. I thought about the ways he could do it. The primary way was to port you onboard. So I wrote a program that overrides any porting between the two ships or using your tracker to end up here, since this is where Natasha and Rivezt port your biological samples. The traitor tried to port you to the dining area, but my program redirected you here. You're in a self-contained isolation area—not even air recirculates to the main ship."

"Traitor?" Lin bit her lip. "The traitor again?"

"Oh, there's so much we need to catch you two up on," Emmy said. "For now, don't discuss this outside of our quarters. Devik, Rivezt, and Wurvez might conduct a meeting about it elsewhere. They'll let us know if it's safe to talk. We're the only ones onboard that know about it. Publicly, we have to keep pretending Talia is suffering from PTSD."

Ava and Lin looked at each other and shrugged.

"Okay, whatever you say," Ava said. "But we want the whole story as soon as you can tell us."

"Rivezt and Lady Natasha are on their way," Tolvex said. "Why was no one in the brig?"

"I'm trying to figure it out, mate." Emmy's impatient snort sounded loud over the tapping on her tablet.

Tolvex' lips twisted like he couldn't decide if he was angry or amused. His comm chimed. "Tolvex."

"Is Talia safe?" Vared's growly voice filled the space.

"Yes. The traitor tried to port her into a main area of the ship, but Emmy's program sent her directly to an isolation area."

"Thank the Goddess. Ask her why she's not wearing her comm."

"Tell him I didn't think I needed it."

"You will wear it from now on, *kirani*. I need to be able to contact you."

"We'll discuss it later, Vared. Right now, there are more important things we need to know. Like why someone should be in the brig." Talia looked at Tolvex.

"Emmy's program should have immediately ported whomever was initiating the porting process to the brig so we could catch the traitor. But it seems it did not work." Tolvex frowned.

"It worked just fine, mate," Emmy countered. "The bastard put the port on a time delay, so there was no one standing near the station when the port began."

"If he weren't a traitor who needed to be caught, I'd be impressed with his ingenuity," Tolvex grumbled.

"When is Talia being ported back?" Vared asked.

"We're waiting on Rivezt and Lady Natasha to give the all clear."

Rivezt's voice sounded over a speaker. "Tolvex, I need you to get blood samples from the females and yourself, so we can ensure none of you are infected. Also, an air sample to see if any of the virus made it outside the isolation area. Everything you need should be in the storage area."

Tolvex moved to collect what he needed. "Should we port Lady Talia back now?"

"Actually, since she's here anyway, I would like to get another full body scan and blood sample," Natasha said over the speaker.

"Did you hear that, Commander?" Tolvex asked.

"I do not like it. How long will it take?"

"Less than an hour, then we can send her back," Rivezt said.

"Comm me before you port."

"As you command."

While Tolvex and the others were collecting their samples, Talia took her blood and watched as it disappeared in a port for the doctors to test it. She hopped up on the med bed. Rivezt conducted a full body scan remotely and extracted some of her damaged eggs.

When Tolvex suggested porting her back to the *Intrepid*, she asked him to wait until they had the results back. Everything came back negative for those on the other side of the med bay. Closing her eyes, Talia murmured a silent thanks to the universe that her friends weren't infected.

Vared was waiting for Talia when she ported back to the *Intrepid*. He ran restless hands over her body, checking for injuries. "Are you alright, *kirani*?"

"I'm fine, Vared." She caressed his face and forced him to meet her eyes. Softening, she said, "Really, truly, I'm fine."

Relief replaced the anxiety on his face. He rested his forehead on hers. "Not knowing what happened or where you were worried me greatly."

She closed her eyes and whispered, "I know, but I'm here now and unhurt."

"How did this happen?" She saw the commander in him as he straightened and clenched his jaw. *Damn, that's sexy.*

"Emmy said the traitor used my tracker to port me."

"If he'd been successful, everyone on *Invictus* would have been infected."

"The traitor doesn't know the virus affects Svesti. Perhaps it's time to tell the crew the truth," Talia suggested.

Vared tilted his head. His expressionless face fascinated Talia. His lavender gaze was unfocused, but it felt like she could see the thoughts behind them as he deliberated.

"I'll have to consult with the king. If we tell the crew, the information will make it back to Costonia. It might affect the king's efforts to find the traitors on the home world."

"I hadn't considered that." Talia frowned. "There are so many moving parts to all of this."

"Yes, but for now, let's eat. I'll contact Traxen after." Vared held her hand as they walked. "I'm glad Lady Emmy had a plan in place for a situation like this and that it worked."

"Unfortunately, we didn't get the traitor." Talia frowned. "He's getting bolder. This wouldn't have been considered an accident."

Vared's chest rumbled angrily. "I'm looking forward to catching him. We need to know who he's working with on Costonia."

"Do you think it's just a few Svesti or is it a whole faction?"

"I hope it's just a few, but I'm concerned it's more widespread than we know."

"What do we do? A faction puts all of us, including humans on Earth, at risk."

"We root them out, *kirani*, as best we can, and we take steps to protect us all."

"I hope that's enough, Vared."

"As do I."

Talia listened to Vared's heartbeat slow as she regained her breath. *Damn, he keeps getting better and better.* The musk of their combined scents tickled her nose. She raised her head and smiled at his peaceful expression. Her fingers reached to caress his face.

"I've never asked you how you got this scar."

Vared opened his eyes. "It was on one of my first missions to a Zuvgran-controlled world. Devik, Karid, Ash'n, and I were in the same unit. Our orders were to capture a Zuvgran commander. According to our intel, he had a small security force at his home. But it must've been a trap. They were waiting for us."

"Oh."

"We were outnumbered almost three to one." A faraway look entered his lavender eyes. "It was the first time our unit saw battle. We lost a number of good Svesti that day."

"I'm so sorry, babe." Talia stroked his chest.

"I received this during the battle. Normally, it would have been healed right away, but someone blew up the building. I was trapped in the rubble for over a day."

"What happened to the Zuvgran commander?"

"He got away, but we tracked him down not long after."

"Good." Talia traced the lines of his clan marking. "I like this. It suits you."

Holding her finger, he outlined the portion of his clan marking that belonged to his father. "This is House Ruxila."

"And the starburst one is your mother's house?"

"Yes, House Davelk."

"That's the same house as the king, isn't it?"

"Yes, Traxen's father and my mother were siblings."

Talia glanced at him in surprise. "I didn't realize you and the king were related."

"We're cousins. Traxen is a good male, and an excellent leader. That reminds me, I have something for you." Vared reached around her to a drawer and pulled out something wrapped in paper. "I bought this for you on Theron."

Talia opened the gift and smiled when she saw the necklace. "It's the one with stones that match your eyes."

"Is that why you liked it?"

"It was one reason. I also liked the starburst."

Taking the necklace from her, he sat them up and moved her hair over one shoulder. She shivered at the cold metal touching her skin as he wrapped the light chain around her neck before engaging the clasp. Turning her upper body, she kissed him. "Thank you, Vared. It's beautiful."

Gently, he lifted the pendant to look at it, before dropping it to rest just above her cleavage. "Not as beautiful as you, *kirani*." Sliding his hand into her hair, he drew her closer for another kiss. "I spoke to my father about us."

"You did?"

"He suggested we might consider my going back to Earth with you."

Talia stared at him. "You would do that?"

He nodded. "I've thought about it, and I want us to remain together. If Earth is where you will be happiest, then I'll return with you."

Tears filled her eyes. "Oh, Vared. That means so much to me, but I can't let you do that. It's not fair to you. You would have to give up being a warrior. What you do is important." She drew in a shaky breath. "And, truthfully, I don't trust humans not to mistreat you."

"Are you suggesting I can't take care of myself?"

"No, but humans have a long history of fear-based actions. It wouldn't surprise me if there were those that would want to capture you and perform experiments on you. Or torture you for information about the Svesti."

His eyes narrowed. "They would act like the Zuvgran?"

"I don't think they'd be as bad, but, yes, we have some that would delude themselves into thinking they were protecting humans. The fact that you're different and an unknown would be enough for them to convince themselves and others that it was necessary."

"The more I learn about humans, the more I wonder how your race has survived as long as it has." He shook his head in disbelief.

Talia laughed sadly. "You're not the only one who wonders that, babe. We have some wonderful, caring people, and we also have some total assholes. Unfortunately, fear is a powerful motivator and clouds people's judgment." She tilted her head. "Although it seems the Svesti are experiencing a bit of the same thing themselves with this traitor business."

He hummed in thought. "You may have a valid point. So you don't believe my returning to Earth is feasible for us?"

"I wish I did, but no. I would have more fear that something awful could happen to you than I do now."

"What are we going to do, *kirani*? I don't want to give up on us." Tugging her closer, he rested his forehead on hers.

"I don't know, babe. I just don't know."

Crek! As far as the Svesti male could tell, the human female never made it to the *Invictus. What happened? The coding was sound.*

The traitor punched the training bot hard enough that it tipped over. Growling low, he turned it off before yanking it upright. As he cooled down, his thoughts circled the problem. Then he smiled.

If I can't get her here, maybe I need to reverse it. In a much better mood, he left the training area. *It'll take a day or two to arrange it, but perhaps it will be worth it.*

Personal Journal - Day 28.

Shit's getting real. Vared offered to return to Earth with me. He doesn't believe it, but I'm sure he would end up resenting me if he gave up everything for us to be together. I don't think I could handle it if that were to happen, because, once again, I wouldn't be good enough.

If his cousin agrees to some of my suggestions, maybe Vared could be stationed on Earth part of the time. Would it be better or worse for us to only see each other part time?

I'm frustrated. In my books, I can weave complicated scenarios and solve them with a happy ending. But for the life of me, I can't seem to find an answer for us.

Chapter 23

"WE'RE SENDING OVER a vaccine for you," said Ash'n.

Vared looked at the healers. "You've developed one?"

"With a lot of help from Lady Natasha and the Master Healer, yes. We think this will work." Ash'n smiled.

"It won't correct the damage already done," said Lady Natasha. "However, it renders the virus inert so that you can't transmit it to others."

"What if the Zuvgran infect more people? Will they lose their fertility, too?" Talia bit her lip.

"If this works as we hope, once someone is vaccinated, it would render the virus ineffective if that being is subsequently exposed to it," Ash'n said.

"The issue then becomes how do we ensure humans on Earth receive the vaccine before the Zuvgran release the virus," said Lady Natasha.

"We send it to Earth with instructions," Vared said. He looked at both females when they sighed.

"Yeah, well, remember what I said about some humans being total assholes?" said Talia. "The problem is getting them to believe it's necessary and that we're not trying to do some weird alien stuff to them."

"Talia is right. Some humans are contrary, even when presented with facts." Lady Natasha frowned, her brown eyes serious.

"Well, we can decide on how best to handle that with the king," said Vared, his tail swaying. "First, we need to know if it works."

"True," said Ash'n. "We're not positive how long it will take to render the virus inert if someone is already infected. We believe it will occur within several days."

"How do we determine if it protects people without exposing them to the virus?" asked Talia. "What if it only keeps us from spreading it, but doesn't protect someone from getting it?"

Ash'n frowned. "That is a concern. The only way to test it is to expose someone to you before you receive the vaccine."

"I'm not comfortable with that," Vared said at the same time Talia said, "No."

"We need to, Vared. Devik has already received the vaccine and volunteered. I was going to do it, but he convinced me the *Invictus* needed a healer more than a security officer."

"I don't agree." Vared's growl filled his chest and his tail flicked in short, fast snaps. "We cannot expose anyone else."

"Too late," said Devik from behind them. "I'm already here."

"Why would you do this, Devik?" Vared yelled at his friend.

"Because I am the logical choice, Vared," Devik said calmly. "Ash'n is needed as a healer, Karid is needed to command the *Invictus* if the vaccine doesn't work, and we all agreed that potentially infecting the human females is unacceptable. I have three brothers to continue my father's line if this doesn't work."

Talia laid a hand on Vared's forearm. "Why weren't we involved in this decision?"

Lady Natasha said, "Because we knew both of you would disagree."

"Last I heard, I was still the Commander of the *Invictus*." Vared's angry roar echoed off the walls.

Devik nodded. "Yes, you are. That is why we went over your head to the king."

"You did what?" Talia's arms wrapped around Vared's waist. He looked down and saw tears in her eyes.

"This vaccine better work. I don't know if I can handle the guilt if you become infected, too, Tolvex," she said quietly.

"Lady Talia, I trust the healers, and I believe it will work. But if it doesn't, it is my honor to sacrifice my fertility for both our worlds." Devik's teal eyes softened. "Guilt is unnecessary. My life is not in danger, and it is my choice." He looked at Vared, his face hardening. "I'll say it again, Vared. It's my choice."

Vared worked to control his temper. After a few long moments, he blew out a harsh breath. "My friend, I am going to take pleasure in causing you great pain when we spar."

Devik and Ash'n both laughed. Devik clapped Vared on the back. "I look forward to it."

"Vared, we'd like you to have the vaccine, but wait until tomorrow for Lady Talia's turn," said Ash'n.

"Why wait?" Vared asked.

"We want to ensure that Tolvex's exposure is for more than a few minutes," said Lady Natasha. "We'll also need blood samples from you and Tolvex every hour to track the vaccine's progress. And sperm samples from both of you in eight hours."

Vared watched Talia toy with her necklace as he injected himself with the vaccine Devik handed him. He drew his blood and gave the vial to Devik to port.

When they were alone, Vared gently pulled Talia into his arms, smoothing her hair behind her ear. "It looks like we have a shuttle guest."

Smiling, she rested her hand on his cheek. "So no more sex in public areas, huh?"

He turned his head and kissed her palm, then grinned at her. "You'll have to control yourself."

Laughing, she pushed at his chest with her other hand. "Oh, like you're going to find it so easy. I seem to recall you're the one who gets handsy pretty much everywhere we are."

Caressing her back, his hands drifted lower to squeeze her ass. "I have no idea what you're talking about, *kirani*." Dropping his eyes, he enjoyed the sight of her soft breasts pressed against his bare chest.

"I know that look, Vared. Don't get started." She giggled when he lowered his head to rub his cheek against her mounds. "Knock that off."

Hearing Devik returning, Vared straightened and flashed his fangs in a wide grin. "What is that Earth saying? Check on the rain?"

"Rain check, babe."

"I'm still not happy with you," Vared said as he sparred with Devik.

"It was the right decision. You know that," Devik said as he dodged Vared's fist.

"That doesn't mean I agree with it." Vared feinted right, then punched Devik's stomach with his left.

"Ooomph." Devik's teal eyes narrowed. "Well, you don't have to be happy. You just have to accept it and let it go." He landed a blow on Vared's chin.

Vared shook his head, sweat flying off his face. "You went over my head, you *naroon*." He dodged the next punch.

"You know why I did." Devik blocked the uppercut. "You and Lady Talia were too close to the situation to make the decision. It needed to be made dispassionately."

Vared's angry growl rose in his chest and he surged forward to tackle Devik. He threw a rage-filled punch into the mat to the right of his friend's head. The loud whack sounded over their heavy breathing. "Next time, show me the respect of telling me you're going to the king before you do it."

Silently, Devik searched Vared's face. Then he nodded. "You're right. We should've presented the plan to you first, then gone to the king if you didn't agree. I apologize."

Vared grunted and stood. He held out his hand to help Devik up. "Don't do it again."

Devik slapped his hand into Vared's and got to his feet. "I won't, brother."

They were silent as they wiped the sweat from their bodies and rehydrated. Then Vared said, "I have no problem sending you into battle, Devik, but the thought that you could lose your chance at young upsets me."

"Because the virus is an enemy our skill and determination can't fight, Vared. Our warrior skills mean nothing to it."

Vared let his friend's words settle into him. He nodded slowly. "Perhaps you're right. I still wish you hadn't done it."

"I understand your concern, but you need to respect my choice." Devik smiled. "So you and the Ambassador?"

"We're making good progress on a tentative agreement between our races."

Devik laughed. "That's not what I'm talking about, and you know it. I do have a nose." His face became serious. "Have you mated her?"

"No, we haven't decided what we're going to do. I offered to return to Earth with her, but she refuses to have me give up my career. She also has some other valid concerns about my living on Earth."

Astonishment coated Devik's voice and showed on his face. "You would leave Costonia? Isn't it too early in your relationship to make such an enormous change in your life?"

Vared locked eyes with his friend. "Talia is everything to me. I want to be with her, no matter the sacrifice."

"So you're happy?"

"Absolutely. I only wish that we could find a solution for the future that will make her happy."

"I'm curious. How do your feelings compare to those you had with Shazeen?"

Vared felt his brows knit. "I can see now that Shazeen was a youthful infatuation. It pales in comparison to what I feel for Talia."

"If the vaccine works, your time together grows shorter." Devik frowned.

"I'm aware." Vared's shoulders drooped slightly. "I don't know the best course of action."

"Whatever you need, brother, I will help."

Drawing in a deep breath, Vared sighed. "For now, let's clean up. Then you can tell me all that is happening on the *Invictus*."

The next day, Vared sat with Talia and Devik in the dining area sharing the midday meal. The conversation flowed easily and Vared enjoyed watching two of his favorite people interacting. Talia's animated gestures as she spoke drew his gaze as he remembered her hands on his body earlier in the morning. His grin widened as he listened to Devik debate with her about her ideas for an agreement between their races.

"It does not matter what the intent is, Lady Talia, only what is written," Devik said.

Her brown eyes narrowed. "On Earth, intent is a large portion of arbitrating a disagreement of a contract. I wrote a book once that included negotiations of an agreement. I specifically spent time with lawyers and negotiating parties to ensure accuracy."

"Well, if you check your knowledge of Svesti law, you will find that most judgments are for the strictest interpretation of the written word," Devik countered.

Frowning, she said, "Another difference between our races that could create problems."

"Could you include an explanation of the intentions to the treaty?"

She smiled and turned to Vared. "What do you think? Should we include a more detailed addendum outlining what we are attempting to achieve?"

"I think it's an excellent idea, *kirani*," Vared said as his tail wrapped around her ankle.

She opened her notebook and began writing. Under her breath, she said, "To account for potential differences in law between the two parties, this addendum is to clarify the intent of each party for..." The sound of her pen moving over the paper sounded louder than her mumbles.

Devik looked at him. "What just happened?" He tilted his head at Talia. "Is she even paying attention any longer?"

Vared chuckled. "When she has an idea and begins to write, the outside world no longer exists for her. If she hasn't set an alarm, she'll go until she tires or is interrupted."

"Fascinating. Why doesn't she use a tablet?"

"She says she likes to put her thoughts on paper before entering it digitally anywhere."

"It seems like it would be twice the work." Devik shook his head.

"According to her, she is an anomaly on Earth as well, as most choose to use their computers to write. But she claims it helps her frame her thoughts."

"Have you read any of her fiction?"

"No. Have you?"

Devik looked sheepish. "After that pink-haired human with the Wing Raiders mentioned Lady Talia's books, I searched the human internet for them. Fortunately, we downloaded a number of library collections and I found them."

"And?"

"They are surprisingly good stories. The characters feel believable, even in unbelievable circumstances. And there are warriors."

"Then why do you look uncomfortable?"

"There are a lot of detailed descriptions of mating in the books, much more so than in our literature. However, I do feel I've learned a lot about human anatomy when it comes to mating." Devik laughed.

"Really?" Vared smiled. "Send me the titles so that I may read them and see if there is anything I should learn myself."

"*Kirani?* It's time for us to meet with the healers," Vared said as he gently brushed her hair from her face.

"Huh?" Talia's eyes slowly focused on him as she lifted her head.

"The healers?"

"Oh, that's right." She blew out a breath. "I'm sorry. I wanted to get some ideas down."

He smiled at her. "That's fine. Devik and I kept busy without you. I just wanted to give you a few moments to collect yourself before the meeting." He handed her some water.

"Thank you, babe."

Devik entered the dining area. "Ready?"

Vared nodded. Devik tapped his comm, and the healers appeared.

"Good afternoon, everyone," Lady Natasha said.

They exchanged short pleasantries. Then Ash'n said, "The vaccine appears to be working. None of Devik's samples show any sign of the virus."

Talia murmured, "Thank goodness."

Vared said, "And my samples?"

"The virus is inert. As of right now, your fertility is still non-existent." Ash'n frowned.

"We'd like you to give Talia the vaccine now. You'll be able to..." Lady Natasha's words cut off as she was ported unexpectedly.

"What the hell?" Talia exclaimed.

"Devik, where is she?" Vared growled.

"I'm searching for her tracker now," Devik said as he tapped his tablet. His comm chimed. "Emmy is attempting to contact us."

"Encrypted channel," Vared ordered.

"Devik. The traitor is at it again," Emmy said. "He attempted to port all the women to the *Intrepid*."

"Where are you now?" Vared asked.

"In Talia's quarters. I set up the program to port us here, since we knew no one would be in the way."

"Good plan," said Vared.

"Did the traitor use a time delay again?" Devik asked.

"Yes." Lady Emmy's lips thinned. "He's really starting to piss me off."

Vared saw his confusion mirrored on the other Svesti faces. He looked at Talia.

"Slang for making her angry," Talia said with a half-smile.

Vared nodded. "Devik, get Karid on an encrypted channel."

Karid joined them. "What's going on?"

Vared briefed him. "I want guards with the females at all times."

Talia pulled on his arm. "Slow down, Vared. Let's think this through."

He glanced down at her. "What do you mean?"

"What if we let the traitor think he's been successful?"

Devik said, "How do you mean?"

Talia bit her lip. "Right now, we're operating on the assumption that the traitor may or may not know that I was infected, right? So, if he thinks I've been infected, what is his goal?"

"To infect the other human women," said Vared.

"But it also puts the males at risk," said Karid.

"He doesn't know that," Talia said. "So if Tolvex and Emmy make it look like the women were ported here, then returned to the *Invictus* in a couple hours, he would think he was successful. If they return without a quarantine, then he would believe I wasn't infected. Hopefully, he would stop trying to scare the women."

"There's only one problem doing that, Lady Talia," Karid said as he frowned. "He may not attempt anything else at all. We might not discover who he is before we reach Costonia."

"Talia, I know you are trying to keep the females safe." Vared's tail rubbed her back. "But Karid is correct. We need to catch him, and we cannot do that if he thinks he's won."

Lady Rachel said, "I think there's another way to try to flush him out."

"We're listening."

"Emmy and Tolvex adjust the logs to show us ported, but no destination. Then, in an hour, show another port to our quarters on the *Invictus* without an origin point. We women don't say anything about it at all. We see if anyone asks where we were and just answer that we've been sworn to secrecy, which would be the truth. We note anyone's interest in our whereabouts and follow up with more investigation."

Vared nodded slowly. "I like this idea. Are you females willing to assist us in the manner Lady Rachel outlined?"

"Yes," they all answered.

"Devik, Lady Emmy, are you able to adjust the logs?"

"I'm working on the initial port now," said Lady Emmy.

"I'm setting up the return ports," Devik said as he tapped on his tablet.

"Commander, you can also give Lady Talia the vaccine," said Ash'n. "Once we ensure she has no side effects, and we don't need to adjust it for human biology, we will inoculate the other human females. Lady Talia, we will need hourly blood samples."

"Everyone on the *Invictus* will require the vaccine," said Vared.

"I'm already making enough of the vaccine to do so. I will tell the other healers it is a vaccine against a human flu virus that I discovered when speaking with Lady Natasha. Until the king releases the truth about the Zuvgran virus, it is the best I can do to forestall questions."

"Have we thought of everything?" Vared asked.

"I guess I'll growl and act annoyed when I head back to the bridge, just to keep up appearances that something may have happened," said Karid.

"And is this a departure from your normal behavior?" Vared grinned.

"I'm looking forward to your return, Commander. It's been too long since we've sparred," Karid grumbled, but his eyes were alight with humor.

"You guys really like to beat on each other, don't you?" Talia grinned.

Vared flashed his fangs. "That we do, *kirani*, that we do."

Chapter 24

"IS IT DONE?"

"Unknown," the Svesti male grumbled. "I've attempted porting the females to each other twice, but do not know if the ports were successful."

"What do the females say?"

"They are not speaking about any of it, and I cannot ask without drawing attention to myself."

"You must take greater risks, Nephew." A growl echoed through the comm.

"Do you have any suggestions, Uncle?"

"Kidnap the lone female and ensure she returns to the *Invictus*."

"I will be caught."

"There may be a way, Nephew, to have another do your bidding. We've been testing a way to use implants to control others. We haven't perfected it, but perhaps a field test is in order."

"What do I need to do?"

"You'll need an upload device."

As the Svesti male listened to the detailed instructions, he cringed inwardly at the thought of mind control. While it may be effective for achieving goals for their cause, his warrior's honor felt abused by using such tactics.

"Uncle, why are you researching mind control at all?"

"If we wish to keep the Svesti race pure, we must use every means available to us." His uncle growled through the comm. "Do you have a problem following orders?"

"No. I will do as you instructed."

"Be aware that most test subjects went insane when forced to go against their belief systems. It is best to give short, concise instructions and align them as closely as you can with their own beliefs. In this instance, making a warrior believe he needs to save a female in danger should work."

"How long does it take to work?"

"A couple of days for something simple like this."

"I will do as you instruct."

"Always Svesti."

Several days later, Talia was pleased with the progress she had made on the draft treaty and addendum. Having Tolvex, as well as the women, give input challenged both she and Vared to revise and better their work. She also enjoyed watching the two males interact. They were brothers—chosen, not by blood.

Humming softly, she typed their work into her tablet. Goose bumps rose on her arms when she felt Vared's breath on her nape. He kissed the junction of her shoulder and neck. She shivered in delight and turned to kiss him.

"Are you done training with Tolvex?"

"Mmm, we're done for today. I was hoping you might join me for a shower, *kirani*." His tail stroked her thigh. Her breasts felt swollen in his hands.

"I think that can be arranged." She smiled as he lifted her from the chair and carried her to the bathroom. "You do know I'm capable of walking, right?"

"Yes, I know." He turned the shower on and stepped in.

She shrieked. "Vared! I still have my clothes on."

His fangs glinted as he grinned. "Now you'll be motivated to get naked even quicker."

Her shirt made a wet plopping noise when it hit his chest before sliding toward the floor. "You wanting me was motivation enough, you *naroon*."

"Let me help you." He knelt before her and tugged on her leggings. The material stretched, but clung stubbornly to her legs. He growled in frustration. Curling a claw and avoiding her skin, he ripped her pants. Gripping the material, he tore them so she was left in her panties.

Purring, he nuzzled the junction of her thighs. "I love the smell of your arousal, *kirani*."

"Taste me," she said as she thrust her hips forward. Her fingers buried themselves in his hair and tugged him closer.

His rumbled "As you command, *kirani*" sent streaks of pleasure to her clit.

He pulled her panties down while licking at her core. Her legs shook as her orgasm exploded. Large, hot hands gripped her ass. He lifted her up as he stood. He dropped her onto his hard cock, filling her all at once. The small bite of pain from his abrupt movement morphed into bone-melting pleasure as her pussy rippled from his nodes. She couldn't tell if it was the same orgasm or another as he moved in a hard, fast rhythm. He wrapped an arm around her back to protect her body from the wall. His tail circled her clit, and he took a nipple into his mouth.

"Oh, yes!"

Steam rose around them. Her breath caught in her throat, and she threw her head back as her body convulsed with liquid heat. His howl as he came echoed in her ears and her pussy milked his cock with tight, erratic pulses. His movements slowed, and he kissed her.

Resting his forehead on hers, he said, "The things you do to me, Talia."

She returned his happy grin. "You really have to stop destroying my clothes. At this rate, I won't have anything to wear when we get to Costonia."

His lavender eyes twinkled. "The thought of you naked all the time is supposed to deter me?"

She let an evil smile grow on her face. "If you don't mind other males seeing me naked, then I guess not, babe." She giggled at his disgruntled face. She patted his chest. "Let me down so we can finish cleaning up. Then you can have a look at what the draft treaty looks like. I want to be sure we agree on it all before sending it to the king for his reaction."

Grumbling, he lowered her and ensured she was steady on her feet. "As you wish."

"Results look good. I think all of you can return to the *Invictus* in a couple of days. That should give us enough time to inoculate everyone," Rivezt said.

Vared squeezed Talia's hand. "We'll let Devik know."

"We appreciate all your hard work. Thank you," Talia said.

"Have you informed the king? All Svesti need the vaccine," Vared said.

"Not yet," Rivezt said.

"And we still need to determine the best way to present the information to Earth," Natasha said.

"We'll brainstorm with the king and figure it out," said Talia. "I'm expecting pushback." She blew out a breath and shoved her hair from her face impatiently.

"Men, women, and children will need the vaccine. Otherwise, they'll spread the virus," Natasha said, frowning.

Talia met Natasha's gaze. "I know. But you know humans. I'm pretty sure we never reached herd immunity vaccination numbers from that flu pandemic about twenty years ago. And people were dying horrible, painful deaths."

Natasha tilted her head. "You're right. Maybe we can see if we can add it to the water supply or something."

"No, we can't do that. While it might get us better numbers, the fallout from the Svesti doing something like that would make a treaty with them unlikely." Talia grimaced. "Remember how we felt when we woke up and found they'd changed our bodies without our prior consent?"

"You make a valid point," said Vared.

"All we can do is send them the information, offer to provide the vaccines, and make it a requirement that anyone who wishes to emigrate to Costonia or work with Svesti must be vaccinated." Talia tapped her fingers on the table. "As much as I want everyone protected, we have to let it be their choice. That doesn't mean we can't protect the Svesti, though."

"But human fertility rates will suffer," protested Rivezt.

"True, but if that's the choice they make, so be it. There are plenty of people who will follow the science and do the responsible thing. We don't have to like it, but we do have to respect it."

"Humans are difficult to understand sometimes," growled Vared.

"You'll get no argument from me on that, babe," said Talia.

"We'll start vaccinations on the *Invictus* immediately." Rivezt disconnected the comm.

Vared pulled Talia onto his lap. "Humans will not take the vaccine, will they?"

"Many will, Vared. It may take a little time for the doctors to verify the science, but once they do, many people will be happy to be inoculated to protect themselves and others." She rubbed her cheek against his. "We can only do what we can. We can't force it—not if you want human women to have Svesti babies."

He made an unhappy sound. "I don't like it. We know it's the right thing to do."

"I know it's frustrating. You'll have to trust that it will all work out." Talia dropped a warm kiss on his lips. "Now let me up and I'll make the midday meal."

Vared's kiss was hungry. Talia pressed closer to him, kneading his back with restless hands. When light burst behind her eyelids, she opened her eyes in surprise. A Svesti male appeared behind Vared. She gasped when she saw the dagger in his hand. As Vared turned, the intruder stabbed him. Talia screamed.

"Must rescue the female," panted the intruder, sweat dripping from his face. His eyes wild, he continued to stab Vared. "Durek dishonorable. Must save the female."

Vared extended his claws and attempted to slice behind him. He slumped in Talia's arms, his weight almost toppling them both.

She grunted. *He's too heavy. Please don't let me drop him.* Talia ripped her shirt sleeve off and pressed it over the deepest wounds as best she could with one hand. *Shit! So much blood.*

"Hold on, Vared."

Tolvex ran into the room and disabled the intruder, who muttered the same things over and over. He restrained the attacker, then helped Talia lay Vared down on his uninjured side. He comm'd Rivezt. "The Commander has been attacked. Stab wounds. Difficulty breathing. Just lost consciousness."

Rivezt said, "I'm on my way."

After porting to the *Intrepid* and assessing Vared's condition, Rivezt said, "I need to get him to a med bed now. Override Lady Emmy's program and port us, Tolvex."

Talia's tears slid down her face. "I'm going with you." She tightened her grip on Vared's hand as they were ported. *Don't you leave me, Vared.*

Onboard the *Invictus*, the healers worked rapidly to stem Vared's bleeding. Natasha engaged the med bed's scanner and a holographic image appeared above him. Multiple areas of red showed where his body was damaged. Talia drew in a harsh breath when she heard Rivezt say, "We need to operate."

As he pressed some buttons, Markham said, "Step back. Engaging sterile field." A shimmery light formed over Vared's torso. "Lady Talia, do not touch the commander below his neck."

Talia nodded.

Sinoaz hurried to gather instruments. Rivezt sterilized his hands and Markham sprayed them with a sealant. Once Rivezt took over, the other healers and Natasha did the same to seal their hands before aiding in the surgery.

Talia's hands shook as she caressed Vared's hair and face. "Stay with me, babe. The healers will fix you up and you'll be good as new." Her voice became hoarse as the minutes turned to hours.

Her muscles clenched whenever one of them couldn't find the source of a bleed, then unclenched when she heard, "I've got it." She alternated between watching the healers, looking at the red areas reducing on the hologram, and Vared's slack face. It scared her to see Vared looking so pale and lifeless—a stark contrast to his usual larger-than-life personality. Excruciating pain gripped her chest at the thought that he might not wake up. When the healers closed Vared up, they rotated him to fix him from the back.

Finally, she heard an exhausted Rivezt say, "We've done all that we can. Now we wait. He's heavily sedated. I don't expect him to regain consciousness for at least a day. Thank you all for your assistance." Rivezt nodded at everyone.

After washing up, Natasha laid a gentle hand on Talia's shoulder. "Why don't you go get some rest? You look pale and you could use a change of clothes."

Talia looked down and saw Vared's dried blood caked on her shirt. "I'm not leaving him."

"At least take a shower and change, Talia. You won't do him any good if you don't take care of yourself. I'll have someone bring you some clothes and some food."

Talia wearily nodded. "As long as I can stay here, that's fine."

Natasha said, "There was a lot of damage to his internal organs. You need to be prepared for the fact that he might not make it."

Gritting her teeth, Talia said, "He's strong and stubborn. He'll make it."

"I hope you're right."

Talia sighed. "I didn't even think to ask, but is it even safe for us to be back on the *Invictus*?"

"Yes, we finished the inoculations early this morning." Natasha smiled. "The virus becomes inert within an hour of someone getting vaccinated."

"What about the attacker? Something wasn't right about him." Talia frowned.

"What do you mean, Lady Talia?" Rivezt said.

"He kept saying the same things repeatedly, almost like he was in a fugue state. It sounded like he thought he needed to save me from Vared." Her brows creased. "It was like listening to someone who is manic. Who is the attacker, anyway?"

Rivezt said, "Nerid Mantoor. We haven't assessed him, since we were more concerned with treating the Commander. Let me check on him." He comm'd Tolvex as he walked away.

A short time later, Ava showed up with some snacks and clothes. "How's he doing?" Her green eyes shone with concern.

"He's alive, but it sounds like it isn't over yet," Talia said quietly.

Ava squeezed Talia's hand. "I'll sit with him while you get cleaned up."

Talia wanted to argue and stay with Vared, but she also wanted the physical reminder of the attack off her body. "I won't be long," she said as she stood. Her muscles were stiff.

A small smile tipped Ava's lips. "I won't leave."

In the shower, Talia hung her head and let the hot water pelt her body. All the anxiety she felt rose to the surface, and she sobbed. She let the tears flow freely and eventually she felt her tension ease. *He has to be alright. I won't accept anything else.*

Although she'd tried to keep her heart safe, she now knew that she loved Vared and wanted to spend the rest of her life with him. Seeing him so close to death made her realize how much she cared. She didn't know how they would make it happen, but there was no way she could be apart from him for extended periods of time.

She finished washing, dressed, and stared at her tired reflection in the mirror. She straightened her shoulders. Her brown eyes hardened with resolve—she would help Vared convalesce, figure out how to be together, and stay close to Joshua. *Goddammit, I deserve to have it all and I'm going to make it happen.*

"You look much better," Ava said when Talia approached Vared's med bed. "Have something to eat."

"Thanks," said Talia as she took a sandwich. "I appreciate everything you women have done over the past few weeks."

Ava bit into her own sandwich. After she swallowed, she wagged her eyebrows and said, "So you and the Commander, huh? Still think you're boring?"

Surprised, Talia laughed. "I wasn't expecting you to go there." She smiled. "We're good together—really good. Now he just needs to get better."

"He'll pull through, especially if he knows he has you waiting for him."

"What a sweet thing to say. Don't make me cry again." Talia's eyesight blurred. "Fill me in on what's been happening here."

While Ava shared tidbits of gossip, Talia stroked Vared's face, only half-listening to her friend. *Is his color improving?* Ava excused herself when Tolvex came in.

"Tolvex, is Mantoor the traitor?"

"I don't think so. Rivezt found an upload in his implant. It appears the traitor was brainwashing Mantoor to attack the Commander and bring you to the *Invictus*."

"The implants can be used to control people?"

Tolvex frowned, his face stern. "We've never seen anything like this before. If the traitors are experimenting with implants this way, there is great potential for misuse."

Talia bit her lip. "No one should be experimenting with mind control. People are dangerous enough on their own. They don't need others messing with their free will."

Personal Journal - Day 37.

Vared was critically injured in a surprise attack today—or maybe it was yesterday. It's hard to tell what day it is, but it's the middle of the night. He hasn't regained consciousness, but I'm sitting with him now, watching his stats. I just need a few minutes to get all of this out so I can concentrate solely on him again.

Tolvex told me it looks like the attacker was brainwashed. That scares the shit out of me on so many levels. Rivezt was able to remove the offending upload from Mantoor's implant, but Rivezt said he wasn't sure how much damage was done and what long-term effects there might be for Mantoor. The Svesti have no experience with a situation like this. Sadly, Natasha was able to find information on Earth's internet for the healer. I mean it's good that we might be able to help Mantoor, but sad humans do have some experience with brainwashing. What does that say about us as a species?

Watching Vared almost die made it clear to me that despite my best efforts to keep it from being a serious relationship, I somehow fell in love with this big, stubborn, caring brute of a male. I can't leave him and go back to Earth alone. I want to spend the rest of my life with him.

In between worrying about him, I've been running different scenarios in my head. Right now, the best I've got is us dividing our time between Earth and Costonia somehow. Maybe a year or two on each planet? I know he said that the Svesti were building a communications relay, so I would at least be able to talk to Joshua and Krista regularly. It's not a perfect solution, but I think it's one that I can live with. Now he just has to wake up and agree to it.

Please let him wake up.

Chapter 25

S LOWLY, PAIN MADE itself know to Vared—mostly in his back and his right side. Then he felt the darkness lift enough to notice he was lying on his left side. Groggy, he tried to remember what happened. Then he noticed the scent. *Mine, she's close...where is she?*

Throat parched, he tried to speak. *"Kirani?"*

A soft hand stroked his cheek. "Vared? Are you awake?" His shoulders relaxed as her voice came closer.

"Mmm." He forced his eyes open and saw her beautiful face smile.

"Oh, good. You are waking up." Her eyes looked bruised and exhausted. "You had me worried." She lightly kissed his forehead.

With heavy arms, he tried to reach for her. Gently, she grabbed his hands and stopped him. He grunted in annoyance.

"Stop, Vared. You were seriously injured and shouldn't be exerting yourself yet." Her fingers entwined with his. "I don't want you to hurt yourself even worse."

His scar tugged as he frowned. "What happened?"

Talia quietly brought him up to date as she helped him drink some water. His tail flicked when she told him of the brainwashing. "Hush, babe. Everything that can be done is being done. You've been out for almost three days. You need to heal." Her eyes watered. "You almost died."

He unclenched his jaw. His body was responding better to his commands the longer he was awake. He reached for her face. "Were you hurt?"

She shook her head, rubbing against his hand. "No, only you. And Mantoor. We're not sure if his mind will heal."

His thumb softly stroked her cheek. "Right now, I only care about you."

She kissed his palm. "And I only care about you healing. Go back to sleep, Vared. It's the middle of the night."

"I've missed some days with you. I don't want to miss any more."

This time, a tear fell from her eye. "You sweet male. We'll have many more days. Now rest. I'll be here when you wake." She pressed a button on the med bed.

"What did you just do, Talia?" he asked suspiciously.

"I gave you another dose of pain meds, grumpy." She smiled. "You'll be able to rest better."

"Sneaky female," he grumbled. "I want to hold you." The meds began working, and his eyes slowly closed. "I don't want to sleep."

"I know, babe, but you need it." He felt her hands stroke his forehead and face. Her breath mixed with his. "I'm here and I'm not leaving. Sweet dreams."

The next time Vared woke, it was morning. He heard Talia talking to Ash'n and Lady Natasha. He grunted as he tried to shift on the med bed.

"Commander? Can you hear me?"

Vared opened his eyes. "Yes, Lady Natasha."

She smiled. "Good. How do you feel?"

"Like I've been stabbed multiple times."

"Oh, you're one of those patients," she said with a wide grin.

He tried to roll onto his back. Ash'n said, "I'd rather you didn't do that until we check your wounds, Vared."

Vared grumbled. "Well, check them already so I can move as I like."

Talia giggled. He glared up at her. She pursed her lips and blew him a kiss.

The healers took their time checking his body and asking questions, which he grudgingly answered. When he was finally allowed to sit up, he felt his incisions pull.

Ash'n said, "You're healing well. I'd like to keep you here for another couple of days for observation."

Vared growled. "I will rest easier in my own quarters."

"We can't observe you in your quarters," Ash'n countered. "I know you don't like being in a med bed, but you were closer to death than you have been in a long time, Vared. I want you where we can monitor you. You have a tendency to overdo when healing."

Vared was about to argue with his friend when Talia put her hand on his shoulder. "For my peace of mind, would you at least stay here another day? Preferably without making the healers crazy." She smiled at him.

He sighed heavily. "It would ease your mind?"

"Yes."

"Fine, I'll stay until tomorrow morning."

"Thank you." She leaned over and kissed his lips. "If you're okay for a bit, I'll go take a shower, then get some food for us."

"You look tired. Perhaps you should go rest, *kirani*," he said quietly.

She straightened and brushed her hair from her eyes. "I'll make a deal with you. We have morning meal together, then I'll go rest for a while."

He narrowed his eyes. "Meal, rest, then shower."

Her wide grin encouraged him to grin back at her. Her eyes sparkled as she said, "Deal."

When Talia left the med bay to get them food, Lady Natasha said, "I'm glad you convinced her to take a break."

"What do you mean?"

Ash'n said, "She's barely left your side for days."

"And she allowed no one near you she didn't fully trust," said Lady Natasha. "She was very protective."

Vared's heart thumped louder hearing about Talia's actions. Knowing she watched over him when he was unable to do so warmed his soul. Then he ground his teeth when he realized he hadn't protected her, but instead became a liability. *I didn't keep her safe. I never even saw the attacker coming. Maybe she really is safer without me.*

When Talia returned, he said little as they ate.

"Are you in pain?" she asked.

"A little, not too bad," he said.

"You just seem quiet—as if you're thinking hard thoughts."

"I..." He broke off as Karid entered the med bay.

"Commander."

"Wurvez." Vared nodded.

"Good morning, Wurvez," said Talia. She stood and gathered the dishes. "Before you two start talking ship's business, I'll just head out." She lightly kissed Vared's lips. "I'll be back later." He enjoyed the soft sway of her hips as she walked away.

"How are you feeling, Vared?" Karid's concerned eyes scanned his body.

"I'm fine, Karid. Bring me up to date on our status."

After he listened to Karid tell him about shift rotations, updates to and from the king, the continued hunt for the traitor, and the *Intrepid* was now in the hangar bay, he nodded in satisfaction.

"You've done well, Karid. It sounds like I'll be medically restricted for at least another day. Continue as you have. Although if you could arrange for me to have my tablet, I would appreciate it."

"As you will, Vared. Also, the king and your father have requested that you comm them on a secure channel when you feel ready."

Vared sighed. "They know about the attack, then."

Karid nodded. "Of course. I informed the king during my daily reports and he, of course, notified your father."

"I'll contact them when I can," Vared grumbled.

Karid grinned. "No need to pout that so many care about your well-being, my friend." His grin faltered. "Ash'n wasn't sure you'd survive. We were very worried."

Vared saw the concern in his friend's eyes. "I will be fine," he reassured him.

Karid's face lightened with humor. "So, you and Lady Talia? You've been a busy Svesti." He laughed.

Grunting, Vared said, "Yes and no."

Brows furrowed, Karid said, "What does that mean? She was by your side for days. There is no doubt she cares for you deeply."

"I obviously couldn't protect her." Vared's eyes were downcast.

His friend squeezed Vared's forearm. "According to Lady Talia, there was nothing you could have done differently, Vared. Mantoor ported directly behind you and immediately attacked. Even so, you inflicted some damage to him."

"But..."

"No, my friend. Don't do this to yourself." Karid's normally cheerful face hardened. "I've known you a long time, and Lady Talia makes you happier than I've ever seen you. Do not give up your chance to keep her with you. Leave it up to the female." His face lightened. "But you do your best to convince her to stay with you or I might take my chances with her."

Vared growled. "I will rearrange your face if you ever attempt to touch my female."

"And that's why you need to squash those doubts of yours, Vared. If you really wanted to let her go, you wouldn't be so possessive." Karid grinned widely, his arms spread. "I enjoy being right."

Shaking his head, Vared laughed. "I see your point. I would suggest that it's dangerous to play such mind games."

"Oh, but you're injured and too weak to attack from your bed," Karid teased.

"Never that weak." Vared's hand swiftly smacked his friend's arm. They both laughed.

After spending his morning going over reports, performance reviews, and training schedules, Vared was more than ready for a break when Talia returned. She sat next to him, the warmth of her thigh resting next to his. He cupped his hand behind her head to keep her close as they kissed. He rested his forehead on hers.

"You look rested, *kirani*."

She smiled, her brown eyes sparkling. "I feel better. Knowing you were okay allowed me to sleep deeply."

He inhaled, her unique scent settling him. "I missed you."

She kissed him again. "I'm here now." She leaned back. "How are you?"

"I'm good. I feel the wounds when I move certain ways, but other than that, I am fine."

Tilting her head, she stared at him. "Truth?"

He nodded. "I would not lie to you."

"You'd better not." Her lips twitched. She waved her hand at his tablet. "Keeping busy?"

"Catching up on reports." She giggled at his exaggerated grimace.

"I bet you're missing the bridge after all this time." Her understanding smile warmed him.

"Just a little." He gave her a questioning glance. "Did you send the draft agreement to the king?"

She frowned. "Honestly, it completely slipped my mind when you were injured."

He tapped several keys on his tablet. "Done."

Laughing, she said, "Look at you, in a med bed, and still keeping track of everything."

"If I can stay ahead of it, I have more time to devote to you. Speaking of which, I have a question to ask you." Vared held her hand. "Now that we're back on the *Invictus*, I'd like you to move into my quarters."

Her hair brushed her shoulder as she tilted her head slightly and bit her lip. "Are you sure that's what you want?"

"Absolutely certain, *kirani*."

Her face brightened with a wide smile, and she hugged him tightly. She whispered in his ear, "Yes, Vared. I'll move in with you."

His hands stroked her spine as he kissed her reverently.

"It's been two days since I was released from the med bay," Vared growled as he ground his body against Talia.

She giggled as he kissed her neck. "The healers said you could resume light training. I don't remember hearing sex mentioned at all." She moaned as he cupped her breast.

"If I can train, I can pleasure you," he said before his lips closed over her hard nipple. Her breath hitched. Then her hand buried in his hair and tugged him hard. He lifted his head in surprise.

Her face was serious. "We need to talk first, Vared."

"What is wrong, *kirani*?"

"Nothing. I hope." She nibbled at her lower lip. "While you were recuperating, I made a decision."

Heart thumping hard, he sat up on the bed. "What decision?"

Hair awry, she rose to kneel in front of him, heavy breasts swaying with her movements. "I don't want a troth contract with you."

Every muscle in his body froze as her words pierced his heart. His breath felt frozen in his chest. He turned his head to look away so she could not see how much pain her words caused. "I see."

"No, I don't think you do." She scooted between his thighs and leaned close. Gentle hands on his face turned him to look at her. "I want to true mate with you."

Feeling returned to his body as his blood seemed to rush to unfreeze his limbs. "True mate?" His hands gripped hers. "Are you sure?"

Lips tipped up, she nodded. "Yes."

"But what about your son and sister?" He needed her to be certain.

"We'll figure it out. Maybe visit every year or two. I love you and I want us to be together with no reservations." Tears welled in her eyes. "When you almost died, I realized that what we have is worth taking the leap. I don't want to live without you."

His thumbs swiped the few tears that fell as she spoke. "I love you, Talia. I would be honored to true mate with you."

Her blinding smile erased his doubts. Wrapping his arms around her, he held her tight as he kissed her with all the joy he was feeling. Gently, he turned them so she was again on her back. He rose slightly and worshipped her body with his. Soft kisses trailed to her ear, fangs occasionally nipping her skin. Her neck then received his attention. His tongue licked the area where he would eventually bite her. When his mouth left a portion of her skin, his adoring hands took over.

The scent of her arousal surrounded him as he worked his way lower across her chest. Her gasps made him smile in satisfaction as he licked the underside of her plump breasts with long, slow, wet motions before circling her puckered areolas. Sucking on one nipple, he gradually increased the intensity until it was red and engorged. His tail played with it as he moved on to the other. One of her hands clutched the back of his head, while the other moved restlessly along his back.

He raised his head and used his fingers to pull and tug on her nipples. He grinned at how red and hard they were. Her stomach muscles contracted as he kissed and licked his way to her belly button. He rolled her over onto her front.

Talia mockingly complained. "Hey, you were just getting to the good stuff."

Vared laughed. "I'm saving it for last. There is more of you to love, my mate."

He moved her hair off her shoulders and kissed her neck. Her sighs filled him. Spreading her legs, he knelt between them and covered her upper body. His hands caressed her arms to her hands, then fingers entwined as he rested some of his weight on hers. The heat of her skin seared his. He blew into her ear. "I love you. I will adore you for the rest of our lives, *kirani*." Her body became boneless beneath his.

He lifted his body off hers. His tail reached for her wet core, lightly tracing up and down, never penetrating, never quite touching her clit. Between kisses along her back, he said, "All I am is yours. I will love and protect you. I will support you in whatever endeavors you choose. Your family is mine and mine is yours."

Goddess, her luscious ass. Her sighs and moans gained in intensity as his large hands massaged and cupped the globes of her ass. Her scent became deeper and richer as he kissed them, intermittently extending his claws to lightly scrape across her sensitive skin.

The back of each leg received his loving attention before he rolled her over again to work his way up the front of her legs. His tail moved to play with her ass the closer he moved to her dripping core.

"I will strive to be worthy of you each day." He glanced up to meet her heavy-lidded eyes. "You are my home, *kirani*. Let me be your forever home."

She moaned. He licked her slit and groaned at her taste. His tongue played with her clit, slowly and steadily, never increasing in speed or changing his movement. Cock weeping, he took his time, building her pleasure bit by bit.

Her breathing accelerated, and her voice rose. "Right there. Just like that, Vared. Oh, please don't stop doing what you're doing. It feels so good."

His heart swelled as the pitch of her moans became higher and higher. When he knew she was on the edge, his tail breached her forbidden hole and he swiped his fang over her clit and growled. Her thighs clenched around his ears. Back bowing, she screamed his name. Shaking and shuddering with the force of her climax, she almost dislodged his mouth from her clit. He continued licking as her juices flowed freely.

His face wet from her pleasure, he looked up when her body relaxed. "Tears, *kirani*?"

Chest heaving, she lifted her head to look down at him, moisture on her cheeks. "That was the most intense, slow-building orgasm I've ever had, Vared. Breathtakingly beautiful." Her head dropped back. "I've never experienced anything like it before."

He grinned. "I'm pleased you're pleased." Inserting a finger into her cunt, he began licking and sucking again. His tail began short thrusts in her ass and she gasped. By the time she came again, he had three fingers curled inside her. Her cunt squeezed them so tightly, he could swear he had lost blood flow. And the pressure on his tail sent shivers down his spine.

Crawling up her body, he kissed her hard and deep for long moments. Lifting his head, he asked, "Are you sure?"

Talia smiled and caressed his face. "You are my home. Let me be your forever home. Mate me, love."

A rumble rose in his chest and his cock felt like it could dent steel. Slowly, he thrust into her cunt, her wet heat surrounding him. The air was heavy with her scent. Her hands clasped his ass, and she pushed upward to take his full length. They both groaned. He stilled, buttocks clenched, trying to maintain control of his body. Then he withdrew almost all the way and thrust hard. Her hips tipped up to take him deeper. In and out, he kept a steady but pounding rhythm. They gazed into each other's eyes.

Their breathing sped up in time with their rhythm. When he saw her eyes start to roll back, he elongated his fangs and bit at the juncture of her neck and shoulder. The copper taste of her blood hit his tongue. He felt her bite him in a similar manner as she orgasmed. He raised his head when an unfamiliar feeling registered.

Eyes widening in surprise, they stared at each other as his cock vibrated. *Crek! My cock is actually vibrating like a sex toy.*

She gasped, "I didn't know it could do that." Then her cunt spasmed hard around his cock. He roared her name as he came harder and longer than he ever had. He rolled them over so she was resting on him.

He panted, "I didn't either."

As he attempted to catch his breath, his hands stroked her back and head. Her fingers trailed over his torso. She said into his chest, "I love you, Vared."

"I love you, Talia." He kissed the top of her head.

She raised her head and rested her chin on her hands. "I didn't imagine that, did I? Your cock vibrated."

"It's never done that before." Vared knew his confusion had to be showing on his face. "I've never even heard of it."

"Do you think it's because of the bite, or the true mating?" Her brows crinkled as she thought.

"Like I said, I've never even heard of it happening before. I guess I could ask my father."

She laughed. "I bet that will be a comfortable conversation to have."

He smiled ruefully. "You would be correct." He reached down to grab a sheet to cover their cooling bodies, and she gasped. "What?"

"Your clan marking." She pointed at it. "It changed to gold."

Vared looked down, then stared at her in wonder. "Look at your clavicle."

A gold clan marking showed below her left collarbone. It didn't show any of the Svesti clans but was a new one.

"What does it mean?" She rubbed at it.

He caught her hand and kissed her fingers. "Clan markings changing to gold can only mean one thing, *kirani*. We're not just true mates—we are fated mates."

"Fated mates? As in the one person in the entire universe, fated mates?" Her eyes grew large.

He nodded, then laughed. "Now it makes sense why I couldn't resist you. You're my fated mate." Kissing her hard, he hugged her tightly.

"Didn't you say there haven't been fated mates in over a century?"

He nodded. "The fact that humans can be fated mates is going to surprise everyone."

She laughed. "Well, it certainly surprised us. Maybe that's the cause of the vibrating cock." She licked her lips. "I wonder if it's a one-time thing or something we can expect in the future."

He grinned. "Let's find out, shall we?"

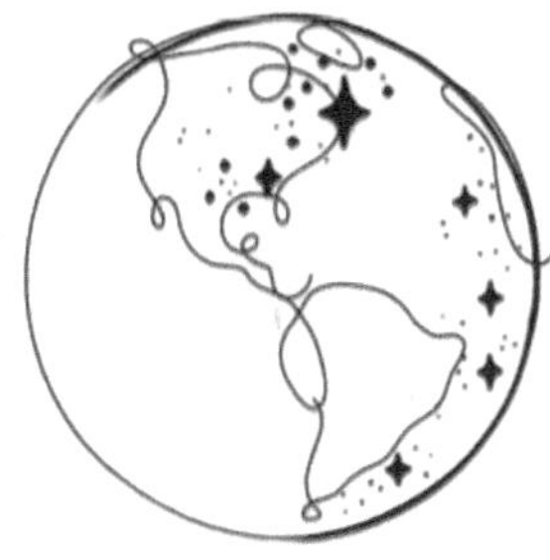

Chapter 26

PERSONAL JOURNAL - DAY 44.

Fated mates. Something I always thought only belonged in romance novels, but it looks like I was wrong. I'm really glad I was wrong.

I told Vared I wanted to true mate. Once we did, the fated mate bond triggered. His clan marking turned gold, I somehow got one and his dick vibrated! I shit you not, it vibrated. And even better, it appears it will continue to do so in the future. <sigh> How lucky can a gal get?

We haven't told anyone yet, not even the king. We're still trying to figure out the potential ramifications. And truthfully? We want to savor it for a bit with no one else involved. There hasn't been a fated mate bond recorded in over a century.

I've been researching the Svesti database, but most of the information about fated mates is in religious texts about the Goddess. It's unclear on the specifics of the bond. From what I can tell, the bond used to make itself known almost immediately somehow. But for us, other than being drawn to each other, I can't recall any specific way we could have known in advance.

Maybe we had to commit to each other freely before the bond would be confirmed? I'm just guessing at this point.

Anyway, I spent a good portion of the morning speaking with Traxen about the draft agreement. There were several changes, as well as a couple additions that he wanted, so we hammered out those. I just need to update the agreement and addendum with the new language. Of course, who knows what the leaders on Earth will do? Vared must've gotten his eyes from his mother's side of the family because Traxen's are very similar.

I told the king I planned on staying with Vared permanently. Traxen seemed pleased with the information and then told me the new communications relays have basic operational capability at this point. They are still working on something to increase the amount of transmissions they can handle, but it sounds like we'll be able to speak with our loved ones on Earth soon, even if we have to schedule time to use the relays.

I'd like that. I still need to talk to Joshua and Krista about my staying with Vared. I'm more than a little worried about how they will take it. They don't even know aliens are real yet. It might be a little much for me to say, "Oh, by the way, I'm in love with an alien and I will not be living on Earth."

"The revisions look acceptable," Traxen said with a smile.

Talia said, "You understand that this is the recommendation I will make to Earth. We still don't have a central planetary government. I don't know if any of Earth's leaders will want to change it. Or even if they'll agree to it all."

"I understand. However, I believe it is a fair agreement for both species. Vared, we may make a diplomat of you yet." Traxen's eyes twinkled with humor.

Vared shook his head. "I believe it was working with Talia that made my efforts successful, Traxen. She is a reasonable being." He grinned mischievously. "Mostly."

She laughed and slapped his bicep. "Be nice."

Traxen's laugh tapered off. "It is good to see you both so happy. Unfortunately, what I have to show you will change that. The *Defiant* sent me the latest transmissions from Earth mentioning the Svesti and aliens. Here's one from your country, Talia." He tapped a few buttons and a video of a White House news conference appeared.

Talia's jaw dropped and her fists clenched as she watched the press secretary state first contact with the Svesti had resulted in kidnapped women from Earth and that Earth's leaders were working together to prepare for war. There was a call for more funding for the military and for the support of the American people. She heard Vared's tail flick rapidly behind her and his growl deepen as he listened to the lies.

She inhaled deeply when the video finished. "Traxen, I have no words. I know many of our politicians play fast and loose with the truth, but this is outrageous, even for them."

Vared frowned. "This information may push more Svesti into wanting to invade."

"I'm concerned about that, too. My question is how do we handle this?" Traxen looked angry. "I want a treaty that will benefit both our species. Not war."

"Let me think," Talia muttered as she started pacing. Both Svesti looked at her, then at each other as she mumbled.

"Does she do this often?" Traxen asked.

"Usually, it's with pen and paper and without the pacing," Vared said with an affectionate glance at his mate.

"Should we wait, or would you like to contact me when she is finished?"

"I think we should…" Vared cut off when Talia spun abruptly.

"I've got a plan," she said. "But I'll need some assistance to make it happen."

Both males listened intently. Their small smiles grew broader as she outlined what she wanted to do. Her plan addressed not only the misinformation but put the vaccine and treaty into play.

"Vared, give her everything she needs. Lady Talia, when do you think you'll be ready?"

She gnawed on her lip as she thought. "Three or four days, maybe? I can get Emmy to help with some of it."

"I'll arrange for the communications relays to be completely available to you in four days. They will be yours until you have finished," Traxen said with a smile. "I like this plan."

Vared's chest puffed with pride. "You have a wondrous mind, *kirani*. Earth's leaders will have to reassess their actions."

"Don't forget, a lot of this hinges on Joshua and Krista. I can get it all ready to go, but they're the ones who will have to get the majority of it into the right hands." Talia shrugged.

"I have no doubt they will help." Vared lifted her hand to his lips. "You are very convincing."

A shiver ran down her spine before she straightened it. "We'll give them a war, just not the one they were expecting."

Personal Journal - Day 45.

This has not been the best of days. Vared told me he's sent Wurvez and Jevax out on a secret mission. Something to do with a Frezzian freighter. I hope they make it back okay. I like both of them.

And then finding out what Earth's governments are saying about the Svesti? A bunch of partial truths and outright lies. This has Newell's prints all over it. What a scumbag. I've got a plan to deal with it, but it's going to require a couple days of work on my part and then some help from Joshua and Krista. I hope those communications relays work.

For the next few days, Talia was busy. She reviewed all the pertinent Earth transmissions, made a long list of things that needed to be done and in what order. She informed the other women about what was going on and they all agreed to help. Emmy and Tolvex helped her with some of the technological items. She even had the *Defiant* take care of some of what needed to be in place. Finally, she was ready to contact her son and sister.

"Is it time, *kirani*?" Vared rubbed her shoulders.

"I think so. I'm pretty sure Joshua should be at my sister's house now, since the semester has finished. If I did the calculations correctly, it's a good time to catch them both together. Traveling in space with our different day lengths and calendars is still a little confusing for me to convert." She took a deep breath. "I had the *Defiant* send a text to Krista with a message that Lee was going to reach her on her computer momentarily."

"Lee?" Vared's nose crinkled in confusion.

"She had trouble saying my name when we were young, so she used to call me Lee. I'm hoping that if the government is keeping track of her communications that they won't realize it's me." Talia smiled.

"Good thinking. Where would you like me?"

"Perhaps on the other side of the desk until I introduce you. Then you can sit by my side." She squeezed his hand.

Giving her a brief kiss, he moved across from her. He tapped his comm. "Tolvex, we're ready. Open an encrypted channel via the comm relays as planned."

"The *Defiant* states they have initiated the link to the computer," Tolvex reported.

"Talia? It is you!" Talia's eyes filled with tears when she saw her sister's happy face.

"Mom!" Joshua pushed close to his aunt. "They're saying you were kidnapped by aliens. Are you alright?"

Talia sniffed and grinned. "I'm great. It's so good to see you both. I've missed you."

"Where are you?" Krista demanded.

"Well, I am on a space cruiser, but I wasn't kidnapped."

"No fucking way. You're in space?" Joshua bounced excitedly.

"Language." Talia and Krista said simultaneously. They looked at each other and laughed.

Joshua mock pouted. "You know I'm an adult, right? I hate when you two gang up on me."

Talia knew the love she felt for her son showed on her face when she said, "You'll always be my baby. But you're right, you are an adult." She met Vared's eyes briefly and saw the love in his eyes for her.

"See? Mom gets me." Joshua knocked his shoulder against Krista's gently.

Krista rubbed the top of his head affectionately. "Yeah, squirt, your Mom is the best." She looked back at Talia. "So what's really going on? It made little sense to me that they're saying you were kidnapped, but you had time to contact us and send me a power of attorney."

"Do you guys remember several years ago when we helped Sally and Bob out of a jam?" Talia asked.

Thoughtful expressions crossed both Joshua's and Krista's faces. "Yeah, Mom. That was something."

"Do you remember how we helped them?"

They both nodded. "Yes."

"Well, it's their turn to help me. They'll be contacting you in exactly one week."

"One week?" Joshua asked.

"Yes, they'll tell you everything you need to know and what to do about it. I don't have complete confidence in this line's security."

"Okay, we'll contain our curiosity until then," Krista said with a smile.

"There's something else. I've met someone. He's very important to me," Talia said.

"An alien?" Joshua said.

Talia nodded. "Would you like to meet him?" She held her breath.

"Can we?" Joshua said. Krista narrowed her eyes and nodded.

Talia let out her breath. "Vared? Could you come meet my family?" She watched her son's reaction when Vared sat next to her."Joshua. Krista. This is Vared Durek. He's the commander of the space cruiser I'm on. Vared, my son, Joshua Sullivan, and my sister, Krista Johnston."

Vared's face looked shocked when he turned to her. "Your sister looks exactly like you with shorter hair."

Krista laughed. "She didn't tell you, did she? We're identical twins."

"No, she didn't. I'm pleased to meet those closest to Talia's heart." Vared smiled.

"Whoa, are those fangs, man?" Joshua's eyes grew wide.

"Joshua—" Talia shook her head. "That is so rude. Apologize."

"Aww, Mom." She glared at her son. Joshua gave a heavy sigh. "I apologize for my rudeness, Mr. Durek."

"Please call me Vared." He leaned forward and said in a low conspiratorial voice, "I also have claws and a tail." He extended the claws on one hand and brought his tail up so it was visible.

"That is so cool!" Everyone laughed at Joshua's antics.

Krista stared hard at Talia. "Does this mean what I think it means?"

Talia met her sister's concerned eyes confidently. "Yes."

Krista turned to stare into Vared's eyes. "Treat her well or you'll deal with me."

Vared nodded solemnly. "I will. The resemblance between the two of you is more than physical, I see." His lips quirked.

"And what does that mean?" Krista said over her crossed arms.

"When Talia arrived on my ship, she took me to task almost immediately." Vared broke into a big grin. "She's quite fierce."

Krista looked between Vared and Talia, then smiled. "Good."

"Mom?"

"What, honey?"

"Are you coming back?" Joshua's face started to lose its excitement.

Talia's shoulders tensed. She felt Vared's tail rub her back in small circles. "Eventually. But it will only be for visits to start. It's still unclear on how the future is going to work out." *Oh baby, please understand.*

"I'll miss you." She could see that Joshua was trying to act brave for her. As much as he'd always told her he wanted her to fall in love and be happy, neither of them had ever considered her living on another planet.

"I'll miss you. Once we get that help, we should be able to talk regularly. It's not like I'm going to disappear from your life." Talia felt the tears well up.

"Are you truly happy?" She could see the man her son was becoming.

"Yes, Joshua, I am. What Vared and I have together is more special than I could have hoped for."

Joshua squared his shoulders and looked at Vared. "If you hurt my Mom, my aunt will have to get in line to kick your ass, because I'll do it first."

Vared gave her son a measuring look, then said, "If I cause your mother pain, I would expect nothing less."

"So we understand each other?" Joshua persisted.

Vared nodded solemnly. "We do, young warrior."

Talia and Krista shared a knowing look. Krista said, "Did you need anything else from us while we're waiting for Sally and Bob to contact us?"

Talia shook her head. "No. Just give hugs to your girls for me. I miss them, too. I'll contact you again as soon as I can."

"Love you, Mom."

"Love you, Sis."

"I love you both." Talia ended the comm and leaned back in her chair. "That went better than I thought it would."

"Who are Sally and Bob?"

"What? Oh, they were characters in a book I wrote a while ago. There was an espionage theme, and I was having some difficulties figuring out how to resolve a conflict. Joshua was taking some computer courses at school and offered some suggestions. Krista was there, and we came up with whole scenarios about what we would do if we suddenly couldn't communicate freely. We made a game of testing out the scenarios until we found one that worked for my book. My mentioning Sally and Bob was to let them know that's how I would communicate sensitive info."

"But you said a week. I thought you were ready."

Talia gave him a satisfied grin. "Oh, that was code. A week means one day. One month means one week."

"I'm curious. What exactly do you expect your sister and son to do?"

"Tomorrow, each will go to a different location that offers public internet. They'll log onto those old email accounts. I emailed the video I made before I left Earth to those accounts already. They'll find a draft email that has instructions in it. How to download the videos we made, what social media video streaming accounts to upload it all to, as well as email addresses to a bunch of news media outlets to copy it all to. Once the *Defiant* tells me that the videos are up and I give the go ahead, the *Defiant* will override all electronics on Earth to play the original video and the new ones, so everyone knows the information was sent to the news media."

Vared shook his head in amazement. "You really do have a devious mind, *kirani*."

"The curse of being a fiction writer, babe. We imagine all kinds of weird shit." Talia laughed.

He pulled her into his lap. He whispered in her ear, "I read some of your books. There was this one where the lovers did..."

She shivered as he recounted the hot scene from her third book. She turned her lips to his. "Wanna try it out?" She wrapped her arms around his neck and laughed in delight when he immediately stood and carried her to the bed.

Hello, again, fellow citizens of the United States and of the world. You may have already viewed the video I made before I left Earth less than two months ago. If not, I am Talia Sullivan, United States Ambassador of Interplanetary Relations.

Contrary to what has been in the news media recently, I was not abducted by the Svesti. Instead, without my knowledge or consent, my government gave me to the Svesti to present at a Choosing where it was expected I would enter a breeding or troth contract. Inflammatory words, I know, but in the videos following this one, you will see I am telling the truth. You will also hear, in their own words, the stories of the five other human women with me on the space cruiser.

I include any documents I mention in this video at the end. They have also been uploaded to the internet and sent to various news outlets. This is to ensure the widest dissemination of information and reduce the chances that any data might be changed without my knowledge or consent.

King Traxen Sovex of House Davelk, the ruler of Costonia, the Svesti home world, hopes to enter into a treaty with Earth where human women may choose birthing and troth contracts with Svesti males to save their race from extinction. While many Svesti wish the same, there are factions that disagree with him. Just as on Earth, there are those that would rather invade and take any women they want, while others believe in racial purity. Unfortunately, the recent actions of some of Earth's leaders make the argument for invasion stronger.

Much has happened since I left Earth. At least one of those factions has been targeting the human women on the ship. One tampered with an information upload, and I was put into an induced coma to recuperate. Two of us were poisoned.

On Theron, a space station along our route, Durelian mercenaries abducted and delivered me to Zuvgran scientists. The Zuvgran injected me with a virus that kills human and Svesti fertility. The Svesti and Jalaxian mercenaries rescued me. I quarantined along with my Svesti companion until a vaccine was developed to protect both humans and Svesti. For me, though, the damage is done. My human eggs are dead. Any Svesti authorized to interact with Earth will be inoculated. Any humans wishing to interact with Svesti will also have to be vaccinated.

I have met other human women who were abducted from Earth by other races. Earth's military capabilities are not even close to what I have seen used by other species out here in space. On the interplanetary stage, Earth barely qualifies as an extra; we're nowhere near ready for a leading role. If you doubt me, ask yourself, could we on Earth simultaneously broadcast on every electronic medium of another world?

The vast majority of Svesti I have been privileged to interact with have been honorable, caring beings. They may look different and have a different culture and belief system than humans, but in many ways we are the same. They are multi-faceted sentient beings who think, feel, disagree, compromise, and love, just as humans do. They are capable of giving respect when it is warranted and they can be worthy of respect. Their personalities range from quiet to boisterous or from ingenue to cynic. They are not perfect, but neither are we.

A copy of what is needed for the vaccinations follows. The Svesti are willing to manufacture and administer the vaccines even without a treaty in place, or Earth can do it themselves. I cannot stress enough that any human being who is not vaccinated will be at risk of carrying the virus and infecting others.

In the interests of transparency, I also have included a draft treaty and a document explaining the intent of each section. President Furman did not authorize my videos, nor the release of the documents. As such, it is highly likely that he will remove me from the ambassador position he has never publicly acknowledged. I am fine with that outcome. It is more important to me that accurate information is given to everyone on Earth.

It is time to ask ourselves how we wish to move forward as a species. If Earth is unwilling or unable to come to a unified agreement, King Sovex is willing to consider treaties with individual countries.

Please take the time to educate yourselves before making any decisions on how you believe Earth should proceed. History is being made as I speak. What will the history books say about humans?

Chapter 27

AMAZED, VARED SHOOK his head as he received another packet of information from the *Defiant*. Talia's plan provoked immediate and constant attention from the humans. There were press conferences, news reports and social media postings coming to him several times a day. He didn't have time to review it all, especially with Karid still on his mission. Fortunately, the females were sifting through it and flagging the most relevant items for his and the king's attention. Their familiarity with their home world benefited them. They knew which outlets were reliable in their reporting and which were biased. The females were working diligently in the War Room with Devik now. He forwarded the latest packet to them.

He cast his gaze over the bridge and allowed a small smile to tug at his lips as he observed his crew. *I am a fortunate male. I have Talia and the best crew. And in ten days, we'll be home. They deserve a break.*

Brauvix interrupted his musings. "Commander. I'm receiving a distress call from Talonka Six."

"Someone refresh my memory," Vared said.

"Talonka Six," said Hozan Crulex, a science officer. "Fourth planet in the Lestanus system. Sparsely populated, mostly by Ermipas to support their mining colonies. Primary export is arbixium."

"Are there any other ships closer?"

"Negative, sir."

"Brauvix, on screen."

Vared looked at the Ermipa with its round furry head and oval eyes. Even though it wasn't obvious on the hologram, he knew the Ermipa was exceptionally short, even shorter than Lady Lin. "This is Commander Durek of the Svesti space cruiser, *Invictus*. What is the nature of your distress?"

"Commander, thank you for answering our call. I am Overseer Roho of the Veba Mine on Talonka Six. An hour ago, we had a collapse at a junction where three tunnels meet. I have 281 beings trapped below the surface. Our engineers are attempting to determine the safest way to retrieve them. We may require help with that, and I know we do not have the resources to treat that many potential injuries and will require medical support."

Vared turned to Crulex. "How long to reach Talonka Six?"

"Eleven hours, twenty-four minutes at maximum speed."

"Lay in a course." Vared turned back to face the Ermipa. "Overseer Roho, we will arrive in under twelve hours. My engineers are available to consult if you would like. If there is anything else you think you may require to treat your people, such as tents, cots, or supplies, please transmit those needs to us as soon as possible so that we can ensure we have it on our shuttles prior to our arrival."

"Thank the Maker," Roho said. His facial fur quivered. "We've never had a collapse of this size. There isn't normally much space traffic in our system. I wasn't sure anyone could help us."

Vared smiled. "We're on our way. You are not alone."

"Thank you, Commander. I will make a list and transmit as soon as I can."

"We'll see you soon, Overseer Roho."

Vared sat in his chair and tapped his tablet. After a few minutes, he said, "Brauvix, open a ship-wide channel."

"Yes, Commander. It's ready."

"Attention all hands. We are currently en route to Talonka Six to answer a distress call." Vared relayed all the pertinent information. "We should arrive in approximately eleven hours. Medical personnel, gather your supplies and coordinate the loading. Section Leaders, prepare your shuttles. Adjust rest periods as needed to be prepared. When we have more information on what may need to be synthesized and loaded, I will send it to you. Commander Durek out."

He spent the next hour coordinating and answering questions. He finally sat back and took a deep breath. *I guess we won't be home in ten days.* He rolled his shoulders to release the tension.

"Uncle, we are responding to a distress call. Our arrival on Costonia will be delayed."

"That works out well. I have a meeting with our co-conspirators in two days. The delay will give us time to put everything in place." His uncle's voice sounded eager.

"What are your orders?" Muscles tense, the male held his breath. *I didn't like using Nerid. While he is weak, the male did not deserve to have his brain muddled. I feel as if I'm too exposed.*

"Take no action, but keep alert for information that may prove useful. You must avoid suspicion. Do not contact me again until you reach the home world. Always Svesti."

The younger male released his breath slowly, and his shoulders relaxed.

"As you command. Always Svesti." Relief filled him as he disconnected the comm.

"No way!" Talia's excited squeal hurt his ears. But it was a small price to pay to see her delight. She squirmed on his lap. "I can't believe the girls didn't tell me."

"Well, we haven't told anyone either, *kirani*," Vared said with an amused smile.

She pouted. "Don't go being reasonable, babe." Then she laughed. "I guess it's time to tell the king."

He nodded. "I thought we'd do that after we talk with your family. We should do it now. Once we reach Talonka Six, we'll be too busy."

"Good plan. Let's get Krista on the horn."

"On the horn?" Vared scrunched his face. "What does that mean?"

She giggled. "It's slang. It just means, let's call her."

He shook his head before tapping some buttons. Her sister answered immediately.

"Hey, sis, how goes it?" Talia said happily.

"We're fine here." Krista grinned. "It seems Sally and Bob knew what they were doing."

"Is that Mom?" Vared heard Joshua's voice approach, then he appeared next to his aunt. "Hey, Mom. You went viral."

"So it seems. How are you?" Talia smiled at her son. "You look good."

"Feeling good, too." Joshua flexed his muscles playfully. "We have some surprises for you."

"Really?" Talia leaned forward. Vared wrapped his tail around her waist to keep her from tipping. "What?"

Krista lightly slapped Joshua on the arm. "Let me go first, squirt." Joshua nodded. She studied Talia and Vared. "When I realized all you had been through, I was upset."

"I'm fine, Krista. And I'm happy." Talia reassured her sibling.

"I know, but you finally found someone who makes you..." Krista waved a hand in a circle. "glow. And the thought that you can't have more kids bothers me, especially now. If you were still alone with no prospects, I don't know that it would matter so much."

"Krista, it's okay."

"From what I understand, it's your eggs that are damaged, not your womb. Is that correct?" Krista's eyes, so much like her sister's, were serious.

Talia nodded. "Yes."

"So if I were to donate some of my eggs to you, you could carry Vared's child if you wanted to?"

"What? No." Talia shook her head violently. "I would never ask that of you."

"You're not asking; I'm offering." Krista smiled. "I have the girls, and since Steve died last year, I haven't even wanted to date, let alone thought about having more children. I can donate a few of my eggs to the cause for you two. Our DNA is exactly the same, Talia."

Tears ran down Talia's face. "Oh, Krista. You're the best. But Vared's fertility was affected, too."

Vared cleared his throat. He couldn't believe the generosity of Krista. "*Kirani?*"

Talia looked at him and cupped his cheek. "I'm sorry that when you rescued me, you lost the opportunity to continue your line."

Vared laid his hand over hers. "There's something I haven't told you." He looked at Krista and Joshua. "This isn't common knowledge; you can't tell anyone." They both nodded solemnly. He turned back to Talia. "When I began warrior training, it was already known that the Svesti might die out. We were given the option to freeze our sperm in case there was another way in the future to save our race, even after our deaths. We keep the knowledge secret so that the Zuvgran never know about those stores."

"Are you saying you donated sperm?" Talia asked.

"Yes. If you decide you wish to have young with me, it is there to use." He watched hope bloom in her eyes.

"Joshua, how do you feel about this?" Talia asked, looking back at her son.

"Uh, Mom, I was the one who suggested it to Aunt Krista," Joshua said with a grin.

"Really?"

"The Svesti haven't had children in decades and you are the best mom there is. You should show them how it's done right." He laughed. "Besides, I always wanted a brother or sister."

"You don't have to decide right now. I can have some of my eggs frozen, just in case," Krista said.

Talia sucked in a shaky breath. "I am incredibly touched and so very lucky to have such a wonderful family."

Vared's chest rumbled with emotion. "We are honored." He bowed his head in respect.

Joshua bounced in his seat. "There's more to tell you." He glanced at his aunt. "Can I tell them this part?"

Krista laughed. "Go ahead. You're about to jump out of your skin."

"Mom, King Sovex contacted us several days ago to thank us for our help."

"That was nice of him, honey." Talia smiled indulgently.

"He also asked if I wanted to finish my schooling on Costonia," Joshua said.

"What?" Talia twisted her torso and pinned Vared with her stare. "Did you know about this?"

Vared shook his head. "No, this is news to me, too, *kirani*. Traxen never said a word, nor did I ask."

"What did you say, Joshua?"

"Hell, yes!" Joshua's face was aglow. "A chance to learn engineering far superior to anything we have on Earth and be close to you—there's no way I could refuse. This is an amazing opportunity, Mom. He also said that he would hire tutors to ensure my base knowledge was what it needed to be before I started my official schooling." He scowled at Vared. "You didn't tell us you were the king's cousin."

Vared suppressed a grin. "An oversight on my part. I apologize."

"There's more."

"I'm not sure I can handle much more excitement." Talia laughed.

"Aunt Krista and the girls are coming, too."

Talia's face was shocked. "Krista?"

Krista smiled. "The king asked me some probing questions. When he found out my profession, he offered me a position."

"What is it you do?" Vared asked.

"I'm a psychologist. I work with people who have suffered significant trauma—like battered women and their children. The king wants my input on how best to provide housing and care for any women and children who suffered domestic abuse and are approved to come to Costonia under a treaty. It's an exciting opportunity. I can be on the ground floor of designing a whole program for this community." Krista's happy expression saddened a little. "I think a complete change of scenery will be good for the girls and me. And with you and Joshua on Costonia, it seems like the best choice."

"I'm so excited that you'll be living on Costonia," Talia said. "But you are aware that I will probably be traveling a lot with Vared, right?"

"Yes, but your home base will be Costonia, not Earth, so we'll see each other more, Mom. And if you do decide to have a baby, you'll probably stick around more." Joshua grinned happily.

"We're still working out when we can make the trip, but we have to pack and sell the houses first anyway," Krista said.

"I love you both and I'm excited for all of us," Talia said. "Talk to you soon."

After the communication ended, Talia hugged him. "I cannot believe how well everything is working out for us, Vared."

"The Goddess is merciful, *kirani*. She has truly blessed us." Vared kissed her reverently.

She drew back, and her eyes traced his face. "What do you think? Should we try to have a baby?"

"What do you want? I'm happy either way, Talia. I have you. I wasn't expecting to have young, but I would never say no if it's what you want."

Her face filled with joy. "I would love to have a child who is part of both of us, Vared. It feels right."

He hugged her tightly. "Thank the Goddess. I was hoping you'd say that."

She laughed at him. "You could've just told me you wanted to continue your line."

"No, *kirani*, this isn't about me. It's about us. You are the one who is giving up your entire world for me. I would not want you to feel you had to give me young." The scar from his bite on her neck was just visible above her shirt collar. He rubbed the scar gently, and the scent of her arousal rose. "Mmm, you're trying to distract me." He kissed her.

"You're the one distracting me." She laughed. "Let's call Traxen. Then maybe we'll have some time to be distracted before we reach Talonka Six."

"You really are a cruel taskmaster," he said. He tapped some buttons, and they both turned to face the king when he answered.

"Vared. Talia. You're looking well." Traxen smiled.

"Thanks, Traxen. I have a couple things to report," Vared said.

"Go ahead."

"First, we are responding to a distress call on Talonka Six. There are hundreds of Ermipas trapped in a mine. So we will be delayed several days."

"Should I try to find another ship to assist?"

"I think we'll be fine."

Talia narrowed her eyes and said, "I understand you've been speaking to my family without my knowledge."

Vared could see his cousin trying to gauge Talia's mood. "Yes, I invited them to Costonia."

"And you didn't think to ask me first before making the offer?"

"I wanted it to be a surprise. Consider it my gift to you for your true mating. We are now family as well," Traxen said carefully.

"Well, that might be a problem since we aren't true mated," Talia said.

Traxen's eyes narrowed and zeroed in on her scar. "I see the mark on your neck."

"Oh, this?" She pointed. "Maybe you should see this as well." She moved to the other side of Vared's lap so his clan marking was visible.

Traxen leaned forward. "Is that what I think it is?"

Talia pulled her collar down to show her new clan marking.

"By the Goddess!" Traxen exclaimed.

Vared grinned. He'd never seen his cousin so surprised. "Yes, cousin, we are fated mates. And better yet, there are two more fated mate pairings with the human females."

"Really?" His cousin sat back, stupefied. "I wasn't expecting this at all."

"Neither were we."

"And there are two others?"

"Yes, they informed me just a little while ago."

Vared watched the thoughts traveling through Traxen's eyes, evaluating, and calculating. They were silent for a long moment.

Traxen straightened. "This is wonderful news. Congratulations. I am glad now, Talia, that you insisted on creating opportunities for natural pairings if fated mate bonds are possible."

"Cousin, you should be aware that the bond did not trigger until we true mated. Unlike the tales I've heard, we did not have an immediate recognition of the bond."

"That is good to know, Vared. We are in forgotten, as well as new, territory now. However, I am concerned those who want to invade Earth might become more eager if they know there's a chance at a fated mate."

Talia frowned. "I've been thinking about it, and I believe the fated mate bond won't trigger for humans immediately."

"Why do you think that?"

"Humans don't have clan markings, so they can't change color for a couple to recognize. I think that unless a human/Svesti couple commits fully to each other, the bond won't trigger at all."

"An interesting theory." Traxen looked thoughtful. "We have much to think about."

"Have you read my reports on the various reactions on Earth to Talia's videos? Her government disavowed her."

"Yes, I'm glad you brought that up. At least two countries want to discuss treaties and have requested Svesti help with the manufacture and distribution of the vaccine. If they don't set up a planetary commission of sorts, I expect more to follow. I am appointing both of you co-ambassadors."

"What?" Vared grimaced. "You know I am not a diplomat, Traxen."

"No, but you are very familiar with the proposed treaty and its intent. We'll discuss it more when you reach Costonia, but I think I'll offer to allow some of the human diplomats to travel here to discuss and ratify any treaty. You and Talia will escort them here on the *Invictus*."

Vared growled, and Talia stroked his tail. She said, "I would advise that you limit their number. If not, they will bring an entire entourage, security, and spies, and it will be a nightmare. I would also suggest you allow a couple of reporters to come along as well."

"Send me all your suggestions. I won't make any offers until we can talk in person." Traxen grinned. "It won't harm them to wait."

Talia nodded. "Are you sure you want me as a co-ambassador, Traxen? I'm not Svesti. It might cause problems with the Council."

"Yes. You know the treaty as well as Vared, and you are now Svesti with your clan marking and fated mate bond. Your leaders attempted to impugn your honor. You'll be in a position above them. It would behoove them to recognize that I trust you and that you are now part of the royal family."

Laughing, Talia said, "So what you're saying is don't piss off the king, huh?"

Traxen laughed. "Exactly."

Chapter 28

P ERSONAL JOURNAL - DAY 55.

We're responding to a distress call from Talonka Six; we're only a couple hours away. Then I'm sure we'll be very busy. I hope the miners are okay.

I've never believed in a higher power, but after today, I'm not so sure. The king contacted Joshua and Krista and in one fell swoop, all the things I was worried about were gone. They're excited to move to Costonia, so we won't be separated by light years. Maybe the change and challenges will help Krista make peace with her husband's death.

Even in her grief, she's thinking about helping me. She offered some of her eggs so Vared and I can try to have a child.

Then Vared tells me about the other two fated mate bonds. I'm gonna have to give those girls some shit for holding out on me. It's good to know that Vared and I aren't the only ones. Maybe the Goddess does have her hand in all of this, and humans and Svesti were supposed to meet.

I know I teased him, but I'm glad Traxen stepped in. I hadn't even considered my family moving to Costonia. Even if I had, I never would have asked. I guess I was too close to the problem to see a potential solution.

Vared's love has taken care of most of my inner "I'm not good enough" self-talk. I still have little moments. It's not like I can get rid of a lifetime of doubt all at once. But I have to admit, Traxen's faith in me as an ambassador and his willingness to back me publicly beat down a little more of the negative self-talk.

I have a surprise for Vared. I think he'll...

Talia put down her pen when she heard the door to their quarters open. She stood and smoothed her gown and smiled.

"*Kirani*? Thank you for understanding while I took care of..." Vared's words trailed off as he saw her.

The sheer lavender gown she wore was embroidered with a design covering her breasts and her pussy that mimicked their clan markings. She had synthesized it to look like typical Svesti evening court dress with only one shoulder, leaving the one with her clan marking bare. However, it was much shorter than an evening gown, barely covering her genitals and cupping under her ass. She'd even made some 5-inch heels which pushed her pussy forward.

She smiled as she spun slowly in front of him, arms extended. "Do you like it?"

His licentious smile baring his fangs made her thighs clench. "You are a vision, Talia. You take my breath away."

She stepped back as he reached for her, playfully wagging her finger at him. "Oh, no, no touching just yet." His growl sent a pulse to her swollen clit. "If you promise not to touch, I'll undress you. But if you can't keep your hands to yourself, you can undress yourself."

He narrowed his eyes, licking his lips as his eyes traveled over every inch of her. His nostrils flared as he momentarily closed his eyes, and she knew he was smelling her arousal. When he opened his eyes, they were the deep amethyst color she loved. He held his arms out. "Undress me, love."

Consciously swaying her hips, the silky gown brushed her upper thighs and buttocks as she walked toward him. She removed his weapons harness, taking care not to touch him. He still wasn't wearing a shirt, so she knelt in front of him to unfasten his boots and loosen them.

"Sit." She pointed to the bed.

Once he was seated, she turned her back to him and bent from the waist, keeping her legs straight and pulled off one boot. His sharp, indrawn breath made her smile.

As she tugged on his other boot, she said in a seductive tone, "Can you see how wet I am for you?"

"Yes," he groaned, his voice deep and raspy. She looked back to see his hands with extended claws gripping the sheets.

Spinning slowly, she cupped her breasts as she straightened and pulled on her engorged nipples. "Lie back, babe."

In a single motion, he fell back. Then he lifted his head and propped himself up on his elbows to watch her unfasten his pants. She nibbled her lower lip when his abs contracted. His eyes stayed glued on her as he wiggled and raised his hips to help her pull down his clothing. She squatted in front of him, enjoying the sight of his aroused body. His taut muscles were straining with the need to reach for her.

"Move up higher on the bed, Vared. I need room to work." Deliberately, she licked her lips. *Oh, yes, he was mesmerized.* Using his elbows, he inched back.

She slowly stood, running her hands over her body, causing the gown to flutter and shift, revealing and covering her at random. That dark, decadent aroma of his that she loved so much was heavy in the air. She smiled when she saw the first drops of pre-cum on his hard cock. She leaned over and licked it off, only her tongue touching his body. His deep groan encouraged her to taste him, her tongue circling each node lightly. Short, erratic licks to the underside of his member caused it to jump. Swiping her tongue on each of his balls, she straightened and walked to the side of the bed.

Crawling on the bed so he could see her breasts hanging and her pussy, she kissed and licked her way down his stomach to revisit his cock, standing straight. She lifted her leg to straddle his torso. *Let's see how long he can hold out now.* He couldn't see her evil grin, but it was there just before she lowered her mouth onto him and sucked hard. Her mouth relaxed as she moaned around him, loving his taste.

"You naughty, filthy female." His chest rumbled against her clit. She moaned louder and rubbed her wetness on him. "Teasing your male, keeping your delights from him as you parade your sexy self around." His tail slapped her on the ass. She jerked and tried to take his cock deeper into her throat. "Look at that beautiful cunt, flowing its juices for me. I bet it feels empty. Should I fill it with my tongue, *kirani*? Or am I still supposed to keep my hands to myself?" She wiggled her bottom, wanting his mouth on her, but unwilling to stop sucking him.

His hands gripped her waist and pulled her off his cock. It released with a pop and she groaned. He pulled her cunt to his mouth and voraciously licked her. His tail found a nipple and slapped it. She sucked in a breath. He stopped just before she orgasmed, and she raked his stomach with her fingernails in protest.

He rolled and spun them so her feet were on the floor and her face in the sheets. He entered her pussy in one hard thrust. She came hard. She didn't have enough breath to scream as her pussy clutched at his cock repeatedly. Slowly coming back to awareness, she felt him still rigid inside her, his hands and claws kneading her ass, her gown pushed up to her waist. He withdrew almost all the way out. She made a sound of protest.

"Look at you, spread wide for your mate. Those shoes make your legs look like they go on forever, especially with you bent over to take me. And that pretty pink cunt sucking at my cock. It wants more, doesn't it?" He slapped her ass. "Answer me, mate."

She gasped. "It wants everything you can give it, mate. Fuck me hard. Please."

He leaned forward and licked her mating scar. She shivered. "What my mate wants, my mate gets." Straightening his body and withdrawing his cock almost all the way, he paused, then slammed into her, his nodes rippling her cunt and his balls slapping her flesh.

"Yes! More!"

He set a punishing pace, as hard and as fast as he could. He gripped her hips to keep her in place while his tail played with her clit. She tried to hold on longer, but when his tail slapped her clit, she screamed as her body spasmed inside and out with the force of her pleasure. Vision dark, she heard him roar as he came, filling her to overflowing with his seed. Their harsh gasps sounded loud in the aftermath. He pulled out and fell to the bed, gathering her close.

"I love you, Talia." He kissed her, long and deep, their tastes mingling.

She burrowed deeper into his arms. "I love you, Vared."

Running her hands tenderly over his body and feeling his hands and tail reciprocating, Talia felt like she was floating. As much as she loved making love with Vared, she also loved this quiet time with him. Soft utterances and being surrounded by him and his love brought her a sense of peace after all the excitement.

She really was a lucky woman. She finally had it all.

Recap

Races thus far

Human - Enough said.

Svesti - Warrior Race. About seven feet tall, skin in various shades of bronze, semi-retractable fangs, tails, and retractable claws. Ruled by a King. Honorable race protecting many regions of space from the Zuvgran, including near Earth. Most Svesti females died or were rendered infertile thirty Earth years prior due to a virus released by the Zuvgran. Plural is Svesti.

Durelian - Mercenary Race. About seven feet tall, orange skin, three bulbous black eyes.

Ermipa - Mining Race. About four feet tall, furry, round head, oval eyes.

Frezzian - Mercenary Race. Adverse to personal risk. Considered dishonorable.

Jalaxian - Warrior Race. About seven feet tall, blue skin, fangs, retractable claws and tail. Considered honorable. Many work as mercenaries after the Zuvgran decimated their world fifty Earth years ago.

Zuvgran - Warrior Race. About seven feet tall, gray skin, fangs, claws and horns. Ruled by an Emperor. Dishonorable race that invades planets to strip them of their resources and take the inhabitants as slaves. Considered violent. Plural is Zuvgran.

Planets and Space Stations thus far

Earth - Really not the center of the universe as humans might believe.

Costonia - Svesti Home World.

Talonka Six - Mining world closer to Costonia than Earth. Fourth planet in the Lestanus system.

Theron - Space Station approximately one quarter of the distance from Earth to Costonia.

XB9428B - Uninhabited planet, home to a Zuvgran lab.

Svesti Houses

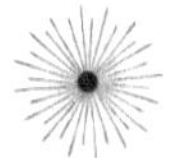 **Davelk** - Ruling House of Costonia.

 **Binova** - Primarily merchants.

 **Fresida** - Primarily educators and scientists.

 **Glixon** - Primarily merchants.

 **Kreliz** - Primarily scientists.

 **Midnar** - Primarily agriculture.

 **Nuxar** - One of the two Houses that strictly adhere to the old ways of worship.

 **Ruxila** - Primarily agriculture.

 **Srotix** - One of the two Houses that strictly adhere to the old ways of worship.

 **Troliv** - Primarily merchants.

 **Vramel** - Primarily warriors and educators.

 **Yula** - Many Svesti healers come from House Yula.

 **Terran** - New human clan marking.

Characters

Humans

Talia Sullivan - American, U.S. Ambassador of Interplanetary Relations, author.

Lin Chang - Chinese, botanist.

Rachel Llewellyn - British, MI-6.

Emmy Norton - Australian, hacker.

Natasha Petrov - Russian, medical doctor.

Ava Taylor - Canadian, chef.

President Leo Furman - United States President.

General Abram Johnson - United States Secretary of Defense.

Krista Johnston - Talia's sister, American, psychologist.

Rick Newell - American, President's Chief of Staff.

Joshua Sullivan - Talia's son, American, college student.

Tim Sullivan - Talia's ex-husband.

Svesti

King Traxen Sovex of House Davelk - King of the Svesti.

Commander Vared Durek of House Ruxila - Commander of the space cruiser, *Invictus*, the flagship of the Svesti military. First cousin to the king.

Lieutenant Triv'n Brauvix of House Kreliz - Communications officer on the *Invictus*.

Lieutenant Hozan Crulex of House Yula - Science office on the *Invictus*.

Canaan Durek of House Ruxila - Vared's father, House Ruxila representative in the King's Court, manages the family estate.

Grulen Jevax of House Midnar - Warrior.

Nerid Mantoor of House Glixon - Warrior.

Rexus Markham of House Yula - Healer on the *Invictus*. Rank - Captain.

Talen Previv of House Fresida - Warrior, Head Cook on the *Invictus*.

Ash'n Rivezt of House Yula - Head healer on the *Invictus*. Rank - Captain.

Klero Rovex of House Glixon - Warrior.

Nerob Sinoaz of House Troliv - Healer on the *Invictus*. Rank - Captain.

Lerix Sproid of House Kreliz - Warrior.

Lieutenant Devik Tolvex of House Vramel - Head security officer on the *Invictus*.

Lieutenant Leriv Volax of House Kreliz - Supply Master on the *Invictus*.

Lieutenant Karid Wurvez of House Binova - Head tactical officer on the *Invictus,* second in command of the space cruiser.

Wing Raiders

Captain Makai - Leader of the Jalaxian mercenary group, Wing Raiders.

Crax - Jalaxian Wing Raider, specialty is weapons.

Kara - Human female in the Wing Raiders, specialty is technology.

Lezon - Jalaxian Wing Raider, specialty is medical.

Rain - Human female in the Wing Raiders, pilot.

Tren - Jalaxian Wing Raider, engineer.

Yaz - Jalaxian Wing Raider, pilot.

Other

Overseer Roho - Ermipa on Talonka Six, head of the Veba Mine.

Svesti Words thus far

Brellia - Small, rumik-filled pastry.

Cold season - Comparable to Earth's winter in the northern hemisphere.

Crek - Fuck.

Harvest season - Comparable to Earth's autumn/fall in the northern hemisphere.

Hot season - Comparable to Earth's summer in the northern hemisphere.

Kirani - Female feline found in the wild. Similar to Earth's lioness.

Leringa - Fruit that has a hint of spice when ingested.

Lunar - Month.

Maxiem - A large animal that resembles a hybrid between Earth's ox and cow. Used as a source of meat, milk and beasts of burden.

Mentok - Similar to Earth's myna bird, but larger and with plumage reminiscent of an Earth's peacock. Chatters incessantly.

Naroon - Large furry animal, similar to Earth's ape, with blue fur. Gregarious and known to be silly in their family groups.

Pertiza - Creamy yellow sweet yogurt made from maxiem milk.

Renewal season - Comparable to Earth's spring in the northern hemisphere.

Rulah - Small, furry animal similar to Earth's cat.

Rumik - Meat similar to Earth's ground beef. Comes from maxiem.

Shurlix - Similar to Earth's tomato, but yellow.

Solar - Year.

Woolah - Red flower that blooms on Costonia during Harvest season.

Young – Baby/infant.

Youngling – Child.

Thank you for reading Vared and Talia's story. If you enjoyed this book, please leave an online review where you purchased it. This lets other readers know whether they might enjoy it, too!

If you'd like to hear about Wavy's other books, you can sign up for her newsletter or find her social media links at wavymartin.com.

9 781735 300887